DOGS, LIES, AND ALIBIS

Also by Wendy Delaney

DOGS, LIES, AND ALIBIS

A WORKING STIFFS MYSTERY
BOOK 5

WENDY DELANEY

DOGS, LIES, AND ALIBIS

Cover by Lewellen Designs

Printed in the United States of America

First Edition
First Printing, 2018

ISBN-13: 978-0-9969800-9-8
ISBN-10: 0996980091

Sugarbaker Press

For Mom

Acknowledgments

None of my books happen by themselves, and that was certainly the case with this "puppy."

First of all, I must thank my husband, Jeff. Not only are you my "guy stuff" advisor, you are my best guy in every way possible, *and* you can cook. I'm keeping you.

Jody Sherin, you were with me every step of the way on this book. Thanks for the encouragement and support even when they were baby steps accompanied by a bit of whining.

To "K," my "cop stuff" advisor, I'm so appreciative of your timely feedback. Without you, I surely would have gone astray on this one.

Jacquie Rogers, Kate Curran, and Diane Garland, thanks for your support. I'm grateful I can call on you when I need another brain.

Elizabeth Flynn, you're a brilliant woman, and you have excellent taste in socks. Thanks for lending me your expertise.

Thank you, Sean Dwyer. Mi amigo, you saved me from making a major oops.

Lastly, I offer my heartfelt thanks to my dream team of beta-readers and supporters: Denise Keef, Lori Dubiel, Susan Cambra, Brandy Jones, Denise Fluhr, Heather Chargualaf, Cindy Nelson, Vicki Huskey, Corie Carson, Kimber Hungerman, DeAnna Shaikoski, Jan Dobbins, Amber Lassig, Mattie Piela, Hope Goodlaxson, Deidre Herzog, Jana Buxton, Connie Lightner, and Karen Haverkate.

Chapter One

I HAD PROMISED myself this week would be different.

I was determined I would see results. And after almost a month on a diet that had stalled, I was willing to shake things up a little. Since I was dodging rain puddles on a soggy Monday morning jog through the streets of Port Merritt, maybe even more than willing.

That didn't mean I didn't hate every minute of it. But despite some serious huffing and puffing, I had been pretty successful in gritting it out and ignoring the stitch in my side until I heard that first rumble of thunder.

Then there was a second one followed by a third, and the skies opened up, dousing me and my fledgling resolve.

Although it might not always appear that I have the good sense to get out of the rain, I actually do. Especially when I see flashes of lightning in the pre-dawn gloom hovering over Merritt Bay.

Fortunately, my great-uncle Duke's diner was a couple of blocks away, and with my misery index starting to red-line I couldn't have been more grateful that the detour was all downhill.

Another clap of thunder echoed the bang of the

Duke's Cafe kitchen door announcing my drippy arrival.

"Land sakes, Charmaine," my great-aunt Alice said, aiming a scowl at me while she rolled out pie dough at her worktable. "You're soaked. You heard the news and decided to run right over?"

Huh? "What news?" I asked, huddling in front of an industrial oven venting the mouth-watering aroma of Alice's award-winning chocolate chip cookies.

She shook her head. "I didn't believe it at first, but..."

My heart, laboring after its first workout in months, thumped with anticipation. "But what?"

Before she could answer, Lucille, Duke's longest-tenured waitress, race-walked over in her squeaky orthopedic shoes and shoved a white towel into my hands. "So? What do you know?"

"Nothing." I ran the towel over my face. "What happened?"

"Little Dog's been arrested," she said, pursing her coral-painted lips as if the words had left a foul taste in her mouth.

"Arrested! For what?"

"Don't know, but I think something really bad happened."

Duke's Cafe's chief gossipmonger had to have been mistaken, or this was an April Fool's joke a day early. And since my high school buddy, George Bassett, was the butt of this joke, I didn't find it one bit funny.

I searched Lucille's face for telltale cracks in her solemn expression. A little flicker, the tiniest quirk of amusement at the corner of the busiest mouth in town.

That's what I do as a deception detection expert for the county. I read people's body language, keying in on the tells that even the best poker face will eventually reveal.

I knew from experience that Lucille couldn't hold back her glee when she held a winning hand. She also couldn't hold back the fear currently glazing her pale blue eyes, so like a snap to the face with the towel in my hands, I knew that this news about Little Dog was no joke.

But that didn't mean that Lucille had her facts straight. "Tell me everything you've heard."

"It ain't much," she said. "One of the long-haul guys came in, asking what was up with the cop cars at Bassett Motor Works. I figured there must have been a break-in or somethin', but Howie told me that Little Dog was taken into custody."

Fresh-faced Patrolman Howie Fontaine was the newest member of the fourteen-person Port Merritt police force. In the eight months at my job, our professional paths had crossed a handful of times, typically with him deferring to a superior when it came to disclosing information.

How come he was making an exception with the queen of Gossip Central, of all people? "He told you that?"

"I wouldn't serve him until he told me what was going on up there, but that's all I was able to get out of the kid."

"When?"

"Just after we opened, so around six-ten."

I glanced at the wall clock mounted above a vintage red and white Coca Cola sign. Six-forty-two. A little early for my boyfriend to be at work. Unless Detective Steve

Sixkiller had wanted to be the individual to take one of his best buddies into custody, which knowing him as well as I did would have been a safe bet.

I didn't have my cell phone on me, so I headed for the wall phone behind the cash register.

"You're dripping on my floor," Duke grumbled as I passed where he was frying a couple of eggs on the grill.

I waved my towel at the old coot. "I'll clean it up in a minute."

"Why were you out in the rain at this hour anyway?"

"I was jogging."

"You?"

"Yeah, I exercise every once in a while," I muttered, punching in Steve's phone number.

Duke chortled. "Your elbow, maybe."

In no mood for any jibes about my dieting woes, I turned my attention to the recorded message playing in my ear. "Hey, you home?" I paused to give Steve a chance to pick up. "Okay, I'll catch you later." At the precinct.

That called for reinforcements, so after I mopped up the floor, I grabbed a white bakery bag and dropped three apple fritters into it.

Duke glowered at me. "You gonna pay for those?"

"Put 'em on my tab."

The salty Navy veteran with the crew cut muttered a few choice words about where he'd like to stick my tab.

I blew him a kiss from the coffee station, where I filled two to-go cups with the steaming crude oil Duke passed off as coffee.

Lucille squeaked up and took the carafe from my hand. "I can make some fresh if you want to wait a few minutes."

"I gotta go talk to a man about a certain dog," I said, placing the coffees in a carrier.

She threw a few creamers into the bag. "I want details, so hurry back."

"I'll see what I can do."

"And bring money," Duke shouted as I headed for the front door, "like a normal person!"

Running toward the police station in the driving rain didn't feel the least bit normal, with or without the apple fritters. But once I rounded the corner of 3rd and Main and spotted Steve's unmarked police cruiser, I had hope that some normality would soon be restored.

Assuming that I could get someone to buzz me in to see him.

Given the fact that I'd been known to make Duke's Cafe deliveries for over half of my thirty-four years, it shouldn't have appeared overly suspicious for me to show up with a breakfast order for Steve. Except for the fact that I was in rain-drenched sweats.

Dodging a car heading past the station, I made my way to the door of the brick building and quickly realized it wouldn't open until the Chief's secretary arrived around seven.

"Well, crap." If I waited until then, I and the apple fritters would be water-logged.

I picked up the phone next to the door with the hope that Steve might answer.

After several seconds a reedy male voice I didn't recognize came through the receiver. "May I help you?"

"Yes, I'm here to see Detective Sixkiller."

"Do you have an appointment?"

"No, but he'll want to see me." Maybe.

"Your name?"

"Char Digby."

Several seconds of silence followed.

"Who is this?" I asked.

"Officer Fontaine, and I don't think—"

"Open the door, Howie!"

More silence.

"I have Steve's coffee and it's getting cold!"

The door clicked open, and waiting on the other side of it Officer Fontaine stood like a human roadblock.

"I can take it to him," he said.

Not a chance. "I'm also here to consult with him on a case."

Howie's eyes narrowed. "I didn't think this was a coroner case."

Since I only worked on the cases that the Chimacam County Prosecutor/Coroner deemed worthy of her budget's limited resources, those cases typically involved an unusual death shrouded by mysterious circumstances. And before they were turned over to the local police or the sheriff's department, one of the deputized staffers—usually me—would launch a fact-finding mission.

My mouth went dry. Not only had Howie just informed me that someone had died in the night, Little Dog had been taken into custody to face criminal charges for causing that death.

"Clearly that determination isn't official," I stated, giving the rookie patrolman my best withering stare. "I mean, really, would I have rushed over in this weather otherwise?"

"Uh…" His gaze landed on the wet bag in my hand.

Okay, so stopping off to pick up some apple fritters

didn't help my argument. "Either tell him I'm here or buzz me in."

Howie picked up the nearest desk phone and punched three buttons. "Char's here to see you. Yeah, to *consult* with you."

I winced at his injection of sarcasm.

Howie turned to me. "He wants to know what you brought to eat."

Clearly, nobody was buying my consultation angle this morning. "Apple fritters."

He repeated the information and then disconnected. "He'll be right out."

I held the bag out to him. "Want one?"

"Thanks," he said, pulling out the biggest of the three.

"You giving away my breakfast?" Steve called out over the buzz of the security door that led to the restricted domain of the department.

"Nope." I had given away *my* breakfast. Just as well. I didn't need the fat calories. "I had extra."

"In the event you needed to bribe your way in here?"

"It worked, didn't it?" I said as he held the door open for me.

Steve blew out a weary breath. "I guess it's safe to assume that you heard the news."

"Yeah. What happened?"

"Not out here."

The hallway leading to his office was deserted. As were the three offices we passed, so it wasn't like there was anyone around to overhear us, but I could sense the tension emanating from Steve like heat waves and knew better than to press.

I followed Port Merritt PD's one and only detective through the open door marked *Investigation Division* and placed the bag and coffees next to his computer monitor.

Watching me take a seat in the hardback chair across from his metal desk, he frowned. "You're soaked. Want me to get some paper towels?"

I reached into the bag for a couple of napkins to sop up the drips cascading from my wet hair. "I'm fine. Can you tell me what happened? Is Georgie okay?"

"He's okay physically."

"What's that supposed to mean?"

Steve's lips flattened into a grim line. "It's not looking good for him."

I shivered, my skin crawling with apprehension. "What on earth happened?"

"We're still sorting that out."

In other words, he wasn't going to tell me.

"Okay," I said, wrapping my hands around the closest coffee cup to soak in some much-needed warmth. "Can you at least tell me who died?"

He popped the plastic top of his cup and dumped in some creamer. "I take it from your attire that you're not heading straight to the courthouse from here?"

"Yeah, it's not mangy Monday."

Leaning back in his black vinyl chair, Steve fixed me with an icy stare that chilled me to my marrow. "You remember Colt Ziegler?"

Mainly as the idiot who got suspended after picking a fight with Little Dog back in high school. "Sure."

"He was found by a tow truck driver delivering a vehicle to Bassett Motor Works early this morning."

I sucked in a breath. "Dead?"

Steve nodded. "From an apparent blow to the head."

"Holy crap. And what... Howie arrested Little Dog because he'd heard about that stupid fight a million years ago?"

"No, he called me, and I took Dog in for questioning."

"You don't think he killed Colt, do you?"

"Doesn't matter what I think. All I know is that a man is dead who shouldn't be, and Dog admitted having a run-in with him last night. So until he gets a bail hearing, he has to remain in holding."

"When's the hearing gonna be?"

"Later this morning."

Reeling with this information, I almost felt like I'd experienced a blow to the head. "Holy crap!"

Steve touched my hand. "Go home and get ready for work. There isn't anything any of us can do now but wait."

Intellectually I understood that he'd dispensed some reasonable advice, but everything about what I had just heard felt very, very wrong.

I leaned across the desk to give him a kiss. "Call me if there's any news," I said, heading for the door. But I knew he wouldn't. This was going to be a long, miserable day of waiting, probably the beginning of an even more miserable week.

And I had wanted this week to be different.

Boy, would it ever be.

Chapter Two

AFTER CHASING AWAY my shivers with a hot shower, I gave my hair a quick blast with my blow dryer, threw on a cotton tunic and black jeans, and drove down the hill toward the highway.

Yes, if I had followed Steve's advice and trotted off to work, I would have turned right out of my apartment complex instead of left, but this way I could do a drive-by of Bassett Motor Works and satisfy... What, I wasn't sure. Morbid curiosity about the scene of the crime?

Maybe in part.

More than anything, I wanted to understand how the heck the lovable doofus Steve and I grew up with could be responsible for the death of Colt Ziegler.

Slowing as I approached the entrance, I was astonished at how normal the auto repair yard appeared. Even the black and white mutt sleeping near the front door of the office seemed oblivious to the fact that Little Dog had been arrested.

I didn't know what I'd expected to see. Cop cars and yellow crime scene tape cordoning off the area? There was none of that. Of course, Steve would have been the one working the scene after he got that early morning call, and the CSI team of one had obviously come and gone.

With a logging truck gaining ground on the two-lane highway behind me, I pulled into the entrance to let it pass. That's when I noticed George Senior poking his head out of the garage. Probably because the Jaguar XJ6 I'd been awarded in the divorce settlement sounded like it was rattling a cowbell—one in a growing list of maladies Georgie was going to fix once I got another paycheck under my belt.

Senior waved, more business-like than friendly.

I figured it would be rude to drive off without an explanation of what I was doing there, so I parked next to an older-model Jeep waiting its turn for garage time and stepped out into what was now a steady drizzle.

I was immediately greeted by barking.

Behind the dog, George Senior, the six-foot-five block of iron from which his ruddy-faced, redhead son had been chipped, gingerly approached me like a man nursing a hangover. His eyes looked the part too—watery, bloodshot. But given the events of the morning, the *Big Dog* of Bassett Motor Works had to be suffering from something much more profound than a hangover.

"Rufus, knock it off. Sorry," he said, turning his attention to me as he wiped his hands on an oil-stained rag. "We're pretty backed up right now, but if you want to drop your car off later in the week, we should..." His voice broke. "We might be able to fit you in."

"Actually, I'm not here about my car."

Nodding, the big man's eyes welled with tears. "You heard about Junior."

"I'm so sorry. Is there anything I can do?"

"You know any good lawyers?"

Yes, but they all worked for my boss. "I'll ask around."

Senior wiped his eyes with the sleeve of his coveralls. "Appreciate it."

I didn't want to pick at an open wound, but since Steve was never in a sharing mood when it came to his cases, I figured this might be my one and only opportunity to glean some details about what had happened. "Did you have a chance to talk to Georgie before he was arrested?"

Senior shook his head. "Didn't even know he'd been arrested until he called from jail."

"Did he tell you what happened?"

"Char, he doesn't know what happened. After he kicked that Ziegler kid off the property—"

"What was he doing here in the middle of the night?"

"Junior said he was breaking into that limo." Senior pointed at the white Lincoln Town Car sticking out in the row of sedans parked between the office and the chain link fence edging the south property line.

"Rufus here started barking—something he never does unless there's someone on the lot who shouldn't be. That's when Junior grabbed his baseball bat and ran down from his apartment to chase him off."

My breath caught in my throat. "So he hit him with the bat?"

Senior scowled. "He barely touched that punk. Gave him a good shove out the front gate and that's pretty much it."

I didn't want to make a worried father's morning worse by pressing the point, but that couldn't have been it. Steve wouldn't have made an arrest, and there would have been one more Bassett to help with the backlog around here.

"Where's the bat?" I glanced over at Georgie's second-floor apartment above the office, hoping against hope that it was mounted on some wall up there.

George Senior heaved a sigh. "Steve has it."

I was afraid he was going to say that.

"I didn't think it was raining that hard," Patsy Faraday said, raking her disparaging gaze over my brown mop of rapidly frizzing hair as I passed her desk.

"It's not." But when one of my friends could be facing some serious jail time, getting rained on is the least of my concerns.

I looked past her at the empty office of the boss we shared. "Is Frankie in yet? I need to speak with her."

The County Prosecutor's legal assistant arched an eyebrow. "She's in a meeting. What exactly do you need?"

The name of an attorney for Little Dog. And in no way, shape, or form was I going to get that from Patsy without having to first choke down a big slice of condescension pie. "Never mind. I'll catch her later."

I headed down the hall, following the worn-down path in the carpeting to the break room, where I was relieved to see an almost full pot of coffee.

After I poured a cup, I dropped my tote off at my desk and then marched straight to Ben Santiago's office.

I knocked and waited for the Deputy Criminal Prosecutor to wave me in. He did without hesitation, but the crinkle of irritation between his thick black eyebrows told me that it would be advisable to make this impromptu visit a short one.

"Good morning," I said, placing the coffee mug well away from the red file folder open in front of him.

Peering over his horn-rimmed glasses, his hooded dark eyes narrowed as they swept over my hair. "Get caught in the rain this morning?"

More than once. "Yeah, I ran into George Bassett this morning." Sort of. "I don't know if you've heard, but his son has been arrested and—"

"I know. I'm reviewing the case right now."

That explained the red file folder—red being the color that distinguished the criminal cases handled by Ben's department.

I swallowed the lump forming in my throat. "Unless you plan to tell Detective Sixkiller to drop the charges and release George Junior, he's gonna need a lawyer."

Ben slowly nodded. "He's definitely going to need a lawyer."

Criminy. "Then could you recommend a good defense attorney?"

He reached into his top drawer and pulled out a short stack of business cards. "This is a little unorthodox since I'm the one who'll be prosecuting this case," he said, removing a rubber band and thumbing through the cards. "But these two are probably the best in the tri-county area."

I quickly scanned the cards he'd handed me. It didn't surprise me that both attorneys had offices in Seattle and Port Townsend, a popular tourist destination a half-hour north of town. A lot of the more high-powered professionals in the region extended their reach by hopping on a Seattle-bound ferry a couple of times a week. And most of us who might need to avail ourselves of their services recognized those services would come at a premium cost.

It was another lesson this former pastry chef repeatedly learned in culinary school. If you want the best outcome, you have to invest in the best.

I just hoped Little Dog and his father would feel the same way.

Chapter Three

WITH THE SEALED subpoena that Patsy had just
handed me to deliver, I felt like I was holding a permission slip. Maybe not to loiter outside of Judge Witten's
courtroom, but at least I had been granted a temporary
reprieve from refreshing the county's webpage for an
update on Little Dog's bail hearing like I'd been doing
for the last two hours.

I put my ear up to the door and heard nothing but
muffled voices. That gave me a decision to make. I could
go in and risk incurring Frankie's wrath if any of her
subordinates tattled on me poking my nose where it
didn't belong, or I could brave some more rain and go
deliver a subpoena. Neither option felt like the right
choice.

"If you have no business inside, step away please,"
said Sheriff's Deputy Mankowitz, the buzz-cut human
security system, standing guard between the two
courtrooms.

With no desire to invite any trouble with Deputy
Mankowitz, I smiled as I closed the distance between us.
"Have you seen George Bassett come out of the court-
room?"

"No, ma'am."

"I have something for him." Not that I needed to explain myself, but I didn't want the next two words out of his mouth to be *Move along*.

He glanced down at the envelope I was holding, and I covered the name with my thumb.

The deputy shifted his gaze to the big brass clock mounted over the main entrance, one of several original nineteenth-century courthouse artifacts still in use. "Shouldn't be much longer."

That's what I'd wanted to believe most of the morning, but at least I'd finally received confirmation from a reliable source.

After almost five minutes of pacing the length of the gold and black checkerboard hallway outside the courtrooms, my cell phone chirped with a text message from Lucille. Like me, she wanted a news update.

"Get in line," I muttered, tucking my cell back in the tote slung over my shoulder.

Just as I thought about cooling my jets on the wooden bench opposite the courtroom, a bailiff opened the door, and a small, somber-looking crowd filed out. Many I knew as long-time residents of Port Merritt.

None of them made eye contact with me, including the large man at the back of the pack heading for the stairs.

"Mr. Bassett," I called out, hurrying to catch up with him just as my phone started ringing. *Give me a break, Lucille.* "May I speak with you for a moment?"

He turned to me and blinked, slightly unfocused.

Since he looked as if he could take a header down the stairs, I took his elbow to lead him back to that bench.

"How'd it go in there?"

Easing himself onto the edge of the seat, George Senior shook his head. "Junior's in a heap of trouble."

"What's he being charged with?"

"Second-degree murder."

"Holy moly!"

He took a deep breath and slowly released it. "Yeah."

"Will he be released on bail?" Georgie had no criminal history and had been an active member of this community, coaching the peewee football team with Steve. That had to count for something, no matter how strong the evidence appeared to be against him.

Senior nodded. "I might have to take out a loan, but I'm getting him out of there today."

I handed him the two business cards Ben gave me. "These two attorneys came highly recommended."

He fingered the embossed cards. "Port Townsend and Seattle, huh?"

"They're supposed to be the best."

"Looks like I'm gonna need a bigger loan."

After I drove to the south end of town and slapped the subpoena into the hand of a disgruntled tax attorney, I stopped at Duke's to get Lucille to stop calling me every ten minutes.

"About dang time," she grumbled the moment the silver bell over the front door jingled to announce my arrival.

I sighed. "Hello to you, too."

Quickly splashing some coffee into the two empty cups at the counter, Lucille squeaked into the kitchen with the carafe and motioned for me to follow her.

Duke eyeballed me while a couple of greasy burgers sputtered on the grill. "You here for lunch or to pay me the money you owe me?"

"Both," I said, not breaking stride.

"What'll you have?"

"I'll make myself a salad in a couple of minutes."

"Salad! You must be trying to stick to that diet."

"Yep." Despite the fact that I was hankering for one of those burgers. Preferably with some bleu cheese and bacon.

I grabbed a bottle of water off a storage rack as I went by to try to drown the craving.

"Sit," Lucille said, pointing at the pine bar stool across the worktable from my great-aunt.

Alice knit her brow as she spread fluffy meringue over the lemon filling of her last pie for the day. "Good grief, Luce. Can't you let the girl have some lunch in peace?"

Lucille glowered at her friend of over fifty years. "Do you want to know what she found out, or not?"

"Oh, yes!" She settled back on her stool and stared at me expectantly. "So, spill it."

"I don't know a lot of details, but here's what's happened so far. As you know, Little Dog was taken into police custody early this morning. He's now facing some serious charges," I said, avoiding the word, *murder*, so that I wouldn't fan the flames of Gossip Central with a blowtorch. "The good news is that he should be released on bail very soon." Assuming that the Big Dog's meeting with his banker went well.

Lucille leaned in. "Arlene Koker came in for breakfast around seven..."

As per usual. You could set a watch by the eating habits of the senior center's activity director.

"She said that she saw Curtis's hearse parked next to a cop car outside Bassett's garage."

I must have just missed it.

Alice reached across the table and wrapped her warm hand over mine. "So, who died?"

I didn't know if notification had been made to the Ziegler family, so full disclosure was off the table. "I'm sure more details about what happened will be made available tomorrow."

I stepped away from the table to signal the end of today's briefing.

Lucille grabbed my arm. "That's it? Little Dog whacks somebody, and that's all you're going to tell us?"

"That's all I know."

"Hon, you're not the only one around here who can tell when someone's lying."

Stifling a sigh, I headed for the refrigerator near the grill, where Duke kept the salad fixings.

Unfortunately, Lucille was in squeaky lockstep with me.

"That boy's in some deep doo-doo, isn't he?" she asked, lowering her voice.

I nodded as I pulled out a bag of lettuce.

"Did he lawyer up?"

"Pretty sure that'll happen later today."

"Order up!" Duke barked in our direction.

Lucille skulked toward the grill. "Well, this week is off to a sucky bang."

I couldn't agree with her more.

❋

Almost an hour later, I was experiencing my more typical source of aerobic exercise, climbing three flights of stairs, when I heard my name reverberating off the courthouse plaster walls.

Catching my breath, I turned to see Ben Santiago coming up the marble steps behind me with a plastic Roadkill Grill cup in his hand.

The Roadkill Grill was a no-frills local dive, but the fries were good, and there was no Lucille there to hang on his every word, so I couldn't blame him for patronizing Duke's competition.

"I'm glad I caught you," he said.

He was? I couldn't imagine why.

Ben flashed me the breezy smile of a politician courting my vote. "Have a minute?"

"Sure."

He led me to the bench seat, where I'd sat with George Senior after the bail hearing. "I had lunch with Detective Sixkiller today."

Okay. It made sense that the criminal prosecutor might want to talk to the arresting officer who just happened to be one of George Bassett Junior's best friends.

But why was he telling me about it?

I nodded, smiling politely.

"He mentioned that when he went out to do the notification, the victim's mother had some choice words about a prior incident between her son and Mr. Bassett."

"That fight back in high school?" That was old news.

Ben's gaze sharpened. "They'd had a previous fight?"

I was just about to give myself a mental head slap for helping to dig Georgie a deeper hole when the significance of what I'd just heard struck me with a wallop. "Tami Ziegler said there'd been a *second* fight?"

"According to Mrs. Ziegler, Bassett broke her son's nose two years ago."

What? "That's the first I'm hearing about this."

"That's pretty much what Steve said."

Not only was no police report filed on the incident, Georgie never mentioned it. Because he had wanted to keep it quiet, or because it never happened?

That same calculating smile passed over Ben's lips. "You know Mrs. Ziegler, right?"

"Yeah?" I also knew that he wanted something beyond some background information from me.

"Would you have time to speak with her this afternoon and assess the veracity of her claim?"

Instead of spending the rest of my day filing in the bowels of the third floor? Boy, would I. "No problem. How about the other family members and friends? I probably know most of them." At least the ones who had lived around here for a while. "Want me to interview them, too?"

He nodded. "Talk to anyone who might have information on the incident. If there was a conflict that had been escalating between them, I want to know about it."

"Got it."

Ben pushed off the bench.

I did the same, and then followed his lead as he headed toward the office to the right of the stairs.

"One last thing," he said, opening the door for me. "I know you're friends with Steve and the Bassetts, but let's keep this between us for now."

This wasn't the first time that one of the prosecutors had warned me about sharing details of a case beyond our office walls. But never before had the instruction made my skin crawl. "Understood."

"Get a copy of the file from my assistant, and reference the case number in all your communications."

"Yes, sir."

With a nod, Ben headed down the hall, leaving me reeling next to the receptionist's desk.

"Char? Are you okay?" she asked.

No. I had just been enlisted to help convict Little Dog of murder.

Chapter Four

AFTER LOOKING UP a few addresses, I set out on my information-gathering mission. My first stop: the Port Merritt Police Department.

I pulled behind Steve's Crown Victoria, turned off the ignition, and called him on my cell phone.

"Let me call you back," he hurriedly said after several rings.

"Better yet, come outside."

"You're here?"

"Parked behind your car."

Without responding, Steve disconnected.

Five minutes later, he opened the passenger door and angled himself in. "What?"

Okay, I understood the frosty reception. Steve was busy with one of the most important cases of his career. But so was I, and I needed to speak with the great guy I'd been sleeping with for the past seven months, not an impatient clone of my ex.

I leaned across the center console and kissed his lips. "How're you doing?"

Pulling away, he stared out the drizzle-coated windshield. "How do you think?"

"Me, too."

"This is bad, Char."

I took his hand in mine. "I know. Ben told me about what happened when you visited Colt's mother."

Steve's grip tightened as he turned to me. "That's not for public consumption at Duke's."

"Give me some credit. I know how serious this is. That's why I'm here."

He pierced me with the intensity of his dark gaze. "Please don't tell me—"

"I'm not here to tell you anything," I said, hoping that he'd get the full measure of my meaning. "I just need to know if she mentioned anyone else who might have been a witness to the fight."

"Why?"

"Trust that I'm asking for a good reason. Did she mention anyone?"

Wordlessly, Steve leaned closer as if he were challenging me to join him in a staring contest, much like when we were kids. "What are you up to?"

"Just doing my job."

"I don't like that you're getting involved in this."

"Not my idea, Detective."

He opened the door and swung his long legs out of the car. "See you around."

"Wait a minute!" I leaned across the console so that I could see his face. "You're just gonna walk away?"

A flicker of a smile crossed Steve's tan lips before he ducked back through the doorway for a kiss. "I meant to do that first, and no."

If he was trying to confuse me, he was doing a good job of it. "No, what?"

"No, Tami Ziegler didn't mention anyone else, so why don't you ask her about that."

I intended to.

The last time I'd seen Tami Ziegler was three weeks ago at Duke's, when we'd sat together at the counter during a crowded lunch hour.

Tami had graduated Port Merritt High in the same class as my actress mother, so I'd anticipated that we'd chat about at least one of the three usual topics: the latest Marietta Moreau teen scream movie, how great my mom looked in her last infomercial, or her engagement to Barry Ferris, my high school biology teacher.

Tami and I managed to hit all three that afternoon. As a bonus, I got to hear all about how Mr. Ferris used to date her best friend and fellow divorcee, Renee Ireland, a newshound for the weekly *Port Merritt Gazette*.

While I hadn't wanted to dig any deeper into the love life of my soon-to-be fourth stepfather, I had squirreled away that little relationship nut as something I needed to be mindful of.

Especially today.

Colt's death and Georgie's arrest made for headline news, and with her tight relationship with Tami, Renee would surely demand the byline. So it came as no surprise when I turned onto K Street and spotted Renee's ice blue Subaru as one of the two vehicles parked in front of Tami's rambler.

It put a monkey wrench in my plans though, because I couldn't very well conduct an interview with a reporter in the room.

But as I parked behind a minivan, I reminded myself that I had something she didn't have: a little badge that made me an officer of the court. About as low on the totem pole of officialdom that one could go, but even my lowly rank had some privileges. I just needed to channel Deputy Mankowitz and insist that Renee *move along*.

Also, keep my comments to a minimum to avoid running the risk of them resurfacing in the newspaper.

With my plan of action in place I approached the white stucco house. That's when I saw Renee step outside, shutting the front door behind her.

At first I was relieved. While my mother wasn't the only one in the family who could deliver a rehearsed line with some authority, Deputy Mankowitz would have been a stretch. But unlike my mother I had no desire for any publicity, and a reporter was rapidly descending upon me.

"Well, hello, Charmaine," she said, greeting me with a smile too gleeful for the reason that had brought us both here.

I didn't want to lead her back to Tami's doorstep, so I stopped to talk. "Hey, Renee."

Standing in front of me in skinny jeans and heels that made her long legs look even longer, Renee Ireland towered over me by at least seven inches.

I'd always assumed she used her size and former model good looks to her advantage when trying to snare an interview. I had just never imagined myself as the interviewee in her sights.

As a cool breeze ruffled her soft strawberry blond curls she thrust a handheld recorder in front of my face. "Are you here in some sort of official capacity?"

"I'm just here to chat with Tami."

"As a representative of the coroner's office?"

"As you can imagine, there are some things having to do with the *body* that must be discussed," I stated solemnly, counting on the fact that Renee wouldn't want to step into the weeds of death and dying.

She blanched as if the Grim Reaper had sent me. "Of course. But can you tell me if there have been any *findings* I can share with my readers?"

I knew it was in my best interest to play dumb. "Oh, I wouldn't know. That's above my pay grade."

Puckering, Renee turned off her recorder. "Okay, I'll call Frankie to schedule an interview."

You're never going to get past Patsy, I thought, watching Renee climb into her Subaru.

I didn't want any more surprises, so I waited for her to drive out of sight before stepping onto the porch to ring the doorbell.

"Tell them to go away," a tearful voice said.

As a death investigator for the county, I had grown accustomed to emotionally fraught home visits. It didn't mean I liked it, but as long as no one on the other side of the door was a media member, I could handle a few minutes of less than gracious company. And based on who just cracked the door open, it appeared that company would include Colt's older sister, Kendra Sparks.

Kendra had been two years ahead of me in school, so we hadn't been particularly close, but she knew me.

Unfortunately, that failed to serve as an equalizer to the level of wariness in her eyes. "If you're here to see my mom, it isn't a good time."

I flashed my deputy coroner badge to *encourage* her cooperation. "I'm sorry, but I'm here on behalf of the coroner's office." Partially true, but I couldn't very well lead this potential witness by admitting that the criminal prosecutor sent me to get more dirt on how Colt broke his nose.

With a sigh Kendra opened the door and I stepped into a house that reeked of a filthy litter box.

One long-haired gray and white cat hovered by the door while twin charcoal kitties darted down the nearby hallway.

Kendra shut the door with a loud thud and the gray and white skittered away to join his buddies. "We have to be careful answering the door because that one likes to make a break for it."

Another partial truth—one that had little to do with her hesitancy to let me in.

I followed Kendra into the kitchen, where Tami was hunkered down at an old Shaker-style table with a plaid dishtowel pressed to her eyes.

"Mom?" Kendra gently said, as if waking her mother from a nap. "Char's here to talk to you."

Tami lowered the towel, revealing angry, swollen eyelids. Shaking her head, tears spilled onto blotchy cheeks. "I can't talk...right now."

I settled into the chair across from her and pulled a pen and notebook from my tote. "I understand. You and Kendra have suffered a terrible loss and I'm so sorry to intrude, but I'm here to help get to the bottom of what happened to Colt."

Yes, I had just presented myself as an ally in what should have appeared to be a quest for justice. Truthfully, that's what I wanted, but not just for the Ziegler family.

While Tami blinked back a fresh round of tears, a dry-eyed Kendra turned to me. "Coffee, Char? I made some fresh."

This caffeine addict never refused free coffee, especially when it bought me an excuse to stick around for a few extra minutes.

"Yes, please." I smiled across the table at Tami. "So, would it be okay if I asked a few questions?"

Sitting up a little straighter, she wiped her eyes with the towel.

I had a feeling that was as much of an answer in the affirmative as she was capable of giving right now. "When was the last time you saw Colton?"

She cleared her throat. "Besides this morning at Tolliver's?"

Curtis Tolliver's mortuary contracted with the county to double as the local morgue, so I had expected that Tami would have gone there to identify her son's body.

I nodded. "I'm mainly interested in when you last talked to him."

"Yesterday. Late in the afternoon. He called to tell me that he wouldn't be coming over for dinner."

I made a note about the dinner. "Was that a usual thing—getting the family together on Sunday?"

"Oh, no." After another swipe with the towel, she cast a disparaging glance at her daughter as Kendra delivered my coffee. "Just Colton and me."

Picking up her mother's empty cup, Kendra heaved a sigh. "You know why Damon preferred to visit when Colt wasn't here."

Ooooh, that sounded juicy. I jotted another note while mother and daughter shot daggers at one another.

Even juicier.

Once Kendra retreated to the kitchen, Tami dismissively waved a bony hand. "Water under the bridge. Nothing you'd want to hear about."

Want to bet?

Taking a ragged breath, Tami squeezed her swollen lids shut. "Where were we?"

"Colton called Sunday afternoon," I prompted. "Around what time?"

"Maybe four-thirty."

"Last minute." Kendra set the mug of coffee in front of her mother. "As per usual."

Tami fired a glare at her daughter that looked much like the warning shot I'd get from Marietta when I bad-mouthed one of her prospective grooms. "Don't start. Not today."

Kendra took the seat separating her mother and me. "I'm just saying."

And I was just hoping for some elaboration. "Did Colton give a reason why he couldn't make it?"

Tami pushed back a wayward strand of salt and pepper hair. "He had to work."

"At the feed store?" Where I'd seen him at the register last month, when Gram sent me to pick up a bale of straw for her vegetable garden.

Kendra smirked. "Hardly."

Sitting very still, Tami stared into the steaming mug in front of her. "No, that job didn't work out."

Clearly. I gave them a chance to explain, but they'd both clammed up.

I added Ray Ortiz, the owner of the feed store, to my interview list. I doubted that Ben would be interested in Mr. Ortiz as a witness, but I would first need to speak with him to rule that out. "So where was Colton working yesterday?"

"He was a limo driver for One Stop Party." Tami's thin mouth twisted into a sad smile. "It's like I told Renee. He liked the job. Wore a chauffeur's hat and everything."

I knew that party supply store—all too well, as a matter of fact. Mainly thanks to a mother who had conscripted me to help her plan her June wedding.

I took a sip of what tasted like Italian roast blended with diesel fuel and longed for some milk to dilute it, but I didn't want to give Kendra an excuse to leave the table, so I pushed the mug to the side. "Had Colton been working there for long?"

Tami blinked. "I don't think so, and—"

"And don't get the wrong idea," Kendra cut in. "This was some easy money that I think my cousin and his wife were tossing his way."

I looked across the table at Tami for confirmation.

She shrugged. "Maybe."

"What's this cousin's name?" I asked.

When her mother hesitated to answer, Kendra jumped in. "Eric Caldwell."

I stared at her in stunned silence for a split second because I'd experienced three years of high school with Eric and Colt, and had never heard anyone mention that they were related.

I added Eric's name to my list. "So, someone must have booked a limo for Sunday and Colton called to let you know that he wouldn't make it for dinner."

Tami nodded.

"Did he mention anything else when he called?"

She shook her head.

"How about before that? Did he say anything about experiencing any trouble with anyone in the last few weeks?"

The older woman shifted in her seat. "Weeks? No."

I slanted my gaze to Kendra, who folded her arms and shifted her focus to her mother's untouched coffee mug.

Since Kendra had checked herself out of this conversation I made a mental note to schedule some time alone with her.

I gave her an out because we both knew that I'd come here to speak with her mother. But Kendra obviously had some strong feelings about her little brother, chief among them enough anger to make my coffee boil. And I wanted to know why.

Tami furrowed her brow, squinting across the table at me like a mole struggling to face the dim light of the kitchen. "But like I told Steve this morning, this problem with George Bassett had been going on for twenty years."

"Problem?" I asked, trying to keep my expression carefully neutral.

"That *menace* using my son like a punching bag."

There was no possible way that could be true of the gentle giant I knew.

Looking for cracks in Tami's conviction, I swept my gaze over her face. She probably had enough tension in her jaw to bite through steel, so I wasn't surprised to hear her lay into Georgie. But as much as she might believe every word she was saying, that didn't make it true.

"You should have seen my boy after that monster broke his nose a couple of years back. He was black and blue for a month."

I gave Kendra a sidelong glance to gauge her reaction to the accusations her mother was making. No escalation of emotion. If anything, Kendra appeared markedly calm compared to her mother.

But also increasingly twitchy.

Something didn't add up.

"Did you see your brother after he was hurt?"

Without making eye contact, she shrugged. "I wasn't...uh..."

"She wasn't talking to him at the time," Tami huffed, aiming her mole squint at her daughter.

Oh?

I angled in my seat to get a better view of Kendra's face. "So you never discussed this incident with him?"

Pressing her pale lips together, she shook her head. "He told me later that it was no big deal. Beyond that, no."

I seriously doubted that was the whole story, but before I could ask a follow-up question, Tami pounded the table with her fist. "No big deal? Your brother's dead!"

Kendra broke into tears for the first time since my arrival. "Don't you think I know that?"

"I'm sorry," I said, fighting to douse the fire burning behind my own eyes as I bore witness to their pain. "I know how difficult this is." I touched Kendra's shirt-sleeve. *And I will talk to you later, when your mother isn't around.*

"Mrs. Ziegler, you said that this thing with George Bassett had been going on for twenty years."

She shook her head as if she couldn't believe it herself. "Off and on since high school."

"Can you give me another example of the 'on'?" Because I was quite confident that no one else in town would be able to come up with one.

"When Colton moved back home." Tami squinted down at her coffee. "This would have been when he was around twenty-five."

I scribbled while she talked.

"For days, he barely came out of his room. At first I thought it was...you know..." She lowered her voice. "Drugs. But after two weeks of him doing nothing but watching TV on my couch, he finally admitted that there was someone he didn't want to run into. I told him that he couldn't live his life in fear, and insisted that he level with me about what was going on."

I waited while she took a sip of coffee, my pen poised over my notebook. "What'd he say?"

"That he owed money to George Bassett—said that big ape was going to kill him if he didn't pay up."

Criminy. "Usually when someone says something like that, it's for effect." Even if Georgie said it, he couldn't have possibly meant it.

She fixed me with her mole eyes. "Colton's dead, isn't he?"

Chapter Five

THE SIX-FOOT INFLATABLE gorilla waving at passing motorists from the corner of the parking lot made One Stop Party's location at the north end of town impossible to miss. I'm sure it wasn't the unofficial greeter the mayor wanted visiting tourists to see as they drove down from Port Townsend. But considering that the gorilla had replaced a blow-up bulldog that lifted its leg every time a car blasted by, no one I knew was complaining.

A chime sounded when I stepped inside, and the middle-aged woman stocking a shelf with glass cake toppers turned to me with a bright smile. "Welcome to One Stop Party."

"Those are pretty," I said, pointing to a heart-shaped one with twin swans at the base.

She set down the box she'd been holding. "Planning a wedding?"

Not voluntarily. "Actually, I'm here to see Eric or Mrs. Caldwell."

The woman's smile slipped. "Eric isn't a store employee."

"Oh, I thought he had something to do with hiring a limo driver."

"I wouldn't know."

"What about Mrs. Caldwell? Is she here?"

"Bethany?" She scoffed as if I had asked a stupid question. "She rarely makes an appearance, but her mother is the store owner. Would you like to speak with her?"

I was already here, so why not? "Yes, please."

I followed her to the far corner of the store where the woman who had booked the limo for Marietta's wedding was sitting at a desk cluttered with paper and framed photos.

"Diana? This young lady is interested in our limo service."

Leaning back in her chair, the attractive sixty-something wearing a cool smile pulled off her glasses and tucked a lock of her silver-blond bob behind her ear. "Excuse the mess." She removed a couple of catalogues from the chrome chair next to her desk. "Please."

I took a seat and grabbed my notebook.

"So, you're interested in our limo service," she said.

"Yes, I—"

"Wait." She pointed a slender finger at me. "Didn't we book a limo for you a few weeks ago?"

"For my mother—her June wedding."

"Ah yes, Marietta Moreau. I must say that we're thrilled to provide the limousine service for her big day."

"About that." I showed her my badge. "I need some information about your driver, Colton Ziegler."

She gave my badge a hard stare. "I don't understand. Has something happened with the limo?"

The limo? "No. I'm sorry to be the one to inform you, but Colton died early this morning after sustaining a head injury."

Flashing a diamond-encrusted wedding band as she covered her mouth, Diana sucked in a sharp breath. "Oh my gosh!"

"My condolences on the loss of one of your employees, Mrs. Ferguson, isn't it?"

"Correct."

"Ma'am, we need to establish a timeline for Colton's whereabouts last night."

She raised her hand like a traffic cop. "You'll need to speak to my daughter about that. She manages our limo service out of her home."

"Her name and phone number?"

After Diana Ferguson supplied me with her daughter Bethany's contact information, she slipped her glasses on and made a few mouse-clicks. "What about the limo?" she asked while focused on her computer screen.

"What about it?"

"We have a booking for this Friday, so was it damaged?"

Steve hadn't mentioned any damage, but that wasn't a question for me to answer. "I'm not aware of any damage, but since it's over at Bassett Motor Works, there must be some issue with it."

Puckering, she tossed her glasses to her desk and turned to me. "Great, that's all we need on top of everything else."

If this woman needed to vent about her inconvenience to a sympathetic ear, she was looking at the wrong girl. I only cared about the *everything else* part.

"Sorry." Standing, I snapped my notebook shut to nip this bitch session in the bud.

"What a dreadful night. First the break-in at the Pembrokes' and now this."

I sat my ass back down. "What break-in?"

"We were at the club for Malcolm Pembroke's retirement party last night, and this morning I heard from Katherine that they were robbed!"

The timing of the break-in caused me to think that someone who knew about the retirement party had been involved. Maybe someone who saw them leave.

Just hours before Colt was killed.

An icy prickle crawled over my skin. "Yes, it was a bad night all around, and I don't want to make today worse by taking too much of your time. But do you happen to know who rented the limo last night?"

"Absolutely. Me. Since my husband was hosting the party, I thought giving them a ride to it in style was the least I could do."

Making Malcolm and Katherine Pembroke two of the last people who saw Colt alive.

I used the navigation app on my cell phone to make my way north to the address Diana Ferguson had provided me. But once I drove past the abandoned farmland just outside of town, the higher I climbed up the bluff the more I wondered if I'd written the address correctly.

By the time I rounded a bend at the crest of the hill, the drizzle had finally let up, and a sign for Willoughby Manor came into view. Behind it perched a sprawling Tudor estate with contrasting brick accents around the dormer windows, giving them the appearance of eyes staring out at the bay.

Like most of the stately homes that had sprung up here over the last twenty years, only the Douglas firs and cedars lining the back of the property remained as native inhabitants of the bluff. Low ornamental shrubs and a putting green quality lawn now dominated the landscaping to afford an unobstructed water and Olympic Mountains view—what I guessed was a multimillion-dollar one.

And according to the app, I had arrived at my destination.

No way. Unless Eric Caldwell had inherited some serious money, how could he afford this mansion?

My answer came when I pulled out my notebook and compared the *102* I'd written down to the *100* carved into the Willoughby Manor sign.

"Nope, I'm only close to my destination." Which made more sense, because the Eric Caldwell I'd known had not been to the manor born. Since he had grown up in one of the clapboard row houses near the old mill, far from it.

I knew better than most that people from modest means could go on to experience tremendous financial success and live in lavish homes. My mother was one of them.

She'd also gone on to make some very poor decisions and almost lost her lavish home.

Okay, so maybe Marietta wasn't the greatest local success story.

If Eric Caldwell had landed on his feet up here and was living his version of happily ever after with Bethany, good for him. It didn't matter that I had never liked the arrogant prick. A man could change, and for his wife's sake I hoped he had.

So where the heck was 102 Willoughby Lane?

I saw no other houses, and the thick stand of trees marking the end of the paved road didn't look promising. But once I passed a weeping willow shrouding the corner of the property, a driveway to what appeared to be a carriage house emerged.

Covered with the same red velvet fudge brick as Willoughby Manor, it looked like someone had replicated the main house as a cozy cottage.

I pulled into a driveway bordered by flowering cherry trees and was immediately greeted by a beagle mix sounding the intruder alert.

"Hello," I said as I got out of the car. I let him sniff my extended hand but he kept barking, especially as I approached the cutie with the Minnie Mouse bike helmet wheeling up to me on a pink tricycle.

She shook a pudgy finger at the beagle. "Bodie, no."

He shut up, seemingly content to wag his tail at her, and she beamed at me. "He's *my* doggy."

"Madison!" called a stunning blonde charging out of the house with a toddler in her arms.

Madison wheeled around. "I got Bodie to stop barking, Mommy."

"Good job. Now go play in the backyard, please."

The little girl waved at me. "Bye."

As she and the beagle took off down a slab of concrete adjacent to the garage, her mom turned a cool gaze to me. "We've been working on how she's not supposed to talk to strangers."

Mom's implication was clear. She wasn't happy that I

was on her property, but I picked up no true sense of alarm. Since she waited expectantly, casually flexing her knees to bounce her increasingly fussy little one, quite the contrary.

Diana Ferguson had obviously called and told her about my visit to the party store.

"I guess it's hard not to show off when you're that cute," I said to diffuse the situation.

She shrugged, as good as saying, *Can we just get on with this?*

Taking that as my cue, I held out my badge. "I'm Charmaine Digby with the county coroner's office. Are you Bethany Caldwell?"

Without so much as a glance at the badge, she nodded. "You're here about Colt."

"You've heard the news."

"My mother called to tell me. Do you know what happened?"

"Maybe we should talk inside." Where it would be easier to take notes.

I got another nod and followed her into a beautiful kitchen of rich cream and gleaming marble, blending classic Tudor architecture with top-of-the-line modern conveniences.

Bethany lowered her son into a pricey-looking high chair that extended the color scheme into the adjoining dining area, and then opened the French door behind her. "Madison, stay where I can see you, please."

Taking a seat at the other side of the table, I pulled out my notebook while Bethany dropped a handful of fish-shaped crackers onto the tray of the high chair.

While the kid proceeded to gleefully chomp on a

little orange fish, Bethany eased into the chair next to him and flipped back the straight hair that had spilled over her shoulders. "What exactly happened to Colt?"

"He died early this morning from an apparent head injury."

She turned to watch Madison through the French door. "A head injury. Like from an accident?"

"The exact cause of death will have to be determined by a forensic pathologist." And when that would happen depended upon the availability of the doctor the county contracted with to perform the occasional autopsy.

"I see," she said on a sigh, staring out the glass.

"I understand that you recently hired Colt as a limo driver."

Bethany's gaze sharpened as it shifted to me. "Yes, and?"

"How had things been going?"

"Okay. We hadn't received any complaints about him, if that's what you mean."

"How about complaints from Colt himself about any of the customers?"

"Nothing like that. He seemed to like driving the limo, so..." With a shaky breath, she clamped her mouth shut and stared out at her daughter.

Bethany Caldwell could hide behind the mask of dutiful mother all she wanted. I didn't need to see her face to recognize a woman who had just censored herself.

"So?" I said over the volume of the clamoring toddler pounding the tray for more fish to stuff in his mouth.

Like an automaton, she reached into a plastic bag and dropped several more crackers in front of him. "I'm sorry, what?"

"You were saying something about the job he was doing for you." She wasn't, but her kid wasn't the only one in the room who wanted *more* from this chick.

"Yeah, well, it seemed to be going better than I thought it would when my husband first suggested hiring Colt."

"Then this had been Eric's idea." Which pretty much matched what Kendra had told me.

Bethany blinked. "You know my husband?"

"I went to high school with him."

"Then you also knew Colt, and how he didn't have the best reputation for being reliable."

"I didn't know him well, but yes."

"As you can probably imagine, my expectations weren't high, but like I said, it had been going okay."

Scribbling, I captured the gist of our conversation in my notebook. "Had Colt mentioned any trouble he was having with anyone?"

She tightened her brown-eyed gaze. "Not to me."

I didn't doubt that she had told the truth, but her tone suggested that I needed to direct my question to the other Caldwell adult living here.

"No issues that you know of with anyone working at Bassett Motor Works?" I asked to see how she'd react to the location where Colt's body was found.

Bethany cocked her head. "Why would there be?"

The reaction was negligible, so I assumed she didn't know anything about the proximity to where Georgie lived and worked.

I forced a smile. "Just asking."

"If anything, I'm the one having issues with that

place."

Oh, yeah?

"The limo was in the shop all week with George assuring me that they'd have it fixed for our weekend booking. And what happens?"

I had a sinking feeling that whatever happened had deadly consequences for Colt Ziegler.

"Colt called to tell me that the engine was making a clunking noise again." She folded her arms tight against her midriff, creating some enviable cleavage exposed by the deep V of her linen pullover.

This information didn't bode well for the removal of the cowbell thunk coming from the Jag, but I was more interested in the time of that call. "When was this?"

"I was already in bed, so it must have been around ten-thirty."

I noticed that she hadn't said *we* were in bed. "Was your husband home at the time?"

"Up with this one." Bethany thumbed at the little guy with the orange cracker-crumb lips. "Connor woke up with a fever and was sick most of the day, so I'd taken the day shift, and Eric took the night. Anyway, since Colt's apartment was near Bassett Motors, he offered to drop it off. Said he could walk home."

Which explained why I saw a white stretch limo when I visited George Senior this morning. "Did you get any other calls or texts from Colt last night?"

Bethany shook her head. "No, after Connor finally got to sleep, it was a very quiet night." Her lips curled into a sad smile. "Here anyway."

I didn't get the sense that there was anything else that she could tell me, so I pulled a business card from my tote and slid it across the table. "If you think of anything else, don't hesitate to let me know."

She nodded.

"Also, I'll need to speak with Eric—tomorrow if possible."

"You should probably call his assistant to set up an appointment." She went into the kitchen, opened a drawer near a cordless phone, and returned with a business card with the Ferguson Ford dealership logo.

I read his title: Sales Manager.

Yep, Eric Caldwell wouldn't be able to afford the mansion next door, but he had been coming up in the world.

"Thanks." Tucking his card into a pocket of my tote, I took what I figured might be my last look at her kitchen. "This is really lovely."

"Thank you. We like it."

"Out of curiosity, was this house a carriage house to Willoughby Manor?"

"No, my parents had it built as a wedding present to Eric and me."

Really. "It's darling—a cozy version of their house."

She squeezed out a smile, and didn't correct me.

Okay, so that explained how Eric and his wife could sit in the lap of this showplace's luxury.

I took a step toward the door. "Well, thank you for the information."

She lifted Connor from his high chair. "I'll see you out."

"No need. I've taken enough of your time."

Opening the front door, I caught a glimpse of sunshine glinting off the hood of a copper-colored vehicle on the other side of the short hedge. Since it had a collection of leaves plastered to the windshield, it looked like it had been there for a while.

"Sorry," I said, returning to the kitchen. "Whose car is out front?"

"Colt's. I figured he'd catch a ride with Eric tonight and...well..."

She didn't finish her thought. She didn't have to.

We both knew why that ride wasn't going to happen.

Chapter Six

BY THE TIME the gorilla greeter came into view it was just after four o'clock. Since Ray Ortiz kept the same early morning hours as Duke, I knew he'd most likely be en route to his ranch in Clatska. I had no desire to make the hour-long round trip this late in the day, so I added the feed store to the top of my list for tomorrow and turned right on Madrone Way.

Having been raised by a grandmother who was an avid gardener, I learned early on that this street got its name from the giant cinnamon-barked tree spreading its twisted limbs over the peeling Madrone Arms apartment sign. She'd also made it abundantly clear that she didn't want me to leave our quiet *uptown* neighborhood and ride my bike down here.

It wasn't that this apartment building or the one I now lived in three blocks away was inherently unsafe. But as I came to realize just days into my six-month lease, if I woke up to the blare of sirens, it was a safe bet that a member of Port Merritt's finest was on the way to my new *downtown* neighborhood.

Such was life in the low-rent district.

But I had my own place for the first time in my life,

and it had come to feel like home to me, sirens and all.

I turned into the Madrone Arms complex, where Colt Ziegler had made his home until yesterday, and wondered if Howie or any of his pals had stopped by this morning.

Switching off the ignition to mercifully silence the Jag's cowbell solo, I scanned the contents of the file Ben's assistant had given me and saw nothing to indicate that any of the neighbors had been questioned.

Not a shocker. Steve had arrested the primary suspect a half mile from here. There was no reason to canvass this neighborhood for witnesses to Colt's murder.

But that wasn't why I was here.

I was supposed to find a witness to the violence Tami claimed had been escalating between Georgie and Colt—an entirely different kettle of fish. My job was to cast out a net and see what I could reel in to strengthen the prosecution's case against one of my childhood friends.

Sometimes I hated my job.

Climbing out of my car, I could almost hear Steve telling me that this was a waste of time.

Part of me agreed with him wholeheartedly. There was no way that anyone living here could have heard Georgie and Colt in a whopper of a heated exchange without word of it getting back to Gossip Central.

The other part of me—the more pragmatic Char who had met plenty of witnesses reluctant to testify—wasn't so sure.

Based on the mostly empty parking lot, I had my doubts any of them would be home. Which meant I was going to have to stick around until well after six to give everyone time to return from work.

My stomach rumbled in protest at the prospect.

Blowing out a sigh, I wished I'd had the forethought to pack a protein bar in my tote. Even a few carrots would be good right now.

I didn't have those either. Dang it.

"I hate today," I muttered, popping a stick of sugar-free gum to give myself something else to chew on as I reviewed the copy of the police report I'd been given.

It didn't mention a roommate, but I figured I'd better start with Colt's apartment—unit 3 on the ground floor.

I knocked.

No answer.

I knocked again.

"He's not home yet," said a youthful voice behind me just as the cell phone in my tote started ringing.

With a more immediate need to find out what else this kid knew, I let the call go to voice mail and turned to see a ten- or eleven-year-old girl holding the collar of a big, furry black dog.

I didn't want to be the one to tell her the reason why Colt hadn't come home. I'd done enough of that today. "Do you live around here?"

She nodded and pointed to the apartment next door. "There."

"Does Mr. Ziegler live alone here?"

"No." She beamed at the dog. "He lives with Fozzie."

The dog's ears pricked up into perfect points at the mention of his name.

"Oh, I thought he was your dog."

"My mom won't let me have a dog, but Colt lets me dog-sit Fozzie, so we're good friends."

Crap. I was going to have to let someone know that

Fozzie now needed more than just a dog-sitter. "Is your mom home?"

She gave me another nod, and I followed her inside a tidy apartment that smelled like chocolate cake.

"Mama, this lady wants to talk to you."

A heavy-set forty-something in form-fitting sweats turned from the bowl of frosting she had been mixing with a wary look in her eyes. By the frown she leveled at the dog I knew I wasn't the only one she wasn't happy to see in her apartment.

"Lily, you know I don't want that animal in here."

"But he's lonely," Lily protested.

Her mother pointed at the door. "Out." The second her daughter shut the door behind her, the woman took a step toward me. "Are you here about the dog?"

The dog? "No, I'm with the coroner's office and I was hoping to talk to you about your neighbor, Colt Ziegler."

Grimacing, she shook her head. "I heard what happened from the police officer who was at his front door early this morning."

"A uniformed police officer?"

She nodded, motioning for me to have a seat on the sofa. "I had to leave for work, but I got the impression that he was waiting for someone."

Probably for Steve to arrive with a warrant to search the apartment. "I assume when you got home from work the police were gone."

She eased into a rocking chair and gave me a sad smile. "You'd never even know anything had happened."

I pulled a pen and my notebook from the tote at my feet. "If you don't mind, I'd like to ask you some questions about how things had been going around here."

"Okay, but I probably don't know much."

Given how observant she seemed, I doubted that. "May I have your name?"

"Anna Maxwell."

"And how well did you know Mr. Ziegler?"

"Not well. We only moved here a few months ago. He seemed good with kids, and Lily loved his dog. Really seemed to fill the void after leaving all her friends in Chicago."

"Any signs of trouble that he might have been having with any of the other neighbors?"

She shook her head. "Not that I'm aware of."

The apartment door opened and I knew that I'd need to choose my words carefully with the smaller pair of ears entering the room. "How about other visitors to the apartment? Any issues that you noticed?"

"No, nothing." Anna's expression softened as her daughter sidled up next to her. "You probably have some homework to do, don't you?"

Lily's long, walnut brown hair hung down over her cheeks as she stared at her canvas sneakers. "This is about Colt not coming home last night, isn't it?"

"Honey, you should go to your room and—"

"Yes, it is," I interjected, meeting the imploring gaze of a mom who wanted to spare her daughter the anguish of losing another friend. "Lily, how do you know that Colt never came home last night?"

She kept her head bowed, enviably thick lashes obscuring her eyes. "I didn't hear his car. It's loud and always wakes me up when he comes home late."

"Really loud," her mother added.

"And I didn't see it parked in front of his apartment this morning." Lily glanced up at me. "So I thought that Fozzie might—"

"Wait a second," Anna said to her daughter. "Where's the dog right now?"

Lily cringed. "I know I'm not supposed to let Fozzie in or out without asking first, but since no one's come to pick him up..."

"I assumed that some family or friends might come get him," Anna explained to me. "You know, because..."

"Because Fozzie got out?" Lily pulled back, her volume increasing. "I'm sure he didn't mean to."

I didn't want to get in the middle of what could develop into a difficult mother/daughter conversation. At the same time I needed this kid to tell me everything she knew. "Those are good questions and sound an awful lot like some of the things I'm wondering. If it's okay with your mom, I bet you could help us sort some stuff out."

Nodding her okay, Anna took Lily's hand.

I locked gazes with Lily. "Are you saying that Fozzie was able to get out of the apartment?"

She shrugged. "I guess somebody let him out."

"Maybe it was Colt. He knew he was going to be late coming home and—"

"No. That's why he asked me to dog-sit last night. I fed Fozzie dinner and then took him for a walk."

"Okay, what happened after you got back from your walk?"

Lily gave me a look as if I'd asked a stupid question. "I brought him back home."

"When was this?"

"I dunno." She turned to her mother.

"After we had our dinner, so probably around six-thirty," Anna said.

I made a note of that for the timeline of last night's events. "Did either of you see Fozzie later? Maybe before you went to bed?"

They both shook her heads.

"How about this morning?" I focused on Lily. "Since you didn't see Colt's car in the parking lot, I imagine you'd want to let Fozzie out to go potty."

"I was going to, but the police officer told me he wasn't there."

Then Colt had either walked back here after he delivered the limo to Bassett Motor Works, or someone who had access to his apartment had let the dog out.

Lily worried her lower lip. "Did Colt have an accident? Was that why Fozzie was up by the school?"

"You saw him near the school?" That was almost a mile away.

She nodded. "When I was walking home. And he was all by himself, so I knew somethin' was wrong."

Something was wrong, all right, and it was feeling more wrong by the minute.

I met Anna's gaze. "When did you get home today?"

"Around three-fifteen. She usually beats me home, but not today."

Lily's lips curled into an impish smile. "Fozzie didn't have his leash on, so he slowed me down."

Which explained why she had been holding the dog by the collar. "I noticed he wasn't on a leash when I got here."

"I looked for it when I let Fozzie in to give him some water, but I couldn't find it.

Anna groaned. "You let yourself into that apartment a second time today?"

Unlike her mom, I didn't care that Lily had violated a house rule. I just wanted to know how she had access to Colt's apartment. "Do you have a key?"

She shook her head. "Colt showed me where he hides it so that I could walk Fozzie when he's not around."

"Would you show me?"

Anna and I followed Lily to where a carved wooden statue of a bear wearing a brown hat stood outside apartment 3.

"It's in Fozzie Bear," Lily said, reaching around its back while the noisier Fozzie barked on the other side of the door.

She fitted the key into the lock and pushed the heavy door open. "It's just me, Fozzie."

The overgrown teddy bear dashed into the kitchen, where two stainless bowls sat empty under the counter, and barked.

"It's not dinnertime yet." She turned to me. "Colt and Fozzie always eat dinner together."

I exchanged glances with her mother because that wasn't going to happen tonight or any other night.

With a nod she stepped out of the apartment. "I'll call animal control."

"What's that?" Lily asked, closing the distance between them.

"Someone who will come pick up Fozzie."

The girl's eyes widened. "What?! Why?"

Anna placed her hand on Lily's slender shoulder. "Because something happened and Colt won't be coming home."

Lily stood very still. "Like ever?"

"I'm afraid not. That's why we need to call someone to—"

"But I can take care of Fozzie," she protested, her voice breaking.

"Sweetheart, you know that won't work." Anna met my gaze. "I have asthma. Can't handle pet dander."

Lily sobbed, her sweet face crumpling like wet newspaper. "But Fozzie needs me!"

The dog came to her side as if she had called him, and Lily wrapped her arms around his neck. "You don't have anyone else now."

That's when he aimed his big brown eyes at me.

Don't even think about it, dog.

A dog needed a yard—a place to run.

I looked around the dump of an apartment—empty beer cans and Roadkill Grill takeout bags littering the stained shag carpeting, dirty dishes in the sink.

Of course, no one could say that Fozzie had anything close to an ideal home here.

He also wouldn't have much of a future.

Unless...

Crap.

Anna touched my sleeve. "I'll go make that call before it gets too late."

It was already too late.

"No, don't," my mouth blurted out before I could put a muzzle on it. "I'll keep him tonight, and then I'll find out what Colt's family would like to do with him."

Lily looked up, blinking away tears. "*You're* keeping him?"

Yeah, I couldn't believe I'd said it either.

Chapter Seven

AFTER I LOADED Fozzie's dog bowls, his toys, and an almost empty sack of dog chow into the trunk of my car, I slid behind the wheel and listened to the voice message from the call I missed.

"You're needed at home as soon as possible," my mother said while the giant fur ball in the passenger seat panted in my other ear.

She hadn't injected much of a sense of urgency into her message. In fact, given Marietta Moreau's flair for drama, the one-liner had been delivered in an uncharacteristic monotone.

"She's up to something," I told Fozzie.

He poked his nose out the passenger window and looked back at Lily, waving to him from the door of her apartment.

"Yep, not our biggest problem at the moment."

I gave Lily a wave as we pulled out of the parking lot. "I'll find out what's going on, and then we'll head home."

Ignoring me, Fozzie sniffed the air, heavy with the food smells venting from all the burger and pizza joints on Main Street gearing up for the dinner crowd.

"I won't be long," I told him a few minutes later,

when I parked in front of the two-story Victorian where I'd grown up.

I cracked the windows to give him plenty of air and then headed up the steps bordered by yellow and violet crocuses. It wasn't until my grandmother stepped out from behind the giant rhododendron blooming in front of the den window that I saw her.

"Hi, Gram. What's going on?"

She set the watering can she was holding on the white wooden porch and planted her hands on her ample hips. "Don't tell me your mother called you."

I kissed her on the cheek. "Okay, I won't tell you."

Scowling, she squinted at my car. "What the heck is that in your front seat?"

"A dog."

"And *why* is there a dog in your car?"

I sighed. "It's a long, sad story." One that I didn't want to bring to my grandmother's doorstep. She had enough aggravation with my mother as an uninvited houseguest until her wedding. "I'm helping out a friend who can't take care of his dog right now."

Sort of true.

"Oh, that is sad. Anyone I know?"

Probably. "It's just a guy I know through work."

She gave my shoulder a pat and resumed watering the two baskets of pink and white impatiens hanging from the porch eaves. "You're a nice girl to help out."

Not that nice. I'd just lied to my grandmother.

And I needed to change the subject. "So, what's the emergency?"

"As far as I'm concerned there isn't one, but perhaps you should speak with your mother." Gram opened the front door for me and then went back to watering her flowers.

"Aren't you coming in?"

She shook her head, carving creases into her upper lip as she puckered. "Not on a bet."

Stifling a sigh, I stepped inside and shut the door behind me. "Mom?"

"Oh, good. You're home," the former Mary Jo Digby said, padding barefooted down the stairs in black leggings and a belted leopard print tunic. Since I usually saw her in five-inch stilettos, she seemed atypically short.

Short could also be used to describe the way she whisked past me, leaving me in a vapor trail of musky jasmine.

"What's going on?" I asked, following my mother to the kitchen table.

She picked up a white envelope and held it out to me. "See for yourself."

The thick linen envelope appeared to have been addressed in an elegant female hand, and not to anyone who lived here. "Why do you have Steve's mail?"

That my boyfriend lived across the street from my grandmother was very inconvenient at times. And this definitely qualified as one of those times.

"Never mind that." She tapped the back of the envelope with her finger. "Look at who it's from."

I turned it over. "G. Campanella." I locked gazes with Marietta. "So?"

"*Gina* Campanella," she said like I should recognize the name.

I shrugged.

"The Los Angeles news anchor."

I tossed the envelope onto the table. "I haven't been living in LA like some people, so forgive me for never having heard of her."

Marietta ran a tongue over her glossy red lips like a vampire savoring the taste of fresh blood. "She used to be a reporter for one of the Seattle stations. I guess that's how she and Steve met, when she interviewed him about some high-profile case he was working."

I didn't like the direction this was going.

"How do you know this?" Because there was no way that Steve would have gone out of his way to chat with her about when he worked for Seattle PD.

"Your grandma. She met Gina when he brought her home to meet his mother."

Holy cannoli! Gina Campanella had to be the ex-girlfriend Steve almost married two years ago.

And I'd had no idea that the feisty old bird outside knew anything about her. Which had to be by design, because Gram was the world's worst when it came to keeping secrets from me.

Or so I had thought.

"Anyway," Marietta said, inspecting a lacquered nail. "Gina's quite the rising star in the LA market. And now that she's marrying Chad Cornell—"

"The actor?"

"Director now, too, so her star is going to be so very shiny down there."

"Good for her," I said, hoping that we could now stop talking about her fabulous life.

"No kidding. The wedding will surely be quite the who's-who affair." Marietta picked up the envelope, her green eyes gleaming as she ran her fingers over it. "So, do you think you'll be going?"

"I have no idea."

She tucked the envelope into my tote. "Perhaps you could find out."

"Because you'd like Steve to make this a plus-two." And add a little luster to her star.

Averting her gaze, she smoothed her cropped auburn hair. "I never said that."

Not directly, anyway.

"But I do have business that requires me to be down there next month, so depending on the date of the wedding...I might be available. You know, to get together while you're in town."

I didn't want to say *Liar, liar, pants on fire* to my mother, but flames should have been coming out of her butt by now.

"I'll give Steve the invitation." Having no desire to join Gina as the newest member of Steve's ex-girlfriends club, that's all I was going to do.

"I look forward to hearing what he says about it," Marietta said, following me to the door.

Me, too.

After I crossed the street to drop Steve's mail in his box, I texted him to find out what his plans were for dinner, and then drove to the Valu-Mart to pick up a new leash.

I'd be the first to admit that dating the only detective in town required a measure of flexibility when it came to meal planning. But a girl on a diet who has had a really bad day can be fresh out of flexibility when that cop finally calls her back after two hours of ignoring her texts and phone calls.

As had become Steve's typical greeting, the first word I heard was, "Sorry."

But he had nothing to be sorry for, because his day had to have been worse than mine.

"Don't worry about it," I said, trying to keep up with my temporary roommate on a post-dinner walk toward a certain auto repair shop.

"Did you eat?"

"Yep." Didn't mean I wasn't still hungry after wolfing down some leftover chicken, but I didn't want his company at the moment. "How about you?"

"I ordered a pizza. I know you're on that diet of yours, but I could come over and you could watch me eat it."

"You really know how to tempt a girl."

"Hey, if you're lucky I'll let you lick my fingers."

"Now you're just being mean," I said over the motor-cycle rumbling past me on the highway.

"Where are you?"

Within sight of the Bassett Motor Works sign, and there was no way I was going to mention that to Steve. "Out on a walk."

"When are you gonna be home?"

"In an hour, and I'll expect your fingers to be grease-free when you show up."

"Spoilsport."

Maybe, but I pocketed my phone knowing that I'd bought myself some time at Bassett Motor Works without Steve asking me the inevitable question: *What do you think you're doing there?*

Much like this morning, I wasn't sure of the answer.

Was it simply to gain some understanding about what happened to the guy who should have been the one taking his dog for a walk?

Did I need to bolster my faith that Georgie couldn't have had anything to do with Colt's death?

Or did I just need to get a clue as to what to do next?

As I stood in front of Bassett Motors' padlocked gate and tried to glean some sense of the scene that played out early this morning, Fozzie looked up at me like he wished I would hurry up and get that clue.

"I know they're closed. We're just going to look around."

Sounding eerily like a bored Marietta, he huffed a breath.

"Come on," I said, leading him toward the front corner of the yard, where the police report had indicated Colt's body had been found.

If the patch of weeds I found there truly was the crime scene, it sure didn't look like much.

Fozzie lingered over a rusty nail next to some old dog poo. Other than that, he seemed disinterested until his nose led him to a scrubby sapling bordering the chain link fence that he lifted his leg on.

While I waited for him to finish his business, I listened to a truck's chattering brakes as the driver slowed to make a right onto Madrone Way—pretty much the only sound on the block other than some birds roosting in the stand of fir trees populating the ravine behind the yard.

As could be said about any patch of dirt in Port

Merritt, come nightfall it would be a nice, quiet place to leave someone to die. At one or two in the morning, even quieter, but between the floodlight illuminating the row of cars parked on the other side of the fence and the outdoor light affixed to the auto glass building next door, not completely dark.

The only way it made sense for Colt's body to be found here was if he collapsed at this spot after being injured somewhere out of view from potential witnesses driving by.

I peered through the chain links at a tall SUV that could have afforded Georgie perfect cover to bash Colt in the head with a bat, and shivered.

"No way," I said, tightening my jacket around me.

I'd seen him smash a ball with a bat countless times in high school, but to do the same kind of damage to a human target? I couldn't see that at all.

I also couldn't see what had claimed Fozzie's focus as he pulled me toward the ravine while barking sharp and loud.

"What?"

Not that I had expected some kind of psychic connection between the dog and his former master to manifest itself where Colt had taken his last breaths. But if some bloodhound in Fozzie had picked up a trail...

I ran to keep up with him, almost tripping over a blackberry vine snaking around a short stump.

"Criminy!" I exclaimed, my adrenaline spiking while the barking intensified. "What'd you find?"

No sooner than the words came out of my mouth I saw a squirrel scamper up a tree.

"Really, dog? We have better things to chase after

here than a squirrel."

A barking Rufus, running up to the fence, appeared to echo my sentiments.

That's when Fozzie gave up on the squirrel and upped the volume of the barking chorus at the fence.

"Time to go." Before the six-foot-six *Dog* living in the little apartment above the office came out here with another baseball bat.

I heard a door slam. "Rufus!"

Uh-oh.

"Fozzie, come!" Yanking on his leash while he continued his barking tirade, I tried to pull sixty pounds of dead weight toward the street.

"Shut up, Rufus," Georgie shouted over the decibel level of the dogs.

Crap! It was bad enough that I was sneaking around the scene of the crime with a dog as my witness. I didn't want any humans to see me doing it, especially the one charged with the crime.

"Come on!" I grabbed Fozzie's collar to insert myself between the animals, and he nipped me.

I reared back, the fleshy skin below my wrist burning. "Crikey!"

"Rufus, down!"

While Fozzie growled at the new addition on the other side of the fence, I met the gaze of George Bassett Junior.

"You okay, Char?"

"Yeah, I...uh..." I needed a believable lie, pronto.

Not that I made a habit of lying to my friends, but complete honesty wouldn't serve me well at this moment. "My dog and I are still getting acquainted."

Georgie pointed at my hand. "Let me see."

I held it out to him.

"He broke the skin. You'd better come in." Without waiting for a response, he headed toward the gate with Rufus hot on his heels.

I glared at Fozzie. "Thanks a lot." Not only did I need to come up with a good reason to be on the property, I needed to do it having suddenly acquired a dog. *Colt Ziegler's dog.*

I could only hope that man and beast had never met one another before. Otherwise, this conversation was going to become very complicated.

Fozzie's ears relaxed, his tongue lolling as if nothing had happened.

"You don't look very sorry," I said, leading him to the gate.

He ignored me, probably because he was smart enough to realize that this dog-walker wouldn't be in his life after tomorrow.

As we stepped through the narrow opening, I pulled up on Fozzie's leash to remind him who was supposed to be in charge. "Mind your manners."

Georgie rolled the gate shut and then leaned over to stroke Fozzie's ear. "He looks like a handful. When did you get him?"

"Technically, he's not mine. I'm just dog-sitting."

Georgie nodded. "Part chow, maybe?"

I had no idea. I was just relieved that he didn't seem to recognize Fozzie. "Maybe."

"Where's your dog?" I asked, hearing barking as we made on our way to the garage, but it sounded far away.

"I put him inside the apartment. Didn't want any

trouble in case the two of 'em didn't get along."

I couldn't blame him. He'd seen enough trouble today.

Georgie turned on the water at the utility sink to the left of the sedan with its hood open, handed me a bar of soap, and took Fozzie's leash. "Wash up."

He wrapped the leash around the car's bumper. "Sit."

Fozzie immediately plopped his butt down on the cement floor.

"Wow, I'm impressed." I was also more than a little envious at the quick rapport that had been established.

"You gotta show 'em who's boss."

The bigger dog in this garage was clearly the dominant male. I knew it, Fozzie knew it, and after at least two tussles with him, Colt should have known it too.

So, what had possessed him to go up against Georgie one last time?

It seemed so improbable, much like the two little puncture wounds just below my wrist.

It just shouldn't have happened, today or any day.

"Excuse me, Chow Mein," Georgie said, using the nickname Steve gave me back when the three of us shared the same third-grade classroom.

Shutting off the water, I grabbed a paper towel and stepped aside to let him pull a first aid kit from the shelf above the sink. "It's not like I'm bleeding to death."

Ignoring me, he took the kit to a workbench, where he silently waited for me.

"Okay, if you insist."

Again, no response.

The silence was fine with me. After all the years I'd

known him, it didn't feel the least bit uncomfortable, but as Georgie motioned to the stool next to him, the tightening in my chest told me that feeling was about to change.

He took my hand, bringing it close to inspect the wound. "Doesn't look too bad. Does it hurt?"

Not as much as what I had to ask him was going to hurt. "It's nothing."

Tearing open a packet, he wiped my red, raw skin with an antiseptic towelette.

I flinched a little, but he gently held my hand in place with his big mitt. "Don't want it to get infected," he said. Then, with the skill of a nurse who had dressed the wounds of a thousand patients, he applied ointment and a bandage.

He gave me a goofy smile as if to tell me everything was going to be fine.

I stood to give him a hug. "Thanks, Dog."

Patting my back like a wrestler who wanted out of the hold I had him in, he pulled away. "I should probably get back to work. We're really behind with... Well, you know."

Yeah, and I needed to know more. "Georgie, could I ask you a couple of questions about what happened last night?"

He shook his head. "I have to give you the same answer I gave a reporter who came snooping around here earlier."

"I'm not trying to snoop. I need to know more facts so I can help you."

"Doesn't matter. My lawyer says I can't talk to any-body about it but her."

"I understand, but maybe you could confirm something your dad already told me about Colt Ziegler trying to break into that white limo."

"I don't know." He raked his sausage fingers through his shock of red hair. "My dad probably shouldn't have said anything."

"But he did, so I already know about it. But what I don't understand is why Colt was breaking into the car that he brought here."

"How the heck should I know?"

"Well, did he try to explain?"

Georgie smirked. "He was too busy running."

"From you and Rufus."

"Just me."

"And your bat."

He gave me a chilling stare. "I should get back to work."

I touched the sleeve of his coverall. "I don't care that you had a bat. You were defending your property and the cars that were left in your care. Just tell me, did you hit Colt with that bat?"

"No," he stated, abruptly marching toward the gate.

But George Senior had told me that some contact had been made, so that *No* didn't jive.

"Wait up!" I untied Fozzie and ran to the gate. "Say it to my face. Did you hit him in the head with that bat?"

"No!"

Was that fear pulling at his eyebrows? Fear of being found out? Fear of what he had done?

"Did you get a good-enough look?" he barked, a bead of sweat trickling down his temple "No!"

The whites of his eyes were painted with anxiety, his

pupils twice what they had been when he was bandaging my hand.

Something had happened in the exchange he had with Colt. Something bad that he didn't want me to know.

I wrapped my arms around him while my heart shattered. "Take care, Georgie, and thanks for fixing me up."

A minute later, I stood with Fozzie at the locked gate and watched one of my oldest friends stalk away in deafening silence. "Hope your dad got you a really good lawyer, 'cause you're gonna need one."

Chapter Eight

TWENTY MINUTES LATER, I opened the door to my apartment and Fozzie's thick tail didn't clear the doorway before he started barking at the guy making himself at home on my loveseat.

"It's okay," I said, unhooking his leash. "That man won't bite."

Steve turned off the TV and frowned at the dog growling at him from the parquet entryway. "The heck I won't." He turned that frown on me. "What's with Cujo?"

"His name's Fozzie, and I'm sort of dog-sitting."

Steve's chocolate brown gaze sharpened. "Sort of?"

"Until I find him a new home."

"That wouldn't be because he recently lost his owner, would it?"

"Something like that." With Fozzie anchoring himself to my side, I filled his water bowl at the kitchen sink.

When I turned to set it down, Steve was leaning against the refrigerator and Fozzie had backed into the corner.

"What are you doing, Char?" Steve asked, arms folded across his solid chest.

"I'm giving him some water. Do you mind?"

"I mean, what are you doing with Colt Ziegler's dog?"

Taking Steve by the arm, I led him back to the loveseat. "I had to interview his neighbors, and when one of them mentioned animal control, and her kid started crying, I thought I should see if Colt's sister would take him."

Staring at the big black dog poking his head out of the kitchen, Steve blew out a breath. "This is not your problem to solve."

Maybe then, but it was my problem now.

I rested my head on his shoulder. "It's just one night."

"Uh-huh."

After several beats of silence in which Fozzie inched closer, I reached out my bandaged hand. "Just come over and say hello."

He made it as far as the garage-sale coffee table I had acquired last month, and then crawled under it as if to shelter himself from the more disapproving human in the room.

"I think you're making him nervous," I said to Steve.

He yawned and unfolded himself from the loveseat. "I can fix that problem pretty quickly."

Both Fozzie and I sat up. "You're leaving? You just got here."

"It's been a long day, and it's not over yet."

"You have to go back to work?"

"I had to join the captain at a press conference today, so I've got a bunch of paperwork to finish up."

I pushed off the loveseat. "To process Little Dog's arrest?"

"That's not the only case I've got, Chow Mein."

I wrapped him in my arms. "Sorry. I know it's been a miserable day all around."

He kissed the top of my head. "There's a leftover slice of pizza in the box on the counter, if that will help you feel better."

"Did it help you?"

"Nope."

I kissed Steve good-bye and then turned to the sound of Fozzie's toenails on the parquet kitchen floor.

Short of jumping up on the Formica counter, his snout couldn't reach the small white box, but I also didn't want to ask for any more trouble today.

"Pizza isn't for dogs," I told him as I popped the box into the microwave.

It also wasn't for a girl who needed to lose another five pounds to fit into her bridesmaid dress for her mother's wedding. But it had been a really crappy day, and I wanted to believe that an application of gooey cheese could salve the sting.

A minute later, Fozzie followed me when I carried the box to the dining table sandwiched between the kitchen and the living room, and took a seat.

Staring at the white box, he sat and licked his chops.

"Not dog food. People food."

Surprisingly, I heard no whining or whimpering. He simply appeared to be waiting as if he had been trained that exhibiting patience would pay off in edible dividends.

"This is a familiar routine for you, huh?"

Fozzie answered with a *woof*. Not sounding so much like begging, but more as an appropriate response to a cue he recognized.

"Sorry, boy," I said, reaching for the slice of Steve's favorite pepperoni and sausage combo. "You may have been taught to sing for your supper, but if you'll recall, you already ate."

Technically so had I, and the congealing cheese was rapidly losing its appeal.

I dropped the pizza slice back in the grease-stained box, my imagination conjuring an image of a battered Colt Ziegler as the life slowly oozed out of him.

Recoiling, I clutched the edge of the table to vanquish the picture from my mind and felt Fozzie's rough tongue drag over my bandage.

At first I had thought he was offering me a little comfort. Then I realized that he just wanted to lick the grease from my fingers.

"Not so interested in biting me now, are you?" I asked, enjoying the distraction of his black tongue as it worked.

He wagged his tail, his pointy ears pinned back.

"I know. You're sorry."

I picked up the pizza box and Fozzie followed me into the kitchen, where I dumped my would-be salve in the sink.

His mouth gaped open as if I had committed culinary sacrilege.

"Trust me, it's not going to make anything about today better. We're still gonna have to find you a new home."

He gave me another soft *woof*.

"Fine. You had a rough day, too."

I picked off three of the pepperoni slices and fed

them to Fozzie one by one.

"Happy now?"

I could have sworn I saw him grin before he trotted off to make himself comfy in the living room.

Yeah, he was happy. And I had the feeling that I had just been schooled by a dog.

After tossing and turning for a couple of hours, I padded into the living room around two and watched *Sleepless in Seattle* for the umpteenth time.

Sure, I lived over thirty miles away in Port Merritt.

Close enough.

Like Steve a few weeks back when a Seattle station was featuring films shot in the region, Fozzie fell asleep long before Meg Ryan found her happily ever after with Tom Hanks.

Not me. I may have had a pillow and a nice soft quilt with me on that loveseat, but the moment I'd drift off to la-la land I'd envision Colt Ziegler lying in those weeds. Worse, a tall faceless man stood over him holding a bat.

Dear God, I didn't want it to be Georgie.

But since he couldn't lie to me with any conviction, I feared that Ben Santiago would attack this case like a shark smelling blood in the water. And by the time the prosecution rested, no one would doubt the identity of the batter who was up that night: George Bassett Junior.

I threw back the quilt and scrubbed my face. "Jeez Louise." Georgie was in deeper than deep doo-doo.

When I turned off the TV, Fozzie cracked open an eye.

"Don't even try to tell me you were watching that," I said, stepping around him to get to the kitchen.

I started brewing a pot of coffee and noticed he was standing at the door.

"You realize that it's not even four-thirty yet, right?"

Fozzie didn't budge.

"There's no way that Colt took you out this early."

He pawed at the door.

"Fine. Give me five minutes. Are you a runner? Because we might as well get some exercise while we're out there."

He looked back at me and huffed.

"Yes, I know you're a dog. Stupid question."

❋

Yawning, I parked in front of Ray's Feed and Supply and dragged my butt out of the car.

"Be good," I said, pointing at the fur ball in the passenger seat that had run me ragged four hours earlier. "I'm just going to ask a few questions and then we'll go visit your new mom."

At least I hoped Colt's sister Kendra would be willing to take Fozzie.

I knew that she and her husband owned a house near the south shore of Merritt Bay—a quiet pastoral neighborhood lined with horse and bike trails, and where dogs chased squirrels to their hearts' content.

Fozzie would love it there. Couldn't say the same for the squirrels, but they were the least of my concerns today.

After I talked to Kendra, I needed to schedule an appointment with Eric Caldwell and finish interviewing Colt's neighbors. With any luck, also some of his friends.

But first up was Ray Ortiz.

I'd always liked Mr. Ortiz. All the kids did. He'd have a twinkle in his ebony eyes, and a kindly smile on his shoe-leather face when he'd treat us from the stash of candy he kept under the register for his hypoglycemic wife.

The shoe leather was well-worn now, and I didn't expect to be handed any treats, but the same smile greeted me as I stepped through the door.

"Charmaine," he said, standing at a rotating display of brightly colored seed packets. "What brings you here this beautiful morning?"

Considering the reason for my visit, he seemed a little too chipper.

He doesn't know.

I labored to keep my smile from slipping as I walked past an aisle stacked with pungent sacks of dog and cat food.

"Something for your granny's garden?" He waved a packet of cucumber seeds at me. "We've got a sale running this week that she might be interested in."

"I'll let her know. Actually..." I lowered my voice as a customer headed to the register with Seth, the other employee I'd seen with Colt the last time I was here. "I wonder if I could speak with you in private."

Mr. Ortiz raised a heavy silver brow. "Of course. We can talk out back."

He said a few words to Seth, who shot me a wary glance, and then I followed Mr. Ortiz through a back room filled with mulch and fertilizer to a redwood picnic table covered by a faded green and white awning.

"Something wrong?" he asked, easing himself down

on the bench seat.

I sat on the bench across from him and pulled out my notebook. "I'm afraid so. I'm here on behalf of the county coroner to ask you some questions about Colt Ziegler."

His forehead split into deep furrows. "The coroner. Are you telling me—"

"I'm sorry, yes. His body was found early yesterday morning."

Sounding like he was venting steam, Mr. Ortiz slowly shook his head. "I knew that kid was going to get himself into more trouble."

More trouble? I needed to get him to elaborate.

He leaned in, his voice barely audible as if it were being muffled by his soup-strainer mustache. "So what happened to him?"

I didn't want to get into any details other than what he could tell me. "That's still being pieced together, but we're talking to people who knew him to get a sense of what was going on in his life."

"I'll tell you what was going on with him. Same problem that a lot of kids his age have: entitlement."

I was Colt's age. Not that Mr. Ortiz cared about how I might interpret his editorial comments, but none of my friends acted like the world should cast roses at their feet.

"So, were you having some sort of attitude problem with him here at work?" I asked.

"Kind of. But in the form of some sticky fingers."

"Colt was stealing from you?"

"I guess he got tired of waiting for a raise."

I scribbled *stealing* in my notebook.

"It started with a couple of sacks of dog food." Mr. Ortiz's eyes hardened to onyx. "Then cash started disappearing from the till."

"I assume you confronted him about it."

"Yeah, right before I fired him."

"And when was this?"

"Almost a month ago. Had to get the missus to increase her hours on the weekends. Seth, too. At least he seemed happy to make some extra money."

"Anything else going on with Colt that you noticed?"

"Like what?"

"Issues or problems that he might have mentioned."

"Whatever problems he had were probably of his own making. But no, until stuff started disappearing, I didn't get the sense that anything was wrong."

I didn't see much point in taking any more of his time until I saw his tan lips flatten as if he wanted to block the words at the tip of his tongue. "But maybe there was something you noticed?"

He shifted his gaze to the surface of the picnic table that had been carved with dozens of initials. "It hardly seems worth mentioning."

"I won't share anything you tell me with anyone else." Except for Ben, and maybe Steve if it would get some heat off of Georgie.

"It's just that last month I had to break up a little scuffle between Seth and Colt."

"Define 'little scuffle.'"

Mr. Ortiz's lips made another disappearing act behind his mustache. "It was more of a shouting match than anything else. You know, just two male dogs barking at one another."

Yeah, I'd heard plenty of that last night. Only unlike those two male dogs, Colt Ziegler was found dead not long after. "Do you know what it was about?"

He shook his head. "I couldn't get either one of them to talk, so I put Seth to work in the yard out here to keep them separated the rest of the day."

"Okay. Would you mind if I talked to Seth about this?"

"Sit tight." Mr. Ortiz swung his legs out from under the picnic table. "I'll ask him to finish what he's doing and come on back."

I was in the process of writing down everything I could remember hearing over the last five minutes when I looked up to see Seth step to the table.

Wearing a faded blue T-shirt that revealed tattooed biceps, he spread his long legs in a military stance. "You wanted to talk to me?"

I pointed at where his boss had been sitting. "If you don't mind."

Looking as enthusiastic as a kid who had been sent to the principal's office, Seth slid onto the bench seat.

"We haven't officially met." I reached across the table. "Charmaine Digby."

He gave my hand a quick shake with a firm and calloused grip. "Seth Lukin."

"I work for the coroner's office."

I watched him to determine how much more I needed to explain.

By his solemn nod, I knew that I'd said enough. "May I ask you a couple of questions about your relationship with Colt Ziegler?"

A muscle twitched at the corner of his mouth, his

gaze focused on my notebook. "I guess."

Since Seth had appeared guarded from the outset of my arrival, I figured I should start with something innocuous and asked for his contact information and date of birth.

He recited the particulars in a precise monotone. Definitely former military. Since he was just shy of his thirtieth birthday and appeared to be quite the physical specimen, maybe it hadn't been that long ago that a uniform covered those tattoos.

"How long have you worked here, Seth?"

He pushed back a length of razor-cut brown hair with a left hand that wasn't adorned by a wedding ring. "A couple of years."

"How about Colt? When did he start?"

"Last November."

"How well did you know him?"

Seth glanced up from looking at my notebook. "Well enough."

That told me nothing, which I assumed had been the intent. "Well enough to hang out? Maybe go out for a beer after work?"

The muscle twitched again. "We did that...a while back."

"A while back before Colt was fired?"

"Yeah," Seth said with a sardonic edge.

Clearly, this guy wouldn't be a pallbearer. "I heard you two had some sort of a fight."

"Not really."

More like not anything he wanted to talk about. "What was it, then?"

"It's...complicated."

I pasted a smile on my face. "A lot of relationships are."

"Let's just say we had a disagreement about a mutual friend."

"Who was the friend?"

Seth fixed his gaze on me for the first time since he sat down. "No one who had anything to do with him getting killed."

He obviously believed that to be the truth, but I still wanted to know. "I need a name, in case we need to talk to him."

"Her."

I put my pen to the notebook that he was back to staring at. "Name, please."

"Jessica Tuohy."

I didn't know her. "Does she live around here?"

He nodded. "With me."

"Would it be safe to say that Colt liked her as more than just a friend?"

I got another nod.

Yeah, it was complicated, all right.

"Other than this 'disagreement' you two were having over Jessica, did you have any other beefs with Colt?"

"No," Seth said flatly.

Too flatly, because that mouth twitch was telling me something else was going on in his brain. "No other problems?"

He pressed his lips together and shook his head.

Fine. Maybe Steve could get him to talk. "Any mention of issues he was having with someone else?"

"You mean other than Little Dog?"

Crap.

Chapter Nine

"WHAT THE HECK was his problem with Georgie?" I asked for the third time since hitting the highway.

And just like the other two times, Fozzie wasn't spilling any beans about his former owner.

One of Colt's friends had to know something. Certainly his sister seemed to have been holding something back yesterday.

"We can only hope she'll have a looser tongue without her mother around. Right, Fozzie?"

Ignoring me, he stuck his nose out the open window as I made the left turn onto Morton Road, and didn't move until we passed the horse farm near the five-mile marker.

That's when his sniffer started working overtime.

"What do you think? Like the smell of the new neighborhood?"

He turned to me with the same doggy grin I'd seen last night.

"Good. It'll be better than living in some old apartment." Especially mine.

Slowing as I rounded the next bend, I checked the numbers on the mailboxes and finally spotted one with the name *Sparks* in reflective lettering.

Just past the stand of mailboxes, an arrow on a lam-inated yard sign for Sparks Tree Service pointed the way down a one-lane road bordered by pasture land on the right and ranch-style houses on the left. The fourth house at the end of the road had another tree service yard sign out front.

"This must be the place," I said, parking in front of a tall cedar edging the driveway.

Fozzie whimpered when I reached behind his seat to grab my tote.

I patted his head. "Let me talk to her first, then I'll come back and get you."

Standing in his seat as I opened the driver's side door, he barked, sharp and loud.

"What's the matter with you?"

With his attention focused on the garage of the hon-eydew green house, he answered with more barking.

"Dog, this is not the way to make a good first impres-sion." I climbed out of the car and wagged a finger at him. "If you want to get adopted, be good."

Once again, he ignored me, but as I walked by the cherry red minivan parked in the driveway, I heard the reason why: A chorus of barking from two black dogs at the side yard fence.

The front door opened before I reached the porch. "I guess I shouldn't be surprised to see you here today," Kendra said with the warmth my grandmother typically reserves for door-to-door salesmen.

As I approached I noticed her swollen eyelids. She was also wearing an oversized sweatshirt with plaid pajama bottoms—obviously expecting some alone time to grieve.

Sorry, Kendra. "I was hoping you could help me sort through a couple of things your mom brought up yesterday."

Heaving a sigh, Kendra swung the door open to let me in. "I don't know that there's much more I can tell you, but we can talk at the table."

I followed her into an outdated galley kitchen with scuffed hardwood flooring, honey oak cabinets, and dingy wallpaper. It smelled of burnt coffee and whatever leftovers were clinging to the dirty dishes stacked on the counter.

If the kitchen was the heart of the home, this one screamed for resuscitation. Only the cute factor of the baby pictures hanging next to a corner hutch added a little life to the room.

"How old are your kids?" I asked, over the volume of the dogs barking at me from the other side of a sliding-glass door.

"Five and seven."

Good. They'd most likely be in school, so no need to worry about little ears hearing not so nice things about Uncle Colt.

While Kendra pushed a pile of papers and a laptop to the far end of the dinette table, the two dogs outside continued to loudly protest my existence. "Sorry for the mess. I was trying to get caught up with some bills after being gone most of yesterday."

"No worries."

She pointed at the chair I was standing next to. "Please sit, or they'll never settle down."

While I slipped into a high-backed chair with a

stained seat cushion, she turned to the two dogs. "That goes for you, too. Sit!"

Taking the seat opposite me, Kendra glanced back at the two black fur balls giving me the death stare as they lowered their rumps to the wooden deck. "They don't know you, so they'll probably give you the evil eye while you're here."

Better than getting it from one of Steve's old girl-friends. "They're beautiful animals." The larger of the two looked a lot like Fozzie. "Are they related?"

"Mother and daughter. The mom's the Chow Chow."

I had a feeling I had left her son in the front seat of my car.

Tucking back several strands of brown hair that had escaped her ponytail, Kendra worried her lips. "Could you tell me if there's any news...you know...about...?"

"About the cause of death?"

Kendra nodded, her dark eyes glistening with tears.

From what I'd learned when I stopped at the court-house to check my messages, Colt's autopsy had been scheduled for tomorrow. "Nothing yet. We should know more later in the week."

She grabbed a tissue from the box by the laptop and wiped her eyes. "But you think George Bassett did this."

I didn't want to, but so far, no one had come forward with any information to convince me otherwise. "I honestly don't know what to think. That's why I'm here."

While she blew her nose, I reviewed my notes. "Yes-terday, your mother mentioned that there was a period of time where you weren't speaking to your brother."

Shaking her head, Kendra winced. "He made a big mistake, and looking back on it, I should have done more to help him."

I wasn't following her. "Are you talking about Colt making a mistake with George Bassett?"

"No, that deal with George didn't happen the way my mom thinks it did." Kendra's lashes bounced off her cheeks like nervous butterflies as she cleared the emotion from her throat. "You have to understand my little brother. He was a sweet guy in a lot of ways, but when he started using after high school, everything changed."

So, Tami had been right when she suspected her son of having a drug problem.

"I tried to get him back into rehab, but he kept telling me he had the situation under control." Kendra tightened her grip on the tissue wadded in her hand. "Stupidly, I believed him. Even let him stay here after the girlfriend he was living with kicked him out. It didn't take long before I noticed that money was disappearing from my pocketbook. At first I thought Damon was just short on cash and had taken a twenty to buy lunch that day. When I finally mentioned it to him, he knew exactly where it had gone, and confronted my brother. He apologized, of course, but that was the final straw for my husband, and I had to ask Colt to leave."

She gave me a weary look. "A month later, I noticed that a bunch of charges had been run up on our credit card."

"Uh-oh," I muttered.

"That's putting it mildly. Damon hit the roof. Hunted my brother down for days, and finally spotted his beater Camaro being towed to Bassett Motor Works."

"Was your brother in the—"

"The tow truck? Oh, yeah. I guess it took both the driver and George to pull Damon off my brother."

"So, it wasn't George who broke his nose."

Kendra shook her head. "I didn't want any more family drama, so when Colt showed up for my mom's birthday the next week, I let her think that George beat him up because he didn't have the money to pay his repair bill."

Finally, an explanation of what happened two years ago that made some sense.

"Things were never the same after that. I didn't talk to him for weeks." She blinked away a tear. "But if I had dragged his ass to rehab that night instead of walking out the door, maybe he'd still be alive."

"You can't make someone change." As I well knew from way too many years of waiting for my mother to act like the moms I used to see on TV.

"I couldn't, but I guess my cousin Eric finally convinced Colt to go. He even paid for it." She reached for another tissue. "That's where Colt met his girlfriend."

"Jessica?"

"Pretty, but she had a serious drinking problem. At first I thought she'd be a bad influence on him, but I was wrong. She was great, and he was crazy about her. They even got an apartment together."

Kendra wiped her leaky eyes. "I don't know what happened, but everything seemed to fall apart last month."

It had sounded to me like Jessica and Seth happened. "Did Colt ever mention any trouble with a coworker?"

"If he was having a problem with someone, I didn't

hear about it. I just know that money got really tight for him after he lost his job at the feed store."

Actually, prior to that based on Ray Ortiz's reason for firing Colt. "He didn't say anything about what was going on?"

"Not to me, but you should probably talk to his girl-friend."

The one sleeping with his pal Seth? Yep, I intended to.

I scratched down a couple of quick notes and decided that I had better move on to the other reason for my visit. "Thanks for clarifying what happened. I'll provide your information to the prosecutor." And Steve.

"You don't have to say anything to my mother, do you? It's already bad enough between her and Damon."

I understood Kendra wanting to avoid an uncom-fortable situation with her mother. With Marietta having parked herself across the street from Steve, boy did I understand. "I'll see what I can do."

I tucked away my tote. "One last thing. You know Colt had a dog."

She tightened her gaze. "I know. I let him have his pick of Sarabi's litter."

As if on cue the mama Chow shook her head, fluffing her mane as if to convince me she was worthy of her lioness name.

"He was discovered running loose by one of the neighbors yesterday and—"

"Thank goodness," Kendra uttered, her hand going to her chest. "I got worried when I went to the apartment and couldn't find him."

"I have him right now, but he obviously needs a

permanent home," I said, hoping to appeal to Kendra's maternal instincts.

"Why can't Jessica keep him?"

That didn't sound very mom-like. "I'm pretty sure she moved out of that apartment a while ago."

"Great." Kendra rubbed her temples like I was giving her a headache.

"Since Fozzie can't stay there any longer, I thought that you—"

"That I'd take him?"

I nodded.

A humorless chortle escaped her pale lips. "I have a couple of energetic kids that I can barely keep up with, plus a husband who's not crazy about us having two dogs, much less three. Sorry, not going to happen."

"How about your mother?"

"A cat lady who's afraid of big dogs."

Swell. "Then do you know anyone who might want a dog?"

"Fozzie knows Jessica, so maybe..."

I had to talk to her anyway. "I'll ask."

"He's a nice dog. If not her, I'm sure someone will want him."

I was counting on it.

Chapter Ten

"IS THERE A good reason that dog is chasing squirrels in my backyard?" Gram asked, scowling out her kitchen window.

Yeah. I didn't want my car destroyed by a stir-crazy fur ball. "It's just for a few minutes so that he can run around while I have lunch."

"What's wrong with him running around at his own house?"

"That's a long story." That I didn't want to get into, especially while Fozzie and the German shepherd next door barked at one another through the fence.

Turning away from the commotion outside, Gram narrowed her eyes at me. "That's what you said yesterday."

"And it's still true."

"Just how long does this guy expect you to take care of his dog?"

"Uh...he doesn't exactly."

"Charmaine Digby, what have you gotten yourself involved in?"

I caved under her look of reproach and buried my head in her refrigerator. "What is this?" I lifted the glass cover. "Meatloaf?"

"Yes." She nudged me aside and pushed the refrigerator door shut. "And you're not having any until you tell me what's going on."

I blew out a breath. "Fine."

Leaning against the blue and white tile counter, Gram folded her arms. "So, whose dog is that?"

"Colt Ziegler's."

"Tami Ziegler's boy?"

I nodded.

"I know she's had some *challenges* with him over the years, but what's the problem now?"

There was no way to sugar-coat Colt's problem. "He's dead, Gram."

Her eyes widened. "Dead! What happened?"

"He sustained some sort of head injury early yesterday morning," I said, sticking with the sanitized version of the story I'd been telling most of the last twenty-four hours.

"Oh, my. So, you're involved because the coroner's office is investigating his death?"

No, but that provided the dollop of plausibility I needed without the mention of any names I knew she'd worry about. "Sort of."

Her lips twisted into a pucker of disappointment. "I get it. You can't talk about it."

At least that much was true.

"Sorry," I said, reaching for the refrigerator handle when I heard the upstairs toilet flush.

It was time to scarf down some meatloaf and get back to work before my mother decided to come down and get in on the *Twenty Questions* action.

Gram grabbed my arm. "Not so fast. That doesn't explain why you have his dog."

"I didn't want him to end up at a shelter, at least not before I had a chance to talk to Colt's family."

"That should have happened by now, right?"

I nodded. "No takers so far, but I have a few more people to talk to later today."

Gram shifted her attention to the five-foot-four fireball storming toward us while cinching the belt of her silk robe. "Uh-oh, someone got up on the wrong side of the bed."

And this someone should have bought a sandwich for lunch and taken Fozzie to the park.

"What the heck is going on back there?" Marietta demanded. "That dog next door is raising enough ruckus to wake the dead."

Close. It woke her, and before noon.

She sucked in a breath when she reached the window. "Call nine-one-one! There's a bear in the yard!"

Good grief. Not only did she need some coffee, she needed glasses. "It's just a dog."

"Oh." Turning, my mother frowned as much as her most recent Botox injection would allow. "And why is it in our backyard?"

Our? A declaration of kinship from someone who had been conspicuous in her absence throughout the fifteen years I had lived here?

I exchanged glances with my grandmother, who was giving me a subtle headshake.

I knew what she was telling me. *Let it go.* Easy for her to say—or in this case, not say.

Since I needed to keep the words at the tip of my

tongue from spilling out, I opened the refrigerator to find something else to gnaw on. "I'm dog-sitting for a couple of days. We'll be gone in a few minutes."

Gram reached past me for a bag of French roast. "You might as well stay for coffee. I'm making fresh for your mother."

"Yes, stay." Marietta gave me a quick caress as she passed behind me. "I've hardly seen you for days."

We tended to get along better that way.

Gritting my teeth, I turned to Gram. "You know I was trying to get the heck out of here," I whispered.

She kissed me on the forehead. "I do indeed."

I glowered at her. "I'm eating this meatloaf."

"Be my guest." She pointed at the kitchen table, where my mother was settling into a chair. "Just do it over there. I'll bring you a cup of coffee when it's ready."

"You'd better make it a double."

Marietta's green eyes brightened when I arrived with a ceramic casserole dish of meatloaf, and she promptly plucked the fork from my hand and dug in. "Goody, I'm starving."

"Mama, you still make the best meatloaf," she said between moans of carnal delight.

I stared at her, amazed. It wasn't just that she was devouring the seasoned slab of hamburger and bread crumbs that was supposed to be *my* lunch, but that she could make chewing look so sensual.

Of course, the pouty Cupid's bow lips helped.

I had her eyes, but not her lips. Also, not her boobs, tight tush, or shapely legs. Kinship obviously had its limits in the DNA department, too.

She pushed the fork at me. "Have some, honey. The

protein's good for you on your diet."

I'd adhered to a long tradition of ignoring my mother's unsolicited dieting advice, but my growling stomach insisted that I make an exception this once.

And also not think about all the carbs I was about to consume.

Leaning on an elbow, she rested her chin in her palm. "So, what did Steve say about the wedding invitation?"

"Nothing," I said with my mouth full.

"He didn't even mention it?"

"He had a busy day and probably hadn't looked at his mail."

She picked at my lunch with her fingers. "Hmmmpf, if he doesn't mention it today, maybe you should."

"Mention what?" Gram asked, bringing a carton of milk and a couple of spoons to the table.

I cocked my head at her. "That wedding invitation that no one on this side of the street should have known anything about."

She shifted her gaze to the wood-grain vinyl floor. "Oh, that."

"Charmaine," Marietta said, "it was an honest mistake. I'm sure Steve gets some of your grandmother's mail every once in a while."

Yeah, but I'd bet money that he didn't hold it up to the light to try to read it.

After splitting the last chunk of meatloaf with my mother, I carried the dish to the sink.

Gram followed me. "I wish I'd never shown her that envelope. It was just that I was so surprised to see Gina's name after all this time."

Turning to her, I kept my voice low. "How come you

never mentioned meeting her?"

"Didn't seem important."

The only thing true in what she had just said was the discomfort behind her words. "Want to try again?"

Gram shook her head. "Okay, I knew you liked him, so I didn't want to be the bearer of bad news."

"What do you mean? He didn't come over to tell you they were getting married, did he?"

She pressed her lips together.

"Oh."

While I felt like all the oxygen was being sucked out of the room, this revelation didn't change anything. I'd heard through friends that the relationship had seemed serious, and then weeks later, it was over.

I'd always been curious about what happened, and now I was even more curious. Darn it.

"What did you think of her?" I asked, hating myself for needing to know.

"I thought she was beautiful, and I liked her. She seemed genuinely nice." Gram searched my face as if she were trying to gauge my reaction. "Is that enough?"

"Yep." Since my grandmother tended to be a good judge of character, that was more than enough.

"What are you two gabbing about?" Marietta asked on her way to the coffee pot.

"Nothing important." And not anything I wanted to discuss with the resident wedding crasher.

The corners of her mouth curled into a knowing smile. "It's the fact that Steve hasn't said anything about that wedding invitation, isn't it?"

The volume of barking in the backyard escalated, giving me a timely cue for a hasty exit. "I need to go."

Preferably where an ex-girlfriend's wedding wasn't the topic du jour.

"I'm telling you," Marietta admonished when I turned to retrieve Fozzie's leash. "You need to talk to him about it—tonight."

Maybe.

Probably.

Okay, okay. Steve and I needed to talk.

Crap. I hated it when my mother was right.

After my lunch break, I figured I'd better report in at the courthouse before Patsy put an APB out on me, so I left Fozzie in my car and made my way to the third floor.

"Where have you been?" Patsy grumbled, not looking up from her computer screen as I passed her desk.

"Interviews, and they're not over with." Because I'd barely made a dent with Colt's neighbors.

"Don't make a career out of it."

While Patsy snickered at her own joke, I met the gaze of a watchful assistant clicking on a keyboard across the hall. Like Gram, she shook her head.

Yep. *Let it go.* Pretend I'm a shark and just keep moving. Otherwise, Patsy could make my life miserable here, and this week already had more than enough misery to spread around.

That misery was going to compound if I didn't get that report written. So after I settled into my desk chair and answered a couple of emails, I fished Eric Caldwell's business card out of my tote and made an appointment to see him at noon tomorrow.

If anyone would know if Colt had been battling old

demons, I figured it would be his cousin Eric. Not that a relapse and a cracked skull had to have a direct connection, but I wanted to know what Eric thought on that subject. Even more, I wanted Ben to know, especially if that could lead to charging a suspect other than Little Dog.

I needed to keep Steve in this loop, too, but I didn't want to wait until tomorrow to see him. Not when I had so much to tell him. And when he had a little something I hoped he'd want to tell me.

I sent him a text. *R u free for dinner?*

I had just pulled into the Madrone Arms parking lot when he replied ten minutes later. *Doubtful. Will call you later.*

Dang.

I turned to the dog next to me. "Looks like you're going to be my dinner date unless Jessica will take you."

And since I wanted to talk to her alone, I hoped Seth would be working some overtime tonight.

"Either way, dinner's gonna be late."

Fozzie licked his chops. No doubt because he'd picked up the scent of burgers on the grill a couple of blocks away.

I gently chucked him under the chin while I clipped on his leash. "Sorry, boy. I'm sure you're hungry now. As long as we're here, shall we see if Colt ripped off some nice biscuits for you?"

Fozzie chuffed.

"Sorry," I said to the dog following me out of my car. Who was I to cast dispersions on his former owner? At least he was feeding his dog some quality stuff.

Even if it was ripped off.

Fozzie looked up at me as if he could hear my thoughts.

"I'm not apologizing to a dog one more time today." I gave his leash a little snap. "Let's get you a snack and see if there's anything else of yours we should take to Jessica's."

While Fozzie led the way to unit 3, I scanned the lot for a cherry red minivan.

No minivans, red or otherwise, were in sight. No trucks parked out front either, so either Kendra had come and gone, or she had been in no hurry to clean up after her brother one last time.

Since Fozzie Bear had remained at his post outside the door, I suspected the latter.

To be on the safe side, I knocked on the door. When I didn't hear any noise coming from the apartment, I reached into the bear statue's back and retrieved the key Lily had used yesterday.

Fozzie didn't hesitate to barge in when I swung open the door, but I did.

"Hello?"

I didn't get a reply, so I stepped inside, shutting the door behind me.

While Fozzie explored the kitchen with the dirty dishes still in the sink, I did a quick survey of the living room. It didn't appear that anyone had been here since I locked up last night.

All the same, I checked the bedroom to make sure we were alone.

Yep, the only thing breathing in there was the dog that seemed to be searching for the usual occupant of the apartment.

I scratched behind Fozzie's ear when he paused to sniff the rumpled sheets on the bed. "Sorry, pal. He's not here."

But a scent definitely lingered, a seamy blend of sex, sweat, and flowery perfume.

Since Jessica had moved out over a month ago, I didn't want to know how long it had been since Colt had changed the sheets.

Because he couldn't bear to let go of the smell of her in his bed?

The framed eight-by-ten of a pretty blonde on the nightstand certainly would lend some support to that argument.

I reached for the picture to get a better look at her, and a white envelope that had been propped behind it fell to the carpet.

When I leaned over to pick it up, I noticed that Colt's name had been written in a swirly, feminine hand.

"Think we should check it out?" I asked the dog.

I didn't wait for an answer and unfolded the flap of the unsealed envelope.

Inside was a ruled sheet of paper with a short and not very sweet message.

> *I'm sorry for leaving this way.*
> *I hope you can return the ring.*
> *~ Jess*

Ring? As in engagement ring?

I did a quick check of the bedroom and didn't find any trace of a woman's ring, but that didn't surprise me. It was only reasonable that a guy stealing dog food would take his ex-girlfriend's advice and return the ring he bought her.

Assuming that the thief who used to live here hadn't also stolen that ring.

Chapter Eleven

BY THE TIME Lily arrived home from school, I hadn't learned much new from knocking on every door at the Madrone Arms.

Some guy that Mrs. Melnicke in apartment 2 never got a good look at had pounded on Colt's door Saturday night, and then peeled away in a pickup truck. All she could tell me was that she thought the truck had tinted windows and was fairly new, and there had been no one else at home who could add to the story.

I hadn't wanted to hang around to see who might show up. If that person happened to be Kendra, I didn't want to give her the impression I was waiting for her to let me into the apartment I had searched a couple of hours earlier. Not that there was anything in there of interest besides that note.

As I'd quickly discovered while looking for dog biscuits, Colt's cupboards were pretty bare—and that included his medicine cabinet. I found an almost empty aspirin bottle, but that was it. No needles, no paraphernalia—nothing to indicate that anything other than cheap beer was his drug of choice.

Of course, Steve could have already confiscated the

stuff of a more mood-altering nature.

While I would have loved to go have a chat with him about what he found during his search, I didn't think he'd be too keen on the idea.

I was just about to start my car when I noticed that Lily seemed to be having trouble with her door key, and a better idea popped into my head.

"Want to go say hello, boy? I'm sure there's someone here who would like to see you." And if Kendra happened to pull into the parking lot, it would look like I was trying to find another home for her brother's dog.

Perfect.

Climbing out of the Jag, I held the door open for Fozzie.

"Look who's here," I called out to Lily while a black streak raced toward her.

"Fozzie!" Squealing with joy, she dropped her backpack and wrapped her arms around the wriggling dog. "What are you doing here?"

I hated the idea of lying to this kid, but the reason behind my visit was too depressing for full disclosure. "We thought we'd come visit as long as we were in the neighborhood."

"Awesome!"

I clipped on Fozzie's leash and handed it to Lily. "Want to take Fozzie on a walk around the block?"

"Absolutely." She opened the door and tossed her backpack inside. "Let's go, Fozzie," she said, running off with the dog.

Crap. I should have clarified that I was supposed to be part of this deal. Also, that no running would be involved. I'd had enough running for one day.

I set out to catch up. "Wait for me."

Lily glanced back, the dog straining at the leash.

"I thought I could come too. You know, get some exercise."

She nodded. "Sure. My mom is always telling me how exercise is important as we get older."

I felt like I had just been catapulted to her mother's side of forty.

No matter. Lily could age me as much as she wanted as long as I could have the next fifteen minutes alone with her.

While I waited for a stinky diesel truck to motor past us on Madrone Way, I tried to think of a conversation starter that wouldn't sound like I was pumping her for information. "Did you ever go on walks with Jessica?"

"Nuh-uh."

"I saw a picture of her once." Pretty recently. "She looked nice."

"Yeah, she was nice."

"I got the impression that Jessica and Colt were going to get married."

"I guess. But they broke up and she moved out."

"I bet she missed Fozzie after she left. Did she ever come back to see him?" Or Colt?

"I don't think so." Lily patted Fozzie's back while he watered a thicket of weeds at the base of a stop sign. "I sure would have."

I didn't doubt that for a minute. "Speaking of Jessica, I'm going to see her later and ask if she'd like to adopt Fozzie."

Lily shifted her gaze to me. "Where's she live?"

I hadn't recognized the address Seth provided. "I'm

not sure. Maybe on the other side of town."

"I could probably ride my bike there after school and walk Fozzie."

"Maybe. I'd certainly be happy to let her know about your dog-walking offer."

"Did you hear that, Fozzie?" Lily said as the dog led her across the street. "We'll be able to see each other all the time."

I didn't want the kid to get her hopes up too high and decided that it was time to change the subject. "I wanted to ask about something Mrs. Melnicke told me while I was waiting for you to get home. She said she heard a guy banging on Colt's door Saturday night. I guess it was pretty loud. Did you hear it?"

Lily nodded. "He was *really* loud. He probably scared Fozzie."

"Did you see who it was?"

"Uh-huh. My mom wanted me to stay away from the window because she thought there might be a fight or something, but I knew Colt wasn't home."

"Because his car wasn't parked outside?"

"No, it was there. I saw him leave with that other guy."

My heart started pounding and not because of the brisk pace Fozzie was setting. "What other guy?"

She shrugged a shoulder. "I dunno. Somebody with a ponytail."

"You'd never seen him before?"

"I don't think so."

"Did they seem like friends?"

"I guess."

I wasn't getting the impression she could pick him

out in a lineup, so I thought we might have better luck with his car. "Did you see what he was driving?"

"Some old car. Kinda like Colt's, only different."

"Different how? Like different color?"

"Yeah, it was black. With a little cat on the front."

"Like a stuffed animal in the front window?"

She gave me a look like I was the lamest adult she'd ever had to deal with. "It was *metal*. You know, one of those car things."

A car thing. I had no idea what that meant, so it was time to go back to the loud dude looking for Colt.

"How about the guy knocking on the door? You said you saw who it was."

"Uh-huh," Lily said, slowing down to let Fozzie sniff the fire hydrant near the corner on Main Street.

"So, you recognized the man?"

"Sure. He was the one that helped Jessica move."

It was no wonder that I hadn't recognized Seth Lukin's Pembroke Lane address. When I was growing up in Port Merritt, most of the houses within a four-block radius of Broward Park had been stately, World War I– era homes. Now, much of the property adjacent to the park had given way to upscale bay view townhomes.

For the discriminating renters willing to sacrifice proximity to the park for affordability, half of the dozen houses down the hill between 9th and 10th Street had been carved up into chic apartments. For the far less discriminating who couldn't afford chic, twin cracker boxes had been crammed a half block to the south, where Malcolm Pembroke's family home had stood for over one hundred years.

When I was married and living in San Francisco, Gram had told me that Mr. Pembroke's development company had been transforming this neighborhood, but I hadn't realized that he had pushed a narrow lane through to an assisted living facility on the other side of 10th Street and named it after himself. And that wasn't all, which I found out when I pulled into a visitor parking spot near the *Pembroke Village* sign marking the apartment complex.

"You could do worse," I said, cracking the windows for Fozzie. "You won't have a yard to play in, but the dog park isn't far away." I patted him on the head. "Let's just hope the new boyfriend likes dogs." And wasn't home so that I could talk to Jessica alone.

When I got out of my car, I took note of the two cars parked closer to the buildings. I was pretty sure I hadn't seen either one at the feed store, so that boded well for Seth still being at work.

Unfortunately, after I located his apartment on the second floor and knocked several times, it seemed no one was home.

I heard a baby crying nearby and followed the sound to the unit next door to see what the neighbor could tell me.

After I knocked, the volume of the crying escalated, and I steeled myself for an irate greeting. But when the door swung open, to my shock, the woman seemed genuinely pleased to see me.

"Hey, long time no see," she said, patting the back of the baby on her hip.

I had no idea who she was, but the plump, dark-haired mom definitely looked familiar. Put some blond in her long hair and get rid of the baby weight, and I'd have the vague notion that I went to high school with her.

I turned up the wattage of my smile. "How're you doing?"

Ignoring the wailing going on in her ears, she chuckled. "You don't remember me, do you?"

"Port Merritt High? Maybe a year or two after me?"

"Very good. Alicia—Brandt then, Reboulet now."

"Charmaine," I said in case she needed the reminder.

"I know. You haven't changed a bit."

"Neither have you."

What liars we were. Between the two of us we'd gained at least eighty pounds since graduation day.

"What brings you here?" she asked, trying to interest her little boy in his pacifier, but he pushed it away and collapsed against her shoulder.

"Actually, some business next door." That I didn't want to get into. "Do you know when Jessica typically gets home?"

"Probably close to five most days."

Which would give me almost an hour to kill.

"Do you want to come in and wait?"

With a baby screaming in my ear? "No, thanks. I have someone waiting for me in my car." Who needed to be fed before he started gnawing on the seats of my car. "Let me ask you about the neighborhood, though. It's changed so much in the last few years."

"That's for sure."

"Seems quiet." I smiled at the kid Alicia was bouncing

on her hip. "With one very little exception."

"Yeah, and the trouble with Colt Ziegler." She sharpened her gaze. "You remember him, right?"

My mouth went dry. "I sure do."

"I guess he'd been hanging around on the grounds, stalking Jessica."

Whoa. That was a serious accusation that I hadn't expected to hear. "*Stalking* her?"

"That's what Seth called it." Alicia shrugged, swinging her little boy side to side. "I don't get a lot of sleep while this one's teething, so it's hard not to hear what's going on."

"Do you know if Jessica called the police?"

Alicia shook her head. "I got the impression that Seth was handling the situation. You know—he wanted to do the *guy* thing and convince Colt to stay away from her."

No wonder I had gotten a weird vibe when I asked Seth if he'd been having any problems with Colt. Because this definitely qualified as a big problem.

And if Seth had handled it in a physical way on Sunday, his problems were far from over.

Chapter Twelve

I HADN'T PLANNED on ambushing Jessica Tuohy the second she stepped out of her car, but once Fozzie started barking at her like he wanted his mom, he left me no other choice.

"Jessica?" I said, struggling to keep a squirming dog from leaping into her arms. "Could I talk to you for a few minutes?"

Her eyes widened as she stared down at Fozzie. "What is this?"

"I'm Charmaine Digby with—"

"I know. Seth told me that you'd probably want to talk to me, but what's *he* doing here?" she asked, backing out of Fozzie's reach.

This mother and child reunion sure wasn't starting as well as I had hoped. "Fozzie needs a home, and I thought—"

"Well, it can't be here. There's no way that Seth would..." Censoring herself, she cast a worried glance to the street. "We can't have pets here, and you should go."

Given everything I'd heard today, I shouldn't have been surprised at the cold reception Fozzie and I were getting. But I had no intention of leaving—not until

Jessica Tuohy answered some questions.

I aimed a polite smile at her. "Sorry, I can't just leave. Not when the prosecutor has specifically asked that I speak with you about your relationship with Colt Ziegler."

Yes, I was piling it on as high as the corned beef in Duke's Reubens, and I didn't care. I needed to find out what this chick knew, and if a little embellishment was what it took, I was happy to oblige.

By the bleak look in her baby blues, I knew I had her.

"Would you like to talk here or somewhere else?" I tried to think of a place nearby, where I could let Fozzie out of the car. "Broward Park, maybe?"

"Fine," she bit out between clenched teeth. "Give me a few minutes and I'll meet you there."

Whimpering while he watched her walk away, Fozzie turned to me.

I ran my hand over his back. "Sorry, pal. I wish that had gone better." At the same time, given what I had learned about Seth's actions of the last few days, I was relieved to put some space between Fozzie and Seth's fists.

When Jessica found me at the park fifteen minutes later, she hugged Fozzie and echoed my apology. "I've missed you, baby."

He nuzzled her hand, and I noticed it had an intricate ring tattoo.

"Interesting tattoo," I said, sitting next to her on one of the benches away from where several squealing preschoolers were playing on a jungle gym.

She buried her fingers in Fozzie's ruff. "Seemed like a good idea at the time, but a lot of things do when you're drunk."

I wasn't as interested in her regrets as much as I was who she met after she decided to work on her sobriety. "If you don't mind talking about it, I understand that you met Colt in rehab."

She shot me a sideways glance while Fozzie settled at her feet. "You must have chatted with his mother 'cause not too many people know about that."

Nodding, I kept my mouth shut about my information coming from his sister.

"Yeah, we met in rehab," she said softly. "He was such a sweet guy, really impossible not to like."

"So, you hit it off."

Watching the kids play, she smiled and a tear trickled down her cheek. "It was great. He was great, for a while."

"Did he start using again?"

"No, nothing like that. After I moved in, Colt just got...clingy."

"Would you say that he was the jealous type?"

"He sure didn't like me hanging out with my friends, so I guess."

"Would one of those friends be Seth?"

She shook her head, bleached blond tendrils fluttering in the soft breeze. "If Colt could have just accepted that one of his friends could be nice to me without wanting something..."

Jessica and I both knew Seth didn't truly fit that description. "What about Colt's other friends?"

"He pretty much divorced everyone he didn't think was going to support his sobriety, so I never met anyone outside of his family."

"You never saw him with a guy in a ponytail? Might

drive a black car like Colt's Camaro?"

She turned to me. "No, why?"

"Just asking to get a sense of what was going on in his life."

"That's easy to sum up. *Nothing* was going on in his life," she stated, her blue eyes sparking. "A big fat zero."

Softly whimpering as if to protest her increase in volume, Fozzie sat up.

She stroked one of his pointed ears. "He didn't seem to want to do anything besides spy on me and hang out with his buddy here."

I knew about the recent spy behavior from Alicia, but I wanted to hear about it from the person directly involved. "Spying on you when?"

"It started when I moved out."

"And moved in with Seth."

Jessica stared down at Fozzie. "I know that Colt thought that I wanted the quiet little life that he wanted, but I couldn't do it anymore. I had to get out."

"I understand that he gave you a diamond engagement ring."

I waited for her to correct me.

She didn't. Instead, Jessica nodded solemnly.

"Was he pressuring you to get married?"

"He just assumed I'd want to say yes." She teared up again. "That's when I knew I had to go before it got any more complicated."

"When was this?"

"Valentine's Day."

A tough day to leave a guy. "Did he know about Seth?"

She hung her head. "He'd had his suspicions—even

hassled Seth at work about it, but nothing was really going on between us."

I didn't buy her qualified denial. She moved in with the guy on Valentine's Day. "Did the hassling ever get physical?"

"I don't think so."

Her profile was shrouded in shadow from a nearby Douglas fir tree, but I didn't need a Technicolor view to see she was lying.

"How about with Seth?" I asked, leaning a little closer. "Any physical confrontations?"

"Nothing serious."

"Define serious."

Jessica shrank away from me. "He just wanted Colt to leave me alone."

"Seth told him that directly?"

"More than once unfortunately, but..."

"But what?"

She bit her lip. "Nothing."

I understood her hesitation to get her man of the moment in trouble, but that didn't help Georgie. "Colt came around Saturday night, didn't he?"

"Seth didn't have anything to do with his death," she stated in a clipped tone.

That wasn't what I'd asked. "But he was seen pounding on Colt's door that night, so something must have happened."

She stiffened.

"Seth went over to talk to him, right?"

"It's not what you think. Seth wouldn't hurt him."

She didn't believe that any more than I did.

"What were you doing on Sunday?" I asked with the

hope that she would stop with the defensive posturing and just talk to me.

"Nothing much. We went for a drive."

It rained all day. Not exactly great driving weather, but okay. I didn't care about that answer as much as I did the next one. "Did you see Colt when you were out and about? Maybe near the country club?"

She shook her head. "No. We weren't anywhere near there."

"How about after the two of you got home?"

"I never saw him at all on Sunday."

Maybe, but that didn't account for Seth.

"Jessica," I said, waiting for her to make eye contact with me. "Someone hit Colt Sunday night, hard enough to kill him."

"It couldn't have been Seth. He was with me the entire night."

The fear etched across her face told me that her attempt to provide her boyfriend an alibi was wishful thinking at best.

"Okay, do you know anyone else who might want to hurt Colt?"

Worrying her lips, she lowered her gaze. "I can't imagine anyone doing that to him."

Jessica's cell phone started ringing, and she pushed away from the bench. "I need to get going."

Fozzie sprung to his feet and she leaned over to give him a squeezy hug.

"One last thing before you go," I said, tightening my grip on the leash so that the dog couldn't bolt after her. "Did Colt have a second job?"

She blinked. "What do you mean?"

"Beside working at the feed store, did he have some other source of income?"

"Not that I know of."

"Where'd he get the money for the ring?"

Jessica shrugged. "I have no idea, but it was really pretty so I know it was expensive."

She said it with such conviction I didn't doubt her. "Did you happen to see a receipt?"

"No, it was just the way he told me that I was worth every penny." She started to walk away and then turned to give me one of the saddest smiles I'd ever seen. "I told you he could be sweet."

Sometimes sweet and sometimes a stalker? That made Colt Ziegler seem like he had an angel and a devil perched on his shoulders.

It also made me wonder which was whispering in his ear when someone decided that he should die.

After one last hour of knocking on doors at the Madrone Arms that yielded nothing other than a good riddance comment about Colt's barking dog, I called it a day and texted Steve from the parking lot.

Dinner?

He responded a few minutes later with a suggestion that we meet at Eddie's Place in an hour. Since my cupboards were almost as bare as Colt's, I was happy to take him up on his offer. And also see if my pals Roxanne and Eddie Fiske wanted a dog to add to their growing family.

I had thought about taking the dog in question with me to Eddie's, but after I fed Fozzie and took him on his fourth walk of the day, he was sleeping so soundly I didn't have the heart to wake him. Instead, I took a picture of him curled up like a little bear cub next to my balcony sliding door.

"Cute," I said with satisfaction.

He opened one eye and then rolled over and started snoring.

"We just won't mention that you snore." Or bark at everything that moves.

Ten minutes later, I sat at the bar at Eddie's and held my camera phone in front of Rox when she served my drink order. "Come on, admit it. He's cute."

Resting a hand on her baby bump, she crinkled her brow. "He looks pretty big."

Eddie came up behind her with a bucket of ice from the kitchen. "Am I being replaced?"

"Not yet." Rox pointed at the image on my phone. "And not with something that drools."

"He doesn't drool." Much, anyway.

"What the heck is that?" Eddie asked, emptying the ice into the bin underneath the polished oak bar.

I turned the screen so that he could see it. "The dog that is going to be your baby's best friend."

He smirked. "No, it's not."

"Come on, you guys. He needs a good home." And I was having a heckuva time finding him one.

"Who needs a good home?" Donna Littlefield asked while sliding her perfect little butt onto the bar stool next to mine. "Someone I know?"

Donna was one of my best friends since junior high, but she did have an annoying habit of interjecting herself into the middle of conversations. However, since she lived in an apartment building that allowed pets, I was happy to overlook it and showed her Fozzie's picture.

She snatched my cell phone and held it in front of her nose. "Sweet. Does he come with a rich guy?"

I reached for the mineral water I'd ordered. "Nope."

She promptly placed the phone down. "Then I'm out."

"Fine." I sucked down some water while wishing it was a tall glass of calorie-free chardonnay.

Rox delivered a Chablis to Donna and then set a menu in front of me. "Are you eating?"

"I'm waiting for Steve."

"Not anymore, you're not," he said, tucking back my hair to plant a kiss on my right temple.

From the tap at the far end of the bar, Eddie aimed an index finger at Steve. "You still on duty?"

"I've got the night off, so start pouring." Steve took a seat and then leaned into me to talk to Donna. "What's going on? Are you girls having a meeting?"

"Char's showing us dog pictures." She flashed a dazzling white smile at him. "Hey, you have a fenced yard. Want a nice doggy?"

Steve leveled his gaze on me while Eddie delivered his beer. "Seriously? You still have that dog?"

I sighed. "Colt's sister wouldn't take him."

"That's Colt Ziegler's dog?" Rox asked.

Donna placed her hand on my arm. "Honey, what on earth are *you* doing with his dog?"

That wasn't a subject I wanted to delve into in front of Steve. "I was just trying to keep him out of the shelter."

"Awwww," Donna said, giving me a little pat. "The poor thing. His owner dies and then no one wants him.

How sad is that?"

I stared into the bubbles of my drink. "I know." Everything surrounding Colt's death was sad.

She pointed at my phone. "Send me that picture, and I'll post it at the shop. Maybe we can find a taker for him there."

Donna's shop was Donatello's, the local cut and curl. It tended to be frequented by the more senior residents in town, and I doubted any of them would want anything bigger than a lapdog, but...

I picked up my phone and texted Donna the picture. "Done. Thanks."

"Send it to me, too," Rox said. "I'll put it up in the lobby."

Which connected the eight-lane bowling alley to the tavern. "You got it."

After I hit send, I noticed Eddie and Steve exchanging furtive glances. "Okay, you guys, what's with the looks?"

Steve sipped his beer. "I don't know what you're talking about."

Yeah, right. "The girls are just trying to help me find Fozzie a home."

"I'm sure the pictures will go up tomorrow, but what are you going to do in a week, when no one has called about the dog?"

I hadn't thought that far ahead. "Someone will want him."

"What if they don't? Are you going to be able to take that dog to the shelter?"

I locked gazes with Steve. "*Someone* will want him."

They had to.

Chapter Thirteen

TWO HOURS LATER, I was unlocking my apartment door while Steve pressed himself against me and nuzzled my neck.

Any other night I would have turned around to give him easy access to his favorite body parts, but we needed to have a serious chat before I served up any after-dinner treats.

The second I cracked the door open, Fozzie filled the space, barking as if I were an intruder. "Jeez, dog. It's just me."

"He's a pretty good alarm system," Steve said, following me inside. "I'll give him that."

I ran my hand down Fozzie's side while he took a defensive stance across from Steve. "He's a good boy." Most of the time.

The second I reached for Steve to divert him to the loveseat for a little chat, he pinned me against the wall. Cuffing my wrists with his hands, his lips were so close I could almost taste them. "Now, where were we?"

We were someplace Fozzie didn't like, given the way he was growling with his teeth bared. "Uh-oh."

Steve immediately backed away from me. "It's okay,"

he calmly stated. "No one's being hurt."

Sitting on my heels in front of Fozzie, I extended my hand to see if he'd let me pet him. "What's wrong with you?"

Steve pulled a glass from a kitchen cupboard and filled it at the tap. "Nothing. He probably thought you were being attacked."

While Fozzie sniffed my hand, I watched Steve drain that glass. "Everything's okay. Steve's a friend, so you two boys should learn how to get along."

"Or while you have this *houseguest*, maybe we should plan on going to my place."

I gave Fozzie a pat on the head and then joined Steve in the kitchen. "I could do that, but you're here now, so..." Lacing my fingers behind his neck, I flattened my breasts against him. "We might as well make the most of it."

Drawing back, Steve held my face in his hands, his dark gaze shifting to the dog panting next to my feet. "As long as Cujo here doesn't get any ideas."

"I think you're safe." I angled for a kiss. "Just don't make any sudden moves."

"So I shouldn't rip off your clothes and have my way with you on the kitchen counter?"

Not when there was a comfortable bed in the other room. "Probably not advisable."

"Too bad. That's what I had planned." His eyes gleamed with carnal intent as he started unbuttoning my cotton shirt. "Now we're going to have to think of something else to do."

Goody.

✳

I was lying on my side, watching Steve pull on his blue jeans while Fozzie scratched at the other side of my bedroom door.

"I think your dog needs a walk." He bundled up the clothes he'd peeled off me twenty minutes earlier and tossed them on the bed. "Get dressed and I'll go with you."

Fozzie had been whimpering at the door ever since I'd closed it. I didn't think he wanted out as much as he wanted in. That didn't mean I wasn't happy to accept Steve's offer, so long as we exchanged some information first. "Could I talk to you about something?"

Steve reached for his polo shirt. "I don't suppose I need to guess what you want to talk about."

"Probably not." Sitting up, I pulled on the sheet to cover myself and waited for him to give me his undivided attention.

He sat at the edge of the bed to put on his shoes. "Okay, let's have it."

"You know I talked to Tami Ziegler yesterday."

Steve's gaze cut to me. "And you know I don't want to talk about this."

"Then just listen."

His mouth flatlined, his eyes hard as flint.

"I understand why Mrs. Ziegler believes Georgie had a fight with Colt two years ago, but she's wrong. Colt's sister told me that Damon Sparks was the one who broke Colt's nose because of some issues that were going on at her house at the time."

Steve's expression didn't change as he raked his

fingers through his short, cocoa brown hair. "You've been busy."

"I was asked to verify Mrs. Ziegler's statement."

"Okay."

Expecting to see some reaction, I searched his face. I saw nothing but annoyance staring back at me.

He leaned closer. "Got a good-enough look?"

"You're obviously not surprised, so you already knew about the issues between Kendra's husband and her brother."

Steve pushed off the bed. "I'm not going to talk about this case with you."

"Will you just listen? I think Seth Lukin knows a lot more than he's telling. Plus, he was seen at—"

"Char, what the heck do you think you're doing?"

"Sharing what I've found out from interviewing—"

"That needs to stop right now," he said, looming over the bed.

"But you should hear—"

"No, *you* should hear what I have to tell you."

I didn't much care for the finger aimed at my nose.

"You did your verification, so now you're going to cease and desist." He poked me in the sternum with that finger. "You got me?"

Fozzie barked, sounding like he was getting increasingly agitated with the rising volume in the room.

I couldn't say that I blamed him and grasped Steve's finger. "I hear you, but I was asked to talk to these people."

"Beyond verifying that statement?"

"Well..." I pushed his hand away while I wracked my brain for a better comeback.

"That's what I thought." He leaned over and kissed me while Fozzie scratched at the carpet as if he were trying to tunnel under the door. "Are you getting dressed?"

"Sounds like I'd better," I said on a sigh when the scratching got louder.

"Okay, that's enough." Looking like he was ready to shoot our intruder, Steve swung the door open. "No digging!"

Fozzie skittered out of sight, and Steve looked back at me over his shoulder. "That goes for you, too."

"You're here early," Aunt Alice said as I dragged my weary butt through the Duke's Cafe kitchen door shortly after dawn. "Couldn't sleep?"

Not with Fozzie snoring like a buzz saw after Steve left. But the hours of staring at my eyelids had given me plenty of time to think about the digging I wasn't supposed to have been doing.

Had I come up with enough to cause Ben to question the strength of his case against Georgie? Other than shedding some doubt on an old incident, I didn't think so. But if I could find out what Colt Ziegler had been up to after he left Jessica's on Saturday—even better, talk to that guy Lily saw in the parking lot—maybe we could unravel the mystery of what really happened Sunday night.

"Thought I'd be an early bird and catch that worm." And I hoped it would be in the form of a juicy clue to identify the owner of that black car.

Squeaking to the worktable to fill Alice's empty coffee

cup, Lucille arched her pale eyebrows. "Any news?"

Not that I could share. "Little Dog's out on bail."

She scowled. "I could've told you that."

"That's all I've got," I said grabbing a clean cup from the rack by the dishwasher. "But I do have a question for you."

Lucille's eyes gleamed with interest as she filled my cup. "Shoot."

I took a seat on the stool across from Alice and reached for the gallon jug of milk in the center of the table. "Did you ever see Colt Ziegler come in with any friends—maybe a guy with a ponytail?"

Alice stopped zesting the lemon in her hand. "I don't remember seeing him here other than to get takeout now and again." She turned to Lucille, who had sat next to her. "Do you?"

Lucille shook her head, the points of her platinum bob brushing her jaw. "He came in with Tami a couple of times, but other than that, no."

Since that matched my memories of Colt from having worked here for a couple of months last summer, I took a different tack. "How about a long-haired guy with a black car? Have you seen someone like that in town?"

"Hon, that could probably describe any number of the fellas living around here," Lucille said.

"Order up!" Duke bellowed.

"Be right there." Flattening her palms on the table, Lucille sharpened her gaze. "Why are you so interested in this guy?"

I painted an innocent smile on my face. "No particular reason."

She puckered. "He has something to do with Colt

getting whacked, doesn't he?"

"I doubt it. I just want to talk to him."

"Because he knows something."

I shrugged and slurped my coffee.

"I'm taking that as a yes," she said, squeaking away to deliver her order.

I picked up my coffee cup and followed her as far as the entrance to the kitchen, where I scanned the dining room for the other waitress working this morning, but I didn't see one.

That left me one cantankerous short-order cook to question.

"Good morning." I shot Duke a smile. "Lucille's on her own this morning, huh?"

"Yeah, so I'd appreciate you not distracting her back there," he grumbled.

"Fine, I'll just distract you here." And breathe in the heavenly aroma of the bacon that wasn't allowed on my diet.

"Don't you have a job to get to?"

"Yeah, in over an hour. In the meantime I was hoping that you could help me with something."

"If it means that I don't have to provide you with any free food, I'm in."

"Whatever." He knew I was good for it.

I stood next to him and looked out the front window at the cars being coated with a gloomy mist. "You have a good view of people as they park outside."

The bell over the door jingled, announcing the arrival of a familiar old man in a raincoat, and Duke gave him a chin salute. "I can see the ones coming here on foot, too. So?"

I waved at the sweet ninety-year-old as he made his way to his usual yellow stool at the counter. "Mornin', Stanley."

Peeling off his raincoat, his eyes brightened behind thick glasses. "Looks like the help's getting prettier back there."

Duke elbowed me out of his way as he reached for a couple of eggs. "The only way she can help right now is to get to the point."

I could take the hint. "Fine. I'm trying to locate a guy, probably close to my age, with hair pulled back in a ponytail. The only other thing I know about him is that he drives a black car sort of like an old Camaro."

He cracked the eggs onto the grill. "There's more than a few cars like that in town."

"And it has some sort of cat on the front."

"Did I hear you say 'cat'?" Stanley asked, cupping his ear.

I didn't want to broadcast my lame description of the car to everyone in the cafe, so while Lucille served a table in the back, I came around the corner and placed a mug in front of Stanley. "It might be chrome. The only description I got was that it was a metal car thing that looked like a cat."

While he thought about it, I poured him some decaf.

He reached for the sugar. "Sounds like a Cougar to me. Is that the kind of car you're looking for?"

"I have no idea. Would that look kind of like an old Camaro?"

"The early ones might," Duke chimed in. "At least to someone who doesn't know much about cars."

While Stanley stirred his decaf, he stared into its

murky depths. "One of the crew painting the house across the street from me had a black Cougar."

I set the carafe on the counter. "What'd he look like?"

Stanley frowned, his horn-rimmed glasses slipping down the bridge of his bulbous nose. "Pretty much like you'd expect. Young, paint-stained coveralls, wore a hat. I didn't recognize him."

With the way he was describing the guy, I didn't expect that he would. But at least I had a possible make for the car.

Stanley pushed his glasses back up his nose. "The only one of the three I recognized was that Ziegler kid."

My heart jumped into my throat. "You're sure it was Colt Ziegler?"

"If it wasn't him, then I don't know why his Camaro was parked in front of my house when I got home last Thursday."

Maybe the house-painting gig helped explain how Colt was able to pay his rent. Now, all I had to do was find the guy he had been working with.

Chapter Fourteen

AFTER GIVING FOZZIE a quick potty break, I changed into my black pantsuit, a silk blouse, and three-inch pumps—my power suit ensemble that I'd worn to the settlement hearing for my divorce.

Keeping watch on me from my bedroom doorway, Fozzie hadn't appeared very impressed with my transformation from office grunt to officer-of-the-court-to-be-taken-seriously, but he wasn't Eric Caldwell, the alpha dog I had an interview with at noon.

I'd also flat-ironed my hair and applied an extra layer of mascara for a little booster shot of self-confidence. But nothing had lifted my spirits more than getting on my bathroom scale and being down two pounds.

That even made spending most of my morning trying to come up with creative ways to cram case files into overstuffed metal cabinets bearable. At least until I had to kneel on the dusty floor to make some space in a bottom drawer and noticed a pair of brown oxfords next to the pumps I'd kicked off an hour earlier.

"You look a little overdressed for file duty," Ben Santiago said. "Are you making a court appearance today that I don't know about?"

I didn't want to admit that I had dressed to impress a former homecoming king who had never once given me the time of day. "No, I have a lunch appointment."

Which was mostly true.

Ben's tan lips curled into a measured smile. "You're obviously very busy today, but is there a chance you'll have something for me later?"

I had already known that the criminal prosecutor wasn't a man who liked to be kept waiting. While I thought I'd earned his trust over the past eight months, I knew better than to push my luck—or his patience.

"Absolutely," I said, sitting on my heels. "I have one more person to speak with." Possibly two if Mr. Paradiso, Stanley's neighbor, would answer the voice message I left him before I started my filing marathon. "But I'll have a report on your desk before I leave today."

"Good." He backed away from the file drawer as if some toxic ooze could bubble out to ruin his shoes. "We wouldn't want you to make a career out of filing."

I doubted that Ben cared anymore about my career than Patsy had when she made a similar remark yesterday. He just wanted to win his case.

Understandable.

And I was willing to do just about anything to make sure that didn't happen.

✳

"Charmaine, I'm so sorry to keep you waiting," Eric Caldwell said, entering his office.

Pasting a friendly smile on my face, I rose from the utilitarian vinyl chair I'd been fidgeting in for the last ten minutes, and gripped the hand he'd offered. "No problem. Thanks for making the time."

Eric stepped back and gave me a long look of appraisal that should have been reserved for the trade-ins that drove onto his lot. "Wow, you look great."

Okay, aside from some file cabinet dust, I had cleaned up pretty well today, but it didn't merit the level of male interest he was making a show of generating.

We weren't in a bar, and he wasn't going to buy me a drink. Nor did I want him to. What I wanted was to establish a professional boundary from which to assess him, so I took a seat and hoped that he'd do the same.

"I think the last time I saw you was last summer at Duke's," Eric said, sitting in his desk chair.

Two photos on the credenza behind him—one with Eric proudly holding the trophy salmon he'd caught, the other with his trophy wife—bookended his broad shoulders. Between them stood a half-dozen golf and bowling trophies. If Eric had wanted to make a statement of personal achievement beyond the salesman of the year awards hanging on his office walls, a flashing gold star would have been just the thing.

Eric Caldwell was tall, tan, and ruggedly handsome with an athletic build—a muscled-up version of the teenager I'd shared a few classes with. While Eric the man exuded confidence, the winning smile of this success story was as fake as fool's gold, and I knew he wasn't happy to see me today.

"It's been a while." I handed him a business card. "As I explained to your assistant, I work for the county now."

A smirk tugged at a corner of his mouth as he fingered the card. "*Special* Assistant to the Prosecutor/Coroner.

Well, look at you."

He fixed his cool gaze on me, making me feel a little less special. The jerk.

"Yes, and while it's obvious what brings me here today, let me say how sorry I was to hear about Colt."

Taking a deep breath and slowly releasing it, Eric leaned back in his chair. "My aunt Tami is devastated."

"I spoke with her. Kendra, too. They both mentioned how grateful they were that you were there to help Colt out after he lost his job."

I was laying it on a little thick, but I thought the big man on campus might loosen up with a little ego-stroking.

He shook his head. "I was more of a go-between than anything else. My wife needed some part-time help, and my cousin needed a job. Worked out great...for a while."

"Did Colt mention where else he was working?"

"He said something about picking up some other odd jobs. Didn't give me any specifics about where."

I got the sense Eric knew more than he was letting on, but I decided to let it go for now. "I assume he was making enough to cover his rent?"

Furrowing his brow, he stared across the desk at me as if I'd asked a stupid question. "I guess."

"I ask because Kendra made it sound like you'd helped him out financially in the past."

"He was family. Also one of my best friends. That's what you do."

"Had you given him any money lately?"

"It was important for him to make it on his own."

Maybe, but we were also talking about a guy who wasn't known for living very responsibly.

I wrote a *No* next to the money question I'd recorded in my notebook. "I understand Colt had a problem with drug abuse."

Eric vented a breath as he hung his head. "We all have our demons. That was his."

"Do you have reason to believe that he was using again?"

"If I had, I never would have recommended him to my wife, but after last Sunday..."

I tightened my grip on my pen. "What do you mean?"

"Colt showed such poor judgment, he had to have been on something."

"What do you think happened?"

"He obviously did something stupid that got himself killed," Eric said, giving me a cold stare.

"I know that Colt and Little Dog exchanged a couple of punches in high school, but there was no real bad blood between them, right?"

"I hadn't thought so. At least not recently, but that was before my cousin ended up dead."

Heck, Eric was starting to sound like Tami, and that didn't help Georgie's case one iota. But what he wasn't sounding like was a man who had anything useful he was inclined to share with me.

The phone on Eric's desk rang. He focused on the blinking light with the intensity of a caged lion, and I knew I had only seconds before he'd pounce. "I know you're busy, but I do have a couple more things I want to go over with you."

His gaze slashed back to me with clear irritation. "No problem. I'm here to help."

Only because it would look really bad if he didn't appear interested in bringing Colt's murderer to justice. "Could you give me the names of Colt's closest friends?"

Eric knitted his brows. "There was the guy he used to work with—Seth something. They used to hang out some. Beyond that, I couldn't tell you."

I didn't believe that for a minute. "How about a guy with a black car, possibly an old Cougar?"

"If I'd sold him the Cougar, I'd remember." Eric's lips curled into a smile that didn't reach his eyes. "Speaking of old cars, how do you like that Jag?"

My cowbell on wheels? Not much at the moment, but I was more than willing to play his game of avoidance if I could spin it to my advantage. "It's a nice car—my ex's, actually. But with all the driving I have to do with my job, I've pretty much decided that it's time to get something more fuel-efficient."

He handed me his card. "Let me know when you're ready to do that. You can trust me to make you a great deal."

I wasn't sure I could trust Eric in any respect, but I made a show of pocketing the card. "Thanks, I'll do that."

After a couple beats of silence, he stood, signaling the end of the interview.

I rose to my feet. "Thanks for your time."

"I'll walk you out," he said, stepping out from behind his desk.

"Oh, I almost forgot to ask." Instead of walking to the door, I turned to face him. "Why do you think Colt was trying to break into that limo?"

Eric's pupils dilated. "That's something that doesn't

make a lot of sense. But that's the way he was. Always doing stuff that didn't make sense."

The physical response accompanying the safe non-answer he provided was curious, and I wished I could crack Eric's head open to see what he knew about that *stuff.* "But you must have had some confidence in him to recommend him to your wife."

"We never want to give up on the people we care about."

Or Eric had been hoping for the best when he offered the person he cared about the most some cheap labor.

I extended my hand. "Good to see you. I'm sorry it was under these circumstances."

"Come on. We're old friends," he said, giving me a warm hug. "It was great to see you. Give me a call when you're ready for those new wheels."

Really? I come to his office to ask him about the death of his best friend, and he chooses to focus on the opportunity to sell me a car? Clearly, Eric Caldwell was skilled at compartmentalizing his emotions, but this felt plain weird.

I forced a smile. "I will, and I hope you'll call me if you think of anything else that might be relative to our investigation."

"You'll be the first person I call."

More likely, my card would be round-filed the moment I left his office.

Didn't matter. We'd speak again soon enough.

Because Eric Caldwell knew a heck of a lot more than he'd been willing to admit.

✳

After picking up a protein bar and a copy of this week's *Gazette* from the convenience store near my apartment, I sat in my car and read Renee Ireland's front page story about Colt Ziegler's murder while I ate.

Since Renee was a friend of his mother I wasn't surprised that she didn't go into any detail with his personal struggles, instead portraying him like an underemployed choirboy. What did surprise me was that she had a quote about Colt from Eric Caldwell.

My cousin was a sweet guy. I can't imagine what transpired at Bassett Motor Works Sunday night, but he certainly deserved better than he got.

That was a long way from what he'd told me—that his cousin did something stupid to get himself killed.

Of course, Eric wouldn't want to say anything publicly to upset his family members, but between his comment and those from Tami, the article made it very clear that the family was satisfied that the right man had been arrested.

The only thing I found satisfying about it was that my name hadn't been mentioned.

Other than a summary that included some family members who lived out of state, the last line detailing a funeral service planned for this coming Saturday served as the only bit of real news for me.

After I added that noon service to my calendar, I swung by my apartment to grab some carrots and to give Fozzie a pee break. I then spent the bulk of my afternoon crunching carrots and translating my notes into a five-page summation—a Colt's world who's who that I hoped would remove some heat from Little Dog.

Ben was in a closed door meeting in his office, so I emailed him the report and sent a copy to his administrative assistant.

Twenty minutes later, I was back on the floor, paying homage to that overstuffed filing cabinet when Ben's oxfords made a repeat appearance.

"We need to stop meeting like this," I told him.

A fake smile flickered at the corners of his lips. "Let me buy you a cup of coffee."

Why? Had I done something wrong?

While Ben headed for the break room, I scrambled to my feet and hoped that he'd walk in to find more than just a layer of sludge in that pot.

I could smell the dregs cooking in the bottom of the carafe before I saw it, and I crossed the room to turn off the coffeemaker. "Sorry. Shall I make some fresh?"

"Don't worry about it." Ben settled into one of the chairs at the table and pulled out the chair next to him. "Have a seat."

Uh-oh.

He waited until I had parked my butt before he turned to me. "You know how I asked you to keep the project you've been working on under wraps?"

I didn't know where he was going with this. "Yeah?"

"Who did you discuss it with?"

"No one." With the exception of Steve, and I hadn't told him anything he didn't already know. Plus, there was no mention of my interview with Tami in the paper, so that couldn't have been what had put me in Ben's crosshairs.

"You didn't say anything to a member of the Bassett

family?"

"No. Why?"

"I just spoke to an attorney who had most of the information you included in your report."

"Not from me."

After giving me a hard stare, Ben pushed back his chair. "Okay, then."

That had to have been the lamest attagirl I'd ever received.

I followed him to the door. "Since I was able to disprove Mrs. Ziegler's claim, what does that do to the case?"

He shook his head. "Nothing. It's solid without any ancient history."

Heck. That wasn't what I wanted to hear.

Chapter Fifteen

THE BULLETIN BOARD at the dog park kiosk had the same problem as the file cabinets that had frustrated me most of the afternoon: way too much paper for the available space.

After I rearranged the postings for all the puppies for sale, I managed to free up enough real estate for the FREE CHOW MIX sign I'd printed at work.

Fozzie straining at the leash, barking at every dog in sight, might not make a free dog look like much of a bargain, so I let him lead the way to the nearest bush, where he promptly relieved himself. That's also when the cell phone in my jacket pocket started to ring.

When I saw Steve's name displayed, I hoped he was calling about a dinner date. "Hey."

"Where are you right now?"

"Not that far away if you have dinner in mind."

"Oh, I definitely have it in mind, so perhaps you'd like to join us."

Us?

Stopping in my tracks, I sucked in a breath. "It's Wednesday!" With everything going on, I had forgotten all about our usual Wednesday dinner with Gram.

"Sorry, I'll be right there."

I repeated my apology ten minutes later, when I stepped through the back door and inhaled the mouth-watering aroma of a pot roast in the oven.

Gram aimed a brittle smile at me from behind the stove as my mother rounded the corner.

"About time. I'm famished." Marietta said, giving me a once-over. "I certainly hope that you didn't go to work in that *ensemble*."

"No." I had changed into a long-sleeved pullover and blue jeans before taking Fozzie to the park. Not that it was any of her concern.

Since my mother's ensemble included a designer silk shirt that she wouldn't want to splash pot roast gravy on, I was more interested in what she was doing home. "Aren't you going out with Barry?"

"When your grandmother told me what was on the menu, I thought we could make it a quiet evening at home. But he's at a meeting that's running late, so we're starting without him."

Swell. "Need any help, Gram?"

"No. Why don't you keep Stevie company for a few minutes."

In other words, rescue him from my mother.

Marietta hooked her arm around mine and led me into the dining room. "Excellent idea, because we were just chatting about something I think you'll find very interesting."

It had better not be wedding invitations.

Steve looked up from the cell phone in his hand and nailed me with his cool gaze. "Nice of you to make it."

"Sorry, I got busy and lost track of time."

My mother patted my hand as she deposited me in the chair next to Steve. "Never mind that. You'll never guess who's getting married."

I stared across the table at Marietta. *If you say Gina Campanella I'll never forgive you.* "Someone we know?"

Her emerald eyes sparked. "Kelsey Donovan and Andy Falco."

Whew.

The local couple had been an object of Gossip Central speculation ever since Andy's brother died last fall, so the news of their engagement hadn't come as a surprise as much as it had been a relief. "Good for them."

"Your grandmother received the invitation in the mail today." Marietta aimed a predatory smile at Steve. "I assume you received an invitation."

I tried to kick her under the table and missed. "I'll have to check my mail when I get home, but unless they plan on a really small wedding, I can't imagine that we all didn't receive one."

"It's in June. The weekend before mine." She locked her gaze on Steve. "Think you'll be free?"

He shot me a quizzical glance. "No idea. It'll depend on what's going on at work."

"Such a busy time of year." Marietta took a sip from the wine glass in front of her. "So many June weddings. And the weather can be so iffy here that time of year. Not like, say, Southern California. It's so much easier to plan for an outdoor wedding down there."

"I'm sure your wedding will go off without a hitch," I said to try to make this the last word on the subject. "They always do."

Marietta leveled a frosty glare at me. "I'm sure it

will."

"I hope everyone's hungry," Gram said, carrying a heaping bowl of mashed potatoes to the table. "I made enough to feed a small army."

Good. Maybe that would give my mother something to chew on that had nothing to do with upcoming weddings.

To that end, I fetched the roast beef and gravy from the kitchen and had just settled back into my chair when I heard my cell phone ringing in the other room. "Go ahead and start. I'll just be a minute."

Retrieving my phone from my tote, I didn't recognize the number, so I thought it might be someone calling about Fozzie until I heard the man say my name.

"This is Lou Paradiso. You called me about who I used to paint my house."

"Yes, thanks for calling me back," I said, grabbing my notebook and a pen.

While Mr. Paradiso went into detail about Boynton House Painting's quality of work as if I were looking for a recommendation, I noticed that Steve was standing at the refrigerator, fifteen feet away from me.

I didn't want to invite another lecture about staying out of his investigation so I kept my responses carefully vague, thanked the man, and ended the call.

Tucking away my phone, I met Steve's watchful gaze. "Did you get what you were after?" I asked, trying to act casual.

"Yeah." He lifted the bottle of water in his hand. "How about you?"

I batted my eyelashes at him. "I don't know what you mean."

Steve smirked. "Sure."

"Ready to eat?" I hooked my arm around his. "I'm famished."

Yes, there are moments when I'm not too proud to borrow a page from my mother's playbook.

"Want a beer?" Steve asked when I followed him into his kitchen two hours later.

I'd already blown my diet with the mashed potatoes and gravy. I didn't need to add to my bloat with more carbs. "Nope." I also knew I shouldn't stay too long, not when I had a restless dog in my car. "Want a dog? You have a nice fenced yard here."

"Nope."

Heaving a sigh, I took a seat at the kitchen table and looked up at the French country wallpaper border—a chicken-themed leftover from when his mother owned the house. "He'd be better company than these chickens."

Joining me at the table, Steve set down his beer bottle and tossed the mail he'd collected from his box outside into a fruit bowl two feet in front of me. "At least they're quiet. That dog would be outside all day, barking at the neighbor's cat."

"Probably," I said, wondering how many days of mail that bowl contained.

"So, are you going to tell me what that was all about?"

I shifted my gaze to the cop guzzling the beer next to me. "You know my mother. She has weddings on the brain." And now so did I. Darn it.

Steve folded his arms across his chest. "I meant that

phone call."

"Oh. That was just something that I'm working on for one of the prosecutors."

"Which one?"

Like I was going to tell him. "Never mind which one."

"Because I wouldn't want to hear that it had anything to do with Little Dog's case."

I smiled sweetly. "You won't hear that from me."

He gave me a hard stare. "I'm serious."

"I know, and I have a dog outside who is going to be seriously unhappy if I don't let him out of my car soon. So if you want me to stick around for a while, would letting him into the house be too much to ask?"

"Fine, but if Cujo growls at me in my own house, he's outta here."

I scooted to the edge of my seat to give him a peck on the lips. "Deal."

"Not so fast." Steve pulled me onto his lap and gave me a beer-infused kiss.

"Mmmm," I murmured, savoring the taste of him. "Much nicer."

"Are you sure you want to go get that dog?" He nibbled at my neck. "I have a comfortable couch we could make out on."

"Sounds good to me." I pushed off of him to grab my car keys. "Be sure to save me a seat."

Picking up his beer bottle, Steve headed for his living room. "If you're lucky, I'll even find you a chick movie to watch."

I was feeling luckier by the minute, especially once I heard him start channel-surfing for that movie. And while I knew I should trust the man I loved to pick the right moment to tell me about hearing from the woman he almost married, I felt sorely tempted to rifle through the contents of the fruit bowl I'd been left alone with.

But would I want someone to enter my apartment and start poking their nose into my personal business? Absolutely not.

On the other hand, if I knew that Steve had yet to read the invitation, I could relax in his arms a little easier tonight and stop waiting on pins and needles for that moment to come.

It was a feeble argument at best and I should have walked away.

Seconds later, I wished I had followed my moral compass and done exactly that.

Because I found an opened white linen envelope near the bottom of that fruit bowl.

Chapter Sixteen

AFTER SEVERAL HOURS of tossing and turning with that wedding invitation on the brain, I brewed a pot of coffee and declared a truce on the war of obsession I'd been waging the last two days.

"I mean it," I said, waking the dog curled around my dining room chair. "Either you trust him or you don't."

Fozzie whimpered, and I reached down to chuck him under the chin. "Not you. The other male in my life."

So Steve had withheld some information. It wasn't like he didn't have some preoccupations of his own with the arrest of one of his best friends.

I could only imagine how he felt. And I could barely do that because he couldn't talk to me about Georgie's case. More accurately, wouldn't let me talk to him about Seth Lukin, much to my frustration. Because Steve had his own suspicions about the guy?

That would only be true if Steve were convinced of Little Dog's innocence.

That was the one truth that I'd had the most certainty of this week. Plus, it explained the cease and desist lecture I'd been given. Steve wanted to keep me out of harm's way.

Understandable and explainable.

Breathing a sigh of relief, I wrapped my arms around Fozzie's neck. "I knew Georgie didn't do it."

No matter how emotionally conflicted he had been when I talked to him Monday night, there was no way he could have left Colton Ziegler to die on the other side of that fence.

Georgie might be full of bark, but it wasn't in his nature to be cruel or that stupid.

No. Someone did this who knew about some of the history between Little Dog and Colt.

Someone like Seth Lukin.

I stood, feeling lighter on my feet than I had for days. "I think this calls for a celebration, don't you?" I asked the resident fur ball.

Following me into the kitchen, Fozzie wagged his tail as I scooped a cup of kibble from the almost empty sack I had taken from Colt's apartment.

"I need to buy some more of this today," I said, dumping it into his bowl. "Fortunately, I know a place that carries this brand."

And that would give me the perfect opportunity to have another chat with Seth Lukin.

After I got to work and caught up on the last of the filing, I went to my computer to look up Boynton House Painting. They didn't have a web page, but a home services information site listed their Clatska address and phone number, so I made a note of both and gave them a call. That promptly led to a recording, inviting me to leave a message.

Since I didn't want to tip my hand to the guy with the black Cougar or any of his pals, I disconnected, and glared at the note on top of a stack of files that one of the assistant prosecutors had left for me during my hour-long absence from my desk.

Her request was simple enough. The time it would take to grant it was the problem, especially since she needed the copies made for a meeting this afternoon.

Everyone on the third floor knew that the cranky behemoth humming in the copy room didn't respond well to pressure. Neither did this frequent operator of the finicky machine, but I didn't have the luxury of overheating and shutting down for a power nap during my lunch hour. No matter how much I may have needed one after it jammed seven times and finally quit on me.

What I needed more was information, so I used the short walk to my car as a cooling-off period and headed to the feed store, where Seth Lukin was stocking a shelf near the front counter.

"You're back," he said in a tone that made it clear how he felt about it.

I forced a smile. "I'm out of dog food."

"Was there a particular brand you were using?"

"Actually, it's the one Colt Ziegler was using."

Seth did a double take. "You're feeding his dog?"

"I *have* his dog, for now." I looked around, but didn't see anyone else in the store. "Is Mr. Ortiz here? I wanted to put up a little poster on his bulletin board."

"At lunch."

Good. I wouldn't have to ask permission to talk to Seth.

I nodded. "I'll check back with him later, then. I had

hoped that Jessica might want the dog, but I understand that your apartment manager doesn't allow pets."

A crinkle etched a path between his brows. "No."

"Too bad. He's a nice dog." I turned up the wattage of my smile. "You probably saw him at Colt's apartment."

"I never went into his apartment."

"But you went there, right?"

He blinked. "Yeah. Once."

"Saturday night, right?"

"I don't know what you're trying to—"

"Someone saw you pounding on his door that night."

"I...uh...just wanted to talk to him."

"And did you?"

"He wasn't home."

"How about Sunday?" I asked as a buzzer announced the arrival of a customer.

Seth looked as relieved to see an elderly man shuffling toward the back room as I felt to have a witness in the event this *chat* started going sideways.

"I should probably see if he needs some help," Seth said, his feet already in motion.

"He'll let you know if he does." I pulled him into the dog food aisle. "You were about to tell me when you saw Colt on Sunday."

"What? No, I wasn't. Besides, I wasn't even around much on Sunday, which was exactly what I told the police."

Maybe, but that muscle twitching at the corner of his mouth wasn't helping him sell this story. "But you wanted to deliver a message to Colt on Saturday, so it only makes sense that you'd try again the next day."

"I was with Jessica all Sunday. She can tell you."

She had, and about as convincingly.

"She said you went for a drive. I'm betting that you ended up somewhere in the vicinity of her old apartment."

"You've got this all wrong. It's like I told the detective. Jessica didn't want anything to do with him."

Steve wouldn't have been any more satisfied with that answer than I was. "But *you* did, because you had a few choice words for him."

"Yeah, but I didn't kill him."

And that may have been true. He was getting so twitchy I couldn't tell.

I needed more time with him to make sure, but once Seth bolted to help the customer shuffling up to the counter with a bag of fertilizer, I knew I'd gleaned all I was going to get out of him without someone with a scarier badge standing by my side.

With nothing more to say, I grabbed a small sack of dog food and got in line at the counter.

"Did you find what you were looking for?" Seth asked with obvious indifference as he rang up my purchase.

I pulled out the last of the cash from my wallet. "For now."

While he counted out my change, something that he said the first time I met him niggled at me, and I flashed him a smile. "I thought of one more thing I need. You mentioned that Colt said something about having problems with Little Dog."

He shrugged. "Yeah."

"When did he talk to you about that?"

"A while ago." Seth seemed to be inspecting one of

the many scratches that had been dug into the wooden countertop. "I don't know exactly."

Since his muscle twitch was back, I knew why he couldn't tell me when.

The conversation never happened. But I suspected that something else had happened that gave Seth the impression that he wasn't the only one having trouble with Colt Ziegler.

"You saw Colt at Bassett Motor Works Sunday night, didn't you? Maybe even witnessed him being escorted out the front gate?"

Seth paled. "I told you. I never saw him on Sunday."

I picked up my dog food. "Yeah, that's what you said." *I didn't believe you then either.*

I was driving to my apartment when I spotted Steve's cruiser parked in front of the Roadkill Grill.

The Grill wouldn't offer me the family discount I received at Duke's or let me make my own salad, but since my favorite cop was inside and I wanted to tell him what I'd just found out, that was a good-enough bargain for me.

I pulled into the crowded parking lot and was lucky enough to find a spot near the cruiser. Although I would have felt a heckuva lot luckier if I hadn't emerged from my car to see Steve approaching with a full head of steam.

"What are you doing here?" he demanded, blocking my path.

"Aren't I allowed to grab some lunch?"

He scowled. "Since when do you eat here?"

"I saw your car and thought you might like some company." I tried to match the intensity of his gaze. "Clearly, I was wrong."

Steve's lips curled as he eased toward me. "Nope. It's only bad timing since I was just leaving."

Dang. "Do you have to go? I was hoping to talk to you about something."

"Want to go do that in my office?"

Now I was the one scowling. "But you don't like me to come to your office."

"Because you always show up, wanting something I can't give you."

Okay, he had a point. But that wasn't why he was currently shielding me with his body.

I tried to peek around him. "Is there some reason you don't want to be seen with me?"

He took me by the shoulders and fixed me with his gaze. "Hardly."

Steve could be very persuasive, especially when his warm hands were on me and that mouth of his stretched into a lopsided grin.

And he knew it.

But his smile didn't relax the tension in his jaw, so his powers of persuasion weren't quite as effective as usual.

"Then there's something here you don't want me to see," I said, watching him for a reaction.

Nothing.

"Chow Mein, that job of yours is making you suspicious."

I continued to stare at him. "No, *you* are making me suspicious."

"Don't know why, and as fascinating as it is to have a staring contest with you in the parking lot, I have to go," he said, giving me a peck on the lips.

Watching Steve walk away, I was completely confused. Had I misread him? Had I become so consumed by Georgie's case that I was starting to see problems that didn't exist?

Steve glanced back over his shoulder. "You coming? I have a meeting at two, so if you want to talk it needs to be soon."

I did want to talk to him and as soon as possible. "I'll be right there. I'm just going to grab some takeout."

He nodded but didn't look especially pleased about it.

I was too hungry to spend the rest of my lunch hour trying to interpret Steve's body language, so I stepped inside the Roadkill Grill and breathed in a mouthwatering fusion of all the greasy foods I wouldn't be eating.

"Hiya, Char," said Janine, one of the longtime waitresses, greeting me from behind the register. "We don't see you here very often."

"I was in the neighborhood." I left out the reason why.

After I ordered and paid for a chicken Caesar to go, I scanned the crowd to see who else had been in the neighborhood.

Other than Gloria, the Julia Child lookalike who worked in the county clerk's office, I didn't see anyone from the courthouse. Nor did I see anyone connected with Georgie's case, so I failed to understand what had caused Steve to think that I needed a human shield.

Something had. Of that I was certain, but short of having the man here to explain himself, I didn't think any answers were going to be forthcoming.

Since I wasn't accomplishing much beyond working up a powerful craving for a burger and onion rings, I sat at the counter and checked my email on my phone until a white to-go box with my salad was set in front of me.

Putting away my phone, I thanked Janine and turned to face a guy in paint-stained coveralls standing at the register.

Rather attractive despite a slightly crooked nose, he had two days of stubble, tan skin, and dark hair tied back in a ponytail. Two similarly dressed Hispanic men in line behind him stood a little shorter, one of them in a Seattle Mariners ball cap. And I had a feeling I was looking at what Steve hadn't wanted me to see.

I slapped a smile on my face when Ponytail Guy caught me staring.

He nodded as he reached for his wallet.

"Working on a job in town?" I asked, trying to maintain a calm demeanor while beads of sweat popped out on my upper lip.

Ponytail Guy gave me a quick once-over without registering any interest. Fine by me. I wanted to see what I could find out about him, not a date.

"A few blocks away from here," he said, handing a twenty to Janine. "One of the Victorians up on the hill."

"I'll have to show my grandmother. She's been talking about getting her house painted, but wasn't sure who to talk to about that."

Setting aside his disinterest in sweaty, zaftig women, anyone breathing should have recognized what I had just tossed out as a money-making opportunity and pounced on it like a dog on a pork chop.

He pocketed his change, and then pulled out a business card. "Have her give us a call."

I dropped the card into my tote so that I wouldn't appear too eager to find out who he worked for. "I'll definitely do that. Thanks."

As I made my way toward my car, I cursed the wisdom of that decision because I couldn't find the darned card. But standing next to the Jag as if I were searching for my keys provided me a good excuse to scan the parking lot for an older-model black car.

Nothing appeared to fit that description, but I did see a white cargo van leaving with the guy in the ball cap at the wheel, so I hopped into my car to follow it up 2nd Street.

Once it took a left on J and pulled in front of the two-story Victorian getting a fresh coat of dusty rose, I turned into Mrs. Nolan's driveway three houses to the north.

Mrs. Nolan was a former Duke's pie happy hour customer who was now wheelchair-bound. She was also a little deaf, so I didn't think she'd come out to complain about the cowbell solo taking place in her driveway while I waited for the paint crew to get back to work.

Once I saw Ponytail Guy climb some scaffolding with a spray gun in hand, I figured I could do a slow drive-by without attracting his attention. Because I wanted to snap a picture of the black car parked in front of that van.

Chapter Seventeen

"WHAT EXACTLY AM I looking at?" Steve asked, frowning at the image I was showing him on my cell phone.

"See that?" Standing by his desk, I pointed at the blurry emblem of the cougar on the car's front grill.

"Yeah, so?"

"It's a cat on an older-model black car, which matches a witness's description of a car that she saw Colt Ziegler leaving in on Saturday night."

Steve handed my phone back, the tic pulsing at his jawline warning me that now was not the time to ask that he run the license plate to get an owner name and address. "And why are you still digging into a criminal case?"

"Because you know as well as I do that Little Dog isn't responsible for Colt's death."

"What I know is that you're interfering in a police investigation, and if you keep it up you're gonna get arrested."

"And then you'll have to explain to the criminal prosecutor why you arrested his assistant, who was just doing her job."

"Do you mean the one who asked you to get Tami Ziegler's statement?" A corner of Steve's mouth curled into a smirk. "Yeah, let's show Ben that picture so he can see how far you're trying to insert yourself into this case."

"You can be a real jerk sometimes."

Leaning back in his desk chair, Steve lifted his hands in mock surrender. "Hey, like you, I'm just doing my job."

I hated it when he threw my words back at me.

"The owner of this car could know something about what happened Sunday night," I said, shaking my phone at him.

"Because they hung out together the night before."

"Well, not when you put it that way. But I'm pretty sure that he was the one you didn't want me to see at the Roadkill Grill."

"There's that suspicious mind again."

"Are you going to deny it?" And lie to my face?

Steve shook his head. "What I'm going to do is get back to work, and I suggest you do the same."

"That's not a denial."

He rose from his chair and opened his office door. "Have a nice afternoon, Chow Mein."

After spending the rest of my work day trying to locate potential witnesses for an upcoming case, once the courthouse clock struck five, I raced over to J Street with the hope of catching a certain paint crew taking advantage of some late afternoon sun.

Given the fact that the guy in the ball cap was loading a plastic paint bucket into the van I had just pulled up behind, I knew I didn't have much time.

He turned, staring as I stepped out of the Jag, so I gave him a friendly wave.

Yes, you didn't expect to see me again today.

"Your car," he said with a heavy accent. "Very bad knock."

"I know. I need to get it fixed."

Nodding agreement, he headed toward the house. *"Hazlo pronto."*

I wasn't sure what exactly he'd said, but I understood *pronto.* I had something else that needed to be done even more pronto and ran to catch up with him. "Where's the guy who owns that black car?"

"In back."

Coming around through the side yard, I spotted Ponytail Guy painting the trim of a back door and pasted a sunny smile on my face. "Hello!"

His eyes widened. "Hey," he said after a second of hesitation.

I planted my hands on my hips and gazed up at the crew's handiwork. "The new paint looks great. I'll definitely have to show my grandmother when you're all done."

Applying another brush stroke of dark burgundy, he dished out a sidelong glance. "That'll probably be tomorrow afternoon sometime."

"That's fine. I'm actually here to talk to you."

He stiffened. "Me? What about?"

"I'm hoping you can help me with a problem I'm having at work." I pointed at the stretch of overgrown grass that I'd just walked through. "Maybe you could take a two-minute break and we could talk over there." Where there weren't any picture windows for the homeowner to ask why I was on his property.

I was betting on a hunch that the good manners that should have been drummed into young Ponytail Guy would kick in, and he'd be willing to help a damsel in distress.

After he grumbled a few unchivalrous swear words, he set down his paint and brush, and joined me on the lawn. "Two minutes."

He struck me as someone who wouldn't respond well to a badge or note-taking, so instead of reaching into my tote, I extended my hand. "Sorry, I never introduced myself. Charmaine Digby."

"Rusty Naylor."

Memorable name. For his sake I hoped it wasn't the name on his birth certificate.

He held up his paint-splattered hand for my inspection. "I'm probably a little too dirty for you, Charmaine," he said with a twinkle in his dark eyes.

I picked up his double meaning loud and clear, and tried to channel my flirtatious mother as I took his hand in mine. "I'll take my chances."

His lips curled into a cocky grin as his gaze lowered to my chest. "So, what can I do for you?"

Just keep talking.

"I work in the coroner's office. I'm basically the one on the phone calling to verify employer information, family members, that kind of stuff." Which was true, only this wasn't a coroner's case. "And I haven't been able to do that with Colt Ziegler, but he worked with you guys, right?"

Rusty knit his brows. "Yeah. Some."

"Boynton House Painting, the name of the company on the card, right?"

"Right."

"Awesome," I said, blowing out a breathy sigh of relief so that I'd sound more incompetent than probing.

I touched his sleeve. "I'm sorry. That was insensitive. The two of you were probably friends."

His eyes held a hard edge. "Yeah."

"When did you see him last?"

His jaw tightened. "Saturday night."

"Oh, the night before he passed. How sad."

Rusty kept his mouth shut, his expression unchanged.

Obviously not that sad for him. "Did he happen to mention having any trouble with anyone in town?"

"Nope. Can't say that he did."

"My boss is really leaning on me to come up with a timeline for where Colt was on Sunday. If you talked to him that day, that could really help me out."

"Sorry. Didn't see him. Didn't talk to him."

Liar.

"I gotta get going, but if you have any questions for my boss, you've got the number."

"I sure do. Thanks, Rusty. You've been a big help." *Because you gave me a last name that couldn't be that common around here.* Assuming he lived locally, which would be really good to know for the criminal background check I wanted to run.

"No problem," he muttered, turning his back to me.

"Oh, I should have asked. Is that your Cougar out there?"

He puffed his chest out a little. "Yeah."

"I gotta show it to my dad, but he's out of town right now." Way out of town in France. "Do you live around here?"

"Sorta, but the job brings me into town a few times a month."

Then I'd lay odds that he lived in or near Clatska.

"Cool. I'll tell my dad to keep an eye out."

I was going to keep an eye out in the coming days, too, because this guy was clearly hiding something.

I gave him a wave and dashed to my car.

Twenty minutes later, I sat alone in the clerical wing of the prosecutor's office and stared at my computer screen while I scrolled through all the surnames in the regional database that began with *NA*.

I figured that Rusty had to be a childhood nickname. Someone had taken his given name and playfully twisted it to something resembling *rusty nail*. That told me that his first name would be an *R*-name a kid would want to disassociate himself from.

"Rusty," I said, clicking on the hypertext for Ruslan Naylor, a thirty-one year-old with a Clatska address. "Is this you?"

The age and the description of five foot eight and one hundred sixty pounds matched up well with the housepainter I had been speaking with.

Ruslan had an arrest record dating back over ten years: DUI, speeding tickets, theft in the first and second degree, and a couple of burglary charges. But the one that caught my eye was a residential burglary conviction. I didn't have access to the amount of time Ruslan had served, but he was clearly a convicted felon.

Now, if he were a convicted felon who went by the nickname Rusty and was hanging around for a couple of days, painting my house, I'd want to make sure that I tucked my valuables away in a very safe place. Not to say people couldn't change, but Rusty clearly hadn't wanted to answer my questions about Colt.

Because Colt had been in possession of a diamond engagement ring he wouldn't have been able to afford?

Or maybe Colt knew too much about some break-in that Rusty had been involved in?

I sucked in a sharp breath, recalling what Diana Ferguson had said about the break-in at Malcolm Pembroke's house.

Colt had been the Pembrokes' driver and would have been the perfect lookout man to coordinate the burglary with Rusty. Maybe that's what they met about Saturday night—to put their final plan together.

I shivered with the icy realization that if Rusty Naylor wasn't responsible for Colt Ziegler's death, he knew the person who was.

"Holy smokes," I said, shutting down my computer. This was why Steve wanted to keep me out of the Roadkill Grill. He must have suspected that Rusty Naylor was the link between what happened to Colt and the break-in at the Pembroke house. Since there hadn't been an arrest I doubted he could prove it, but I could at least confirm that they'd had contact on Sunday.

I needed to tell Steve. Immediately. And it needed to be face-to-face so he couldn't hang up on me.

Grabbing my tote, I headed for the exit and had just passed Patsy's empty desk when I heard my name.

I hit the brakes, backed up, and locked gazes with

Frankie, who was waving me into her office.

"Charmaine," she said, "what the heck does Ben have you working on to keep you here so late?"

While the county prosecutor might be very interested in everything I'd learned about my new pal Ruslan, she needed to hear it through proper channels, meaning Ben or Steve, not me.

"I was just catching up on some paperwork." I forced a smile. "You know how everyone around here has to have everything printed out."

She sighed. "Indeed I do."

I knew I should skedaddle before I said anything to get myself into trouble. At the same time, I had been presented with a rare opportunity to talk to Frankie without Patsy sitting outside her office like a guard dog, and I would have been stupid to not take advantage of it.

I inched closer to Frankie's desk. "I understand that Colt Ziegler's autopsy was scheduled for yesterday."

She nodded. "Dr. Zuniga sent me his report a couple of hours ago."

"And?"

"Much as I expected—blunt force trauma."

"From a blow to the head?"

I got another nod.

"Was it conclusive that it was delivered by that base-ball bat?" I asked, my heart pounding with trepidation.

Giving me a quizzical look, Frankie cocked her head. "Since George Junior confessed to striking a blow with the bat that night, it's about as conclusive as we can get."

Chapter Eighteen

AFTER I STOPPED by the apartment to feed Fozzie and give him a short walk, I drove to Steve's house. His Ford pickup wasn't in the driveway and I was too antsy to hang out at Gram's and wait, so I decided to kill some time at the grocery store.

The Red Apple Market down on Main Street had a pretty good deli that catered to the local contractors and business owners who wanted their sub sandwiches piled high, their fried chicken crispy, and their salads packed fresh and ready to go. But by the time I arrived around six-thirty, the deli was unattended, with nothing left but a lowly container of chicken wings under a warmer.

Hungry beggars couldn't be choosers, so I grabbed it and headed to the produce section to replenish my supply of diet munchies, where I spotted Katherine Pembroke.

I didn't know how much useful information she might have from riding in that limo with Colt Ziegler, but I viewed this unexpected meet-up as an invitation to find out.

Pretending to not see her perusing the selection of organic tomatoes, I turned my shopping cart into hers.

"Sorry, Mrs. Pembroke. I'm usually not such a reckless driver." I met her gaze. "Good thing my grandmother isn't here. She'd accuse me of taking after my mom."

As a teenager, Marietta had rear-ended Katherine Pembroke's Mercedes—the incident that introduced the then-newly married Mrs. Pembroke to my grandparents—so I figured my conversation starter would strike a chord.

An easy smile lit her full face, her pale skin bearing only the finest of wrinkles to betray her age. "Your grandmother can be merciless when she talks about your mom."

Oh? I hadn't realized that was a subject that came up all that often. Then again, Marietta was the local celebrity who had recently announced her engagement to one of Port Merritt High's teachers, making her a trending community topic.

I didn't want to add any fuel to the gossip fire that had been raging over the last month, so I stuck to the safer past history. "That's what can happen when you total two of your parents' cars."

Mrs. Pembroke touched my arm with feigned concern. "She's not driving while she's in town, is she?"

"No. Gram and I know better than to let her drive our cars. Speaking of driving," I said, trying to segue to the life and death of the limo driver occupying most of my waking hours this week, "I understand that you and Mr. Pembroke were two of the last people to see Colt Ziegler before…"

She shook her head. "It was so sad to hear the news about that boy."

"I know. It was a shocker. I can't imagine what happened, can you?"

"No. Colt was well-mannered and seemed to really enjoy his role as chauffeur, so his death came as a huge shock. After experiencing such a delightful evening at Malcolm's retirement party, to hear about what happened on top of coming home to find our house broken into... It made me sorry that I helped the Fergusons organize that stupid party."

Mrs. Pembroke's eyes glittered with unshed tears. "If we had just stayed home and had the quiet celebration Malcolm said he wanted, nothing would have happened."

My heart broke for her. "This isn't your fault."

"No, that young man would still be alive."

"I happen to work for the county prosecutor," I said while she wiped her eyes. "And it would be helpful to know if Colt mentioned any plans that he had for after he dropped you off. Anyone that he planned to meet up with—that sort of thing."

"When we arrived at the club, I offered to bring him something to eat later, but he said he was going to grab a burger. It was like when he and two other boys were painting our house."

The house that had been burglarized the night of Colt's death? The fact that he had been a member of the paint crew couldn't be a coincidence.

Mrs. Pembroke gave me a sad smile. "I offered to make them some sandwiches, but he said they were heading over to the Roadkill Grill. I guess a tuna sandwich can't compete with their hamburgers."

I tried to remain calm while my pulse thundered in my ears. "When was this?"

"Two, maybe two and a half weeks ago."

"Not that it's important now, but do you happen to remember if there was a dark-haired guy with a ponytail working with Colt?"

"Rusty?

Holy smokes, they were casing the house while they were there. "Yeah, that's his name."

"Another nice boy. Took great care to cover my azaleas."

He wasn't so nice. He ripped you off.

"I know you don't want to hear it," I said, following Steve into his kitchen. "But I'm telling you with absolute certainty that Rusty Naylor met with Colt before or after that burglary and knows what happened later that night."

Steve pulled a beer from his refrigerator. "What part of 'stay out of this investigation' don't you understand?"

I swallowed the growing lump in my throat. "I thought you'd want to know."

He stared at the hardwood floor like he wanted to throw me down on it, and not in a fun way. "You are giving me no choice."

Leaning over, I tried to make eye contact while the chicken wings in my stomach threatened to take flight. "What?"

"Since you won't listen to me, maybe Frankie can get your attention."

"Seriously?"

"What else can I do to convince you to back off?" Steve asked with an icy calm that chilled me to my marrow.

"You know I'm just trying to help."

"What I know is that you're going to get hurt if you keep this up."

I reached out to him, but Steve sidestepped me to sort through his mail at the table.

Standing in the middle of his kitchen, staring at his back, I hadn't felt this ineffectual since my ex informed me that he wanted out of our marriage.

"I'm not trying to interfere in your investigation," I said after several seconds of awkward silence. "I just want Ben to drop the charges against Georgie."

Steve took a swig of beer. "Do you trust me, Char?"

I found it disheartening that he should even ask. "Of course."

"Then know that I can do my job without the benefit of your assistance."

My cheeks burning from his rebuke, I didn't know what I could say that wouldn't stoke the fire raging behind his eyes. So I kept my mouth shut and reached for the tote I'd slung over the back of the chair next to him.

Steve's hand clamped down on mine. "I mean it. You need to trust me on this."

I did, completely. But I wasn't so sure that I'd still be employed tomorrow.

"Are you sure you don't want the baby to have a big, furry dog?" I asked Rox over the din of the 1970s one-hit wonder wailing through the speakers mounted above the bar.

She tossed a coaster in front of me. "No takers yet, huh?"

"Not only no takers, not even one phone call about him."

"Awwww. Sorry, hon. Maybe it's a sign that you're supposed to keep him."

Leaning on the bar, I cupped my chin in my palm. "I can't keep him. A dog needs a yard to run around in."

"Did he have that before?"

"No. He had an apartment a lot like mine."

Rox cocked her head. "Then what's the problem in keeping him?"

"I don't need or want a roommate right now." Especially one that needed to be walked three times a day.

"Uh-oh. What'd he do?"

"Nothing. What goes in has to come out on a fairly regular basis."

"I meant the two-legged male that you're not spending the evening with."

I sighed. "I just came from his place."

"And?"

"Let's just say that we're not good company for one another tonight."

"Sounds like you'd better tell Roxie all about it over a drink." She pulled out a bottle of chardonnay from under the bar. "Am I pouring, or are you sticking to your water rations?"

I'd already blown my diet with all those chicken wings. What did another couple hundred calories matter? "Pour."

"Hey, Eric," Rox called out, looking toward the other end of the bar as she placed the wine glass in front of me. "Does your place have a fenced yard?"

Sporting a sky blue Ferguson Ford bowling shirt, Eric Caldwell approached with an empty beer pitcher and a wry smile. "Yeah. Why?"

Rox took the pitcher from him and headed to the nearest tap. "Char has a dog your kids would love to have."

"Sorry," he said to me, not looking the least bit apologetic. "I already have a dog that I think you met when you came out to the house."

I was fine with that answer, even with the bit of snark that he had injected into it, because I had no intention of handing over Fozzie's leash to this jerk.

"I did, and while you taking Fozzie would keep him in the family—"

"This is Colt's dog that we're talking about?"

I nodded. "I sort of have temporary custody of him while I try to find him a home."

"That's good news then, 'cause my cousin was worried about the dog running off."

"There's some mystery about how he got out of the apartment, but he's safe now," I said to the back of Eric's head as he directed his attention to the pitcher Rox was sliding toward him.

Not that you care.

"Glad to hear it." He glanced back, dialing up the wattage of his car salesman smile. "Good seeing you. Now, be sure to look me up when you're ready for those new wheels."

"You betcha."

Rox wiped away the few drips that Eric's pitcher had left on the surface of the bar. "Are you getting a new car?"

I reached for my drink. "Not anytime soon." And definitely not from Eric Caldwell.

Chapter Nineteen

"YOU REALIZE THAT you just growled at the only person who's called and expressed any interest in adopting you, right?" I said to Fozzie as we left the dog park after six the next evening. "The next time someone calls, remember that good boys get adopted, and bad boys have to come home with me."

Fozzie glanced back at me with a doggie grin.

"Yeah, that didn't come out right, but you catch my drift. That guy we rushed over here to meet has kids and a yard. You would have had fun there. Instead, you're alone all day in an apartment."

Much like most of the men that had come and gone in my life, Fozzie didn't appear to be listening to me. Instead, he picked up the pace once he spotted my car and we power-walked to the parking lot.

"I'm not saying that you and I aren't good for one another. It's not that at all." As my hips would attest, since trying to keep up with him had been providing me with quite the daily workout. "But I'm more like your transitional girl after a big breakup—the one you might like hanging around with, but you both know it's not meant to last forever."

Crap.

I stopped in my tracks with the realization that I'd just described my relationship with Steve.

Looking up at me, Fozzie barked.

"I know. Guys don't like talking about this kind of stuff, but sometimes things need to be said."

No matter how difficult finding the words for that conversation might be.

Not necessarily tonight, I thought ten minutes later, when I didn't see Steve's truck parked in his driveway. But soon.

My more immediate need was to do something about the knock in my car that Rusty's paint crew buddy had warned me to fix *pronto.* Did I truly expect the Jag to do its cowbell swan song in the next twenty-four hours? No. But I didn't want to be out on some remote county road when that eventuality came to pass.

Since today was Friday, I figured that one of the mechanics at Bassett's Motor Works could look at it over the weekend if I could get it over there before the shop closed at seven. Which should have been no problem since that gave me over thirty minutes, but my grandmother's Honda wasn't parked in her carport, and that was the car I was counting on borrowing this weekend.

Dang it.

Just as I was about to pull out of her driveway, the back door opened and Marietta waved at me.

Her lips were moving but I couldn't hear her over the engine noise.

I rolled my window down. "What?"

"Good heavens, sugar. Is that your car making that horrible racket?"

"Yep. I was just going over to Bassett's to have them fix it."

"What are you doing afterward?"

"Walking home to my apartment since I won't have a car."

My mother's eyes brightened. "I have access to one if you want to have a girls' night out."

I didn't. I just needed to think of a way to let her down gently. "I...uh..." *Need to get up early for work?*

No, tomorrow was Saturday.

I'm expecting an important call?

I'd have my cell phone with me, so that wouldn't work either.

Steve's coming over?

He wasn't and probably didn't want to see me right now, but my mother didn't know that. "Actually—"

"Barry's out with his son tonight and your grandmother is at some garden club function, so it's a perfect opportunity for you and I to spend some time together." She reached through the window and playfully nudged my shoulder. "Come on. It'll be fun."

For whom?

"Just give me two secs to get my purse," she said, dashing to the house in her stilettos.

Shifting in his seat impatiently, Fozzie huffed a breath.

"Don't say it. I know."

A minute later, Marietta glared at him through the open passenger side window. "You neglected to tell me that *he* was with you."

Good grief. "He was sitting right here in plain sight."

"In my seat."

"Which now has dog hair on it, so don't feel like you're obligated to come with me."

Marietta crawled into my back seat. "Don't be ridiculous. I don't get to see you that often, so I'm not about to let a little dog hair stop me."

Swell.

"Drive to Barry's on M Street," she said, flicking her bangle-adorned wrist at me as if I were her taxi driver. "And I'll get the DeLorean and meet you at your apartment after you're done at Bassett's."

I wasn't so sure that her fiancé would be all that keen about her borrowing the car she had driven on her 1980s TV show, especially after making it her engagement present to him. "Are you sure that's a good idea?"

She scoffed at me. "Absolutely. What's the worst that could happen?"

After Fozzie and I walked home to my apartment, I tucked him in for the evening and then headed down to the visitor parking area, where Marietta was showing off the DeLorean to a couple of my neighbors.

"Ah, mah daughtah's here," she said, reverting back to the southern accent she'd used in public since the day she was cast in the Georgia-based show that had made her famous. She flashed her bright white smile at the couple. "Lovely to meet you."

The second they walked away, I held out my hand to her. "Keys, please."

My mother blinked. "Excuse me?"

"I'm driving."

"You most certainly are not."

"For your safety and for everyone out and about in Port Merritt tonight, I think it's for the best."

Folding her arms under her double Ds, she pursed her lips. "I drove this car almost every day for three years, and I'm perfectly capable—"

"That was thirty years ago on a closed set. You've already totaled two cars in this town. Do you really want to crush your fiancé's new toy like a tin can and make it three?"

Marietta fingered the pendant at the base of her throat. "I declare. You weren't even around when those unfortunate incidents occurred, so I don't think you've earned the right to dredge up ancient history."

True enough. But since I was the only one standing between "Mayhem" Moreau and the classic car from her TV series, the task had fallen on me to make sure that history didn't repeat itself tonight.

Like I'd discovered as a teenager accompanying my mother to one of her movie premieres, the most effective way to influence her decisions was to leverage her fear of bad publicity. "I'm sure the regional papers would eat that story up with a spoon."

Heaving a heavy sigh, she dropped her key ring in my hand.

"Good decision," I said, sliding behind the steering wheel.

"Whatever." She wriggled into the bucket seat next to me. "So, where're we going?"

I had absolutely no desire to spend the next few hours with her public persona, so all bars and restaurants were out. "How about if we head back to Gram's and we can open up a bottle of that fumé blanc that you like and maybe watch a movie?"

"Perfect." She did her wrist flick thing again. "Drive on."

"Yes, ma'am."

After taking a minute to familiarize myself with her old car, I eased it out of the parking lot and took the right on 2nd Street as a slight detour so that I could satisfy my curiosity about a recently painted house.

Marietta shot me a sideways glance. "Why are you going this way?"

"I wanted to show you a house up here."

She sucked in a breath. "One that you're thinking about buying?"

On my salary? "No. It's a Victorian that just got updated with new paint."

"Okay, but it's getting dark. We won't be able to see much of anything."

I stepped on the gas as we went up the hill toward J Street. "Then we'd better see what this baby can do."

She gripped the center console. "Sugar, I'm not *that* interested in looking at paint."

"I am." And then some.

"Nice, huh?" I asked, after we parked in front of the house across the street.

There were no vehicles besides ours in the immediate vicinity, but with any luck, I'd find that the owners of the house were enjoying a quiet evening at home. Preferably with some sort of security system in place if Rusty planned to make this an upcoming crime scene.

"Oh, it is nice." My mother pulled out her cell phone. "I'll have to show this to Barry. Give him some color ideas for his house, which is begging to be painted, if you ask me."

I'm sure he hadn't been asking, but she was his home decorating problem, not mine.

But *Marietta Moreau, local celebrity,* could come in very handy when I wanted a stranger to invite me into their home.

I just needed to come up with a good reason for her to join me on their front porch. "Need to go to the bathroom?"

A two-year-old could hold her water better than my mother, so I was confident of the answer.

She snapped a photo through the side window. "Not urgently. I can wait until we get home."

Wrong answer. "Okay, but I'd like to see what they did on the inside, so maybe you'd like to—"

"Actually, I do believe that I could use a comfort station," she said, opening her door.

"Excellent." I inspected the key ring in my hand as I climbed out of the DeLorean. "Where's the remote to lock the car?"

She tsked. "You're so young. Use the key, my darling."

"The key—how quaint," I muttered, manually locking the doors.

Crossing the street, I joined Marietta. "Okay, here's the plan. I'm going to knock on their door and say that we were driving by and you noticed that they painted their house. That's when I'd like you to be your charming self so that they'll invite us in."

She straightened, her nose in the air as she strutted toward the front door walkway. "I'll have you know that I'm always charming."

Sure you are.

I reached for the doorbell button. "Ready?"

Marietta moistened her ruby red lips as if a director was about to shout *Action*. "I'm ready."

I rang the bell but didn't hear anything but a dog barking in the neighborhood, so I rapped on the door.

"Maybe they're not home," Marietta said, watching me press my ear to the door.

"Looks that way." Which made me all the more concerned about Rusty showing up to take advantage of the situation later this evening.

I handed the key ring to my mother. "Why don't you make yourself comfortable in the car while I check out the back of the house." And make sure that the doors I saw yesterday were securely locked.

"Chah-maine, I really don't think we should invite ourselves into their backyard without an invitation."

The owners weren't home to defend their property. That was invitation enough for me.

I shooed her away and proceeded to trace my steps from yesterday. "I'll just be a minute."

"Ooooh," she said, following me. "I love the burgundy trim. It's probably a bit much for Barry's house, but I should get a picture of this to show him."

"Whatever." I was only interested in the door surrounded by the trim and was relieved to find it locked.

"Honey, move out of the shot if you would please."

I stifled a sigh and stepped off the back deck to test the lock of the garage door, but the second I reached for the knob I heard some loud barking next door.

"Hey! What do you think you're doing?" asked the burly sixty-something man standing next to the snarling chocolate lab on the other side of a chain link fence.

I held out my hands while my heart battered my ribcage. "Nothing. I was just making sure that the doors were locked after the paint crew left."

"Right." Sneering, he pulled a cell phone from his back pocket. "Maybe you'd like to tell that story to the cops."

"Oh my," Marietta uttered, her voice mainly breath. "Chah-maine, I think it's time to go."

Understatement of the year.

I pasted a smile on my face. "Sir, you don't need to call the police. We were just leaving."

With his phone to his ear, the neighbor pointed at me. "Stay right where you are."

And spend the next few hours explaining to Steve what I was doing here? No, thanks.

I climbed back onto the deck and grabbed my mother by the arm. "Run!"

While we ran for the car, I could hear the neighbor yelling at us to stop.

"Well, this was a very bad idea," Marietta huffed as I pulled her toward the street.

"You can get mad at me later. Right now, let's just focus on getting out of here."

"I don't think he got a good look at me, so unless he knows you—"

"He doesn't."

"Then we should be home free."

Except a local reporter jogging with a golden retriever on a leash was approaching the DeLorean at about the same pace that we were.

"Act casual," I said, slowing our advance on our getaway vehicle.

Marietta jerked out of my grasp. "My heels are sinking in this grass and you want me to act casual?"

"Yep, because that's a reporter waiting for us over by your car."

She stiffened, uttering a string of obscenities.

I stepped in front of her. "Let me handle this."

Renee Ireland's eyes gleamed with interest as I crossed the street. "Well, fancy meeting you here. Visiting friends in the neighborhood?"

"Actually, we were just admiring this paint job." Of course the neighbor standing at the end of his driveway, telling the nine-one-one dispatcher about us trying to get away in a DeLorean didn't lend any credence to my story.

The reporter extended her hand to my mother. "Renee Ireland. I'm happy to meet you, Ms. Moreau. I'm a big fan."

"Ah'm always thrilled to chat with mah fans—"

"The cops are on their way, so don't you even think about leaving!" shouted the man across the street.

"But Ah wonder if we could do this at a more opportune time."

Renee's eyes widened as the retriever strained to sniff at Marietta's feet. "What's going on?"

"Just a little misunderstandin'," Marietta said, working the key into the lock.

Renee glanced over at the neighbor. "He called the police on you? Doesn't he know who you are?"

No, and I was pretty sure that my mother hoped it would stay that way.

Tittering nervously, she gave me an anguished look over the roof of the car. "The lock seems to be stuck."

I formed a basket with my hands. "Toss me the keys."

While I coaxed the door open, Renee pulled her cell phone from the fanny pack strapped around her waist. "Is this the same car that you drove in your show?"

"Of course," Marietta said, looking back in the direction of the siren getting louder with each thump of my heart.

"Do you mind posing for a quick picture?"

Seriously? Now?

I reached across the passenger seat to unlock the door. "Gotta go, Mom." Immediately.

"It was delightful to meet you, Renee," Marietta said after spending a few more precious seconds posing for a selfie.

"May I call you for an interview? And maybe bring a photographer to get some newspaper-quality pictures?"

Marietta beamed as she eased into her seat. "Certainly. I'll be in town for a couple more weeks and—"

"So you two will have plenty of opportunity to get together. Right now, we need to go." Before a vehicle flashing blue and red lights pulled up behind me.

The instant my mother fastened her seatbelt, I tightened my grip around the steering wheel and hit the gas. "Oh, this is so not good."

For the second time in my short career as Frankie's special assistant, a local resident had called the cops on me. Add that to the chat Steve threatened to have with my boss, and I could probably kiss my job good-bye.

Marietta reached over and patted my thigh. "Everything's going to be okay. We never entered the house, so if Steve happens to hear about this little incident, he'll have nothing to get upset about. You'll see."

She didn't know him like I did.

As if to prove my point, my cell phone started ringing in the tote bag I'd crammed behind my seat.

"Want me to get your phone, honey?"

"Nope." I was quite certain that I'd be speaking to the caller face-to-face soon enough.

Chapter Twenty

"I ASSURE YOU that what happened was perfectly innocent," Marietta said to Steve while I refilled her wine glass an hour later.

He shot me a look that felt more like a glancing blow as I joined her on my grandmother's sofa. "Yeah, that's pretty much the way the neighbor made it sound."

Okay, so what I'd done wasn't so perfect or innocent. "I know this doesn't look good."

Sitting to my left in a cushy arm chair, Steve vented a humorless chuckle. "You think? Especially after what you and I talked about yesterday."

I hugged my arms to my chest to ward against the cold glare he was directing at me. "I can explain."

He shook his head. "Save it."

"Oh, my," Marietta whispered in my ear. "Someone isn't happy with you."

Not helpful, Mom.

I needed the room so that I could clear the air. "Shouldn't Barry be here soon?"

"When he called from the restaurant, Barry said he'd get here around eight-thirty." She glanced at the clock chiming the half hour on the mantel and bolted upright.

"I had no idea it was so late. I need to excuse myself and get ready, assuming that I'm not required to provide some sort of statement."

Steve waved her away.

Leaning over to pick up her wine glass, my mother kissed the top of my head. "I'm sorry our evening together ended the way it did, but I still had a good time."

Given the note this miserable week was ending on, to hear that Marietta thought I was a fun date came as little consolation.

"Be nice to my girl," she said, slanting a pointed glance at Steve as she passed.

He didn't respond to her. Instead, it looked like Steve was trying to burn a hole in the coffee table between us with the intensity of his stare.

When Marietta disappeared from view, he turned that stare on me.

I pasted a smile on my face to lighten the mood. "Are you sure you don't want something to drink?"

He slowly shook his head.

I drained the last mouthful of wine from my glass and pushed away from the sofa. "Well, I'm going to get myself a refill."

Steve stabbed his index finger in my direction. "Sit."

I dropped back down on the seat cushion. "You're supposed to be nice to me, not talk to me like the dog."

"And you were supposed to stick to doing your job."

"I just wanted to make sure that Rusty Naylor hadn't left a door open at that house so that he could sneak in later tonight."

"No self-respecting thief would be stupid enough to

rip off the owners of the house he'd just painted 'cause he'd be the first person I'd take in for questioning."

"Oh." Folding my arms back over my chest, I sunk a little deeper in the sofa. "Still, I'm happy to report that all the doors were locked, so no harm, no foul. Right?"

Steve's lips flattened. "Pull another stunt like that and I'll arrest you."

"For what?"

"Trespassing, for starters."

"You wouldn't."

He shifted to the edge of his chair and leaned toward me. "Take a good look and tell me what I would or wouldn't do."

I studied the disgruntled face of the man I loved. "Okay, maybe you would. But you'd at least feel bad about slapping a pair of handcuffs around my wrists, right?"

The corners of his mouth lifted. "I never have before."

"Why is the DeLorean parked out front?" Barry asked when he arrived to pick up Marietta.

"It's a long story." One that I hoped the impossibly gorgeous woman descending the stairs would tell him.

"Hello, my darling." Marietta extended her bejeweled hand to him as she stepped into the foyer and bussed his cheek. "How was your dinner with Jason?"

"Fine." Frowning, Barry locked gazes with her. "Who drove the DeLorean over here?"

I waited for my mother to start explaining. Instead, she cast a nervous glance in my direction.

Swell. "That would be me." Wanting nothing more to do with this conversation, I handed him the car keys.

Thunder rumbled behind my future stepfather's eyes. "And why were you driving *my* car?"

Marietta patted his hand. "*Our* car."

He gave her a long look. "I thought you gave it to me as an engagement present."

She batted her eyelashes like an ingénue. "I did, but I knew you wouldn't mind if we borrowed it for a little girls' night out."

"So, you were drinking and driving in my car?"

"Certainly not." Marietta heaved a sigh as she swayed her hips toward the kitchen table, where she'd left her purse. "And Charmaine only drove it from her apartment to here, so it's not like we were out joyriding."

"Maybe not, but I'd prefer that this not happen again," he said to me.

He needed to express that sentiment to his bride-to-be, not his former student. "Yes, sir."

When Marietta returned, she peeked over my shoulder into the living room. "Did Steve go home?"

"Back to work."

Pressing her palm against my cheek, she made a pretty pouty face. "I thought he might stay and you two could enjoy the rest of your evening together."

Steve hadn't appeared to be taking much enjoyment from my company when he left. But since I could guess which case was occupying his time, I was perfectly okay with keeping my own company this evening. "He's got a lot going on tonight, but I'll see him tomorrow."

Marietta brightened. "At the funeral, right?"

I was surprised she was aware that Colt's service was

tomorrow afternoon. "Uh…right."

"Not exactly the most fun kind of date to have on a Saturday," she said, wrapping her arm around Barry's, "but it's still quality time."

"You're going?"

"Of course. Tami and I were quite close back in high school."

That was clearly a lie—one that she must have wanted Barry to believe for some reason. Her business, and once again, his problem, not mine.

"Speaking of going," Barry said, reaching for the doorknob. "Shall we?"

My mother flashed him a dazzling smile. "I'm ready. Oh, wait. Charmaine, how are you getting home?"

Not with them. That was for sure. "Steve can take me after he gets off work."

Barry motioned to me with his hand. "I'll take you home."

This was starting to feel like the school dance, when my ride disappeared on me, and Mr. Ferris, one of the faculty chaperones, drove me home. "That's really not necessary."

"I've got two cars out there, and I don't want your mother driving," he said in my ear as he handed me his keys.

That meant that history was going to repeat itself, whether I wanted it to or not. "Fine."

Barry turned to Marietta. "It looks like it's going to rain later, so you might want a jacket."

She nodded. "Good thinking."

The second she dashed up the stairs, Barry pulled me into the living room. "I don't know what your intention was taking the DeLorean for this *girls' night out*, but I'd appreciate it if you wouldn't encourage your mother's impulsive behavior."

I stared at him in disbelief.

Since before I was born, my mother's behavior had been influenced by only two things: the men in her life, and her career.

It had taken me a while, but I eventually learned to be at peace with where I fell in the pecking order of her hierarchy of needs—and it certainly wasn't as a person of influence.

"Since that impulsive behavior led to her giving you that car," I blurted out before I lost my nerve, "if it's a problem, you should be discussing that with her."

He drew back, his cheeks ruddy as if I had slapped him. "I thought I could count on your support to help protect her hometown reputation. I guess I was wrong."

Given the fact that my mother had served as the local cause célèbre ever since she brought her bastard daughter home to be raised in Port Merritt, it seemed a little late to worry about her reputation.

"Okay, I'm ready," Marietta announced from the stairway, glancing first at Barry and then at me. "What's going on? Is something wrong?"

Barry went to her, taking her hand. "Not at all."

My mother had been blinded by love, but even she should have recognized the fact that her fiancé was holding something back.

"Then let's go." Marietta winked at me. "I'm sure Charmaine's ready to get home."

True. I just wasn't looking forward to the ride home.

Chapter Twenty-One

"IT DOESN'T LOOK like Stevie's here yet," Gram said as she and I entered the Tolliver's Funeral Home chapel.

Steve had sent me a text that he'd been called out earlier in the morning, so I had figured it was a given that he would be a little late.

I led the way toward the platinum blonde waving us over to the block of empty folding chairs surrounding her. "We'll save him a seat."

"That probably won't be necessary." Gram tsked. "There's not much of a turnout."

I stood at the end of the aisle where Lucille was waiting for us and scanned the small gathering of Colt's family and friends dressed in somber shades of black and gray. Most were familiar faces.

The most familiar face in attendance belonged to the voluptuous woman wearing a curve-hugging aquamarine dress, stepping into the chapel with Barry Ferris.

"Don't look now, but your daughter's making her entrance," Lucille said to Gram. "And she looks like she's dressed to kill."

Gram plopped down in the seat next to Lucille. "I don't know where I went wrong with that girl."

"You didn't." Just as I wasn't responsible for any of her choices, no matter what Mr. Ferris thought. "Everyone knows she likes to play to her image."

Lucille crooked a finger at me, so I edged past her big feet and took the seat to her left. "Have you been here for a while?" I asked her.

"Yeah. I didn't want to miss anything in case the guy who whacked Colt showed up to have a few last words with him."

Not that I subscribed to Lucille's more outlandish theories, but if anyone went up to ask the guy in the oak casket for absolution, I wanted to know about it. "Anything to report?"

She sighed. "Not yet, but we have a few minutes before the service starts."

Scooting to the edge of my seat, I craned my neck to get a good look at the occupants in the first two rows on the right. Other than Kendra's husband, Damon, and their two kids, and a gray-haired man I assumed was Tami's ex, I didn't see anyone I hadn't spoken with this week.

That wasn't the case for the older gentleman sitting behind Eric Caldwell. "Who's the suit sitting in the same row as the Pembrokes?"

"Glenn Ferguson. You know, the dude that owns the Ford dealership. I don't know the kid who just walked up to him though."

I did. Rusty Naylor.

"Nice-lookin' fella," Lucille said, leaning into me. "A little young for me, but I like his leather jacket."

Alarm bells clanged in my head as I watched a cloud of annoyance darken Mr. Ferguson's face. "How would they know one another?" I asked myself out loud.

"Dunno, but they're shaking hands, so maybe the kid works for him at the dealership."

Given what I knew about Rusty Naylor's record, I doubted it, but their paths had clearly passed once upon a time. "Maybe."

Rusty nodded to me as he took a seat a couple rows back.

Wide-eyed, Lucille turned to face me. "Is this the dude with the ponytail that you were asking about earlier in the week?"

There wasn't much risk that Rusty could hear Lucille's stage whisper over the mournful strains of the organ filling the chapel, but I didn't want to take any unnecessary chances. Not with one of my prime suspects on the other side of the aisle.

"Who?" Gram chimed in.

I put my index finger to my lips to shush them both and searched the room for something to divert their attention.

I didn't have to look far. Marietta and Mr. Ferris were headed our way.

I pasted a smile on my face. "Hi, Mom. Pretty dress."

"Thanks." She gave me a once-over while she settled into the seat next to Gram. "You look nice. New suit?"

Sheesh. She had seen me in my one and only black pantsuit on at least a dozen occasions. The only difference this time was that I'd lost enough weight so that I could fasten the waistband without the aid of a safety pin.

Gram scoffed. "It's the same old suit she always wears."

"Oh?" Marietta leaned toward me, exposing a couple inches of décolletage. "Maybe I need to take you shopping."

Not a chance.

I needed another diversion, immediately. "Oh look," I said, pointing at the reporter walking past our row. "There's Renee."

As I could have predicted, my mother shifted her attention to the tall woman glancing in her direction. "Renee. Hello."

Renee Ireland took Marietta's hand in hers. "This is a surprise." She shot a pinched smile at Mr. Ferris.

Obviously not a completely pleasant surprise.

"Yes, I hadn't realized last night that we'd be seeing one another so soon." Marietta turned to Mr. Ferris. "Barry, have you met Renee?"

"I have," he said, keeping his hands to himself. "How've you been?"

She narrowed her eyes much like my grandmother's cat right before he swats you with his tail. "Swell."

The organist stopped playing, signaling that the service was about to start. But I had a feeling that the tension filling the room had only begun.

Renee jutted her chin. "Excuse me, I should get to my seat."

Lucille turned to me. "Your mother knows about them once being an item, doesn't she?"

"Pretty sure she knows now."

After the funeral service closed with a final prayer, Curtis Tolliver stepped to the microphone to invite us to fellowship in the reception room.

As most of us were well aware, this was our cue to follow the bereaved family into the hall adjacent to the foyer and commiserate with them over some sheet cake and fruity punch.

Only most of the family members filing by our row didn't appear to be overly bereaved or in the mood for commiseration. And judging by the amount of steel in Kendra's jaw as she herded her kids away from her glowering husband, she was flat-out pissed.

Lucille glanced back over her shoulder. "Looks like there's trouble in paradise."

"Maybe." Based on what Kendra had told me about their issues with Colt, I didn't think that trouble was especially new.

"Or maybe she's just ticked off about having to bury her brother today," Steve said, his breath warm against my ear.

I leaned into him. "Sure. That's reasonable." But I didn't believe it for a minute, not with the way Kendra's daughter kept looking back at her father.

Lucille's lips pulled into a tight pucker. "You two can believe that if you want. I'm gonna find out what's going on."

Good. Then she could tell me.

I turned to Steve. "Are you staying for the reception?" Since he had arrived late for the service, I figured the chances of him sticking around any longer than necessary were slim.

"I have to get back to the station and finish some paperwork," he said, shifting his attention to the guy in the leather jacket exiting the chapel. "I assume you're going to hang out here for a while."

Was he kidding? I wouldn't miss it. "You assume correctly because I'm sure Gram will want to stay and chat with some of her friends."

Steve leveled his gaze at me. "Right. Just don't harass anyone."

"I beg your pardon. I'll simply be paying my respects."

"Uh-huh." Taking me by the shoulders, Steve spun me to face the center aisle. "Be good or I'll have to punish you later," he whispered, melting my core with his body heat as he pressed his length against me.

Ooooh. "Promise?"

"That depends on what you have planned for tonight."

I knew what I wanted to plan on. "Dinner at my place?"

"If you make it a late one, you're on."

"Then it's a date." Something we hadn't experienced much of in the last week.

Shuffling my feet behind Lucille, I couldn't wipe the smile from my face. At least, not until we made our way toward the door. Then I spotted a tearful Jessica Tuohy sitting alone in the back of the chapel.

Of all the friends and family members who had attended Colt's funeral, none of them appeared to ache at his loss like the woman he had wanted to marry.

While I didn't find her the most sympathetic female I'd ever met, seeing her sitting all by herself tugged at my heartstrings.

"You coming?" Lucille asked when I stopped at the back row.

"I'll catch up with you." I touched Steve's hand as he stepped around me. "And I'll see you later."

He gave me a hard stare. "Remember what we've talked about."

"Every word, Detective."

The second he disappeared from view, I took a seat next to Jessica. "It was a nice service, wasn't it?"

Sniffling, she wiped her nose. "More than nice. Beautiful," she said, her voice thick with emotion.

I nodded, looking up at the dust motes floating on the sunlight cascading through the narrow windows. "Beautiful day, too. I'll be taking Fozzie out for a long walk later, if you'd like to join us."

"I can't. Seth...won't..." She blotted her eyes with her soggy tissue. "He'll be expecting me to be there when he gets home."

"Is he working today?"

Jessica nodded.

Then it was safe to assume that her new boyfriend didn't know that she was attending her old boyfriend's funeral.

I handed her the pack of tissues I kept in my tote. "Guys don't always understand the things we need to do."

Shaking her head, she blew her nose.

"Sometimes, it's best to just keep it to ourselves." More than sometimes when that guy was a cop.

Jessica's full lips curled into a sad smile as another tear trickled down her cheek. "Colt got me, though. I hardly ever had to explain anything. He just got me."

"But you ended up leaving him."

"We were better friends than lovers."

"That happens sometimes." I just hoped that didn't end up as my fate with Steve.

Jessica stared at Colt's casket for several silent seconds. "Who did that to him?" she finally asked.

"I don't know." But I was certain that Rusty Naylor could help me with the answer to that question.

Chapter Twenty-Two

STANDING ON THE funeral home's front step, I watched Jessica Tuohy take baby steps to the parking lot as if her own funeral awaited her.

I can't say that I blamed Jessica. I knew she had her doubts about the man she was living with. So did I, but while he may have been angry enough at Colt to deliver a solid punch to his nose, I didn't think Seth Lukin was a murderer.

"Whatcha doin'?" asked a little voice behind me.

I turned and smiled at Madison Caldwell, the four-year-old cutie I had met last Monday. "I was just saying good-bye to somebody who had to go home."

I looked through the doorway and didn't see a parent keeping a watchful eye on her. "Should you be out here?"

Pulling at the ruffle on her navy sailor dress, she shrugged. "I'm looking for my daddy."

"Did he come outside?"

"I think so."

I took her hand in mine. "Then maybe we should go look for him. Do you know which way he went?"

"No." She jumped down to the next step and then gazed up at me, beaming. "I made it, but I'm really good at jumping. Can you jump?"

Not in heels. "Not like you can."

"I didn't think so," she said, leaping to the next step. "Because you're so old."

And I was feeling older by the second. "It's a good thing you're so cute."

She gave me a toothy grin. "I know."

"Let's find your dad before he gets worried about missing out on some of this cuteness."

The bench under a shade tree in the parking lot was unoccupied, and other than Jessica, I didn't see anyone near any of the cars. That left one other likely place where Eric could be: the designated smoking area on the south side of the building. So as soon as Madison's feet hit the paved walkway, I followed my nose to the corner of the building, where I heard male voices.

Putting my index finger to my lips, I pulled Madison behind me. "Let me see who's back here first," I whispered. Because it sounded like they were in a heated discussion.

She nodded, but I knew I had just a few seconds before she'd run out to see if one of the men was her father.

Flattening myself against the exterior wall of the reception room, I peeked around the corner and spotted Glenn Ferguson stubbing out a cigarette.

"I don't care. I want you out of here," he told Rusty Naylor, who appeared to be more interested in the smoke rings he was blowing.

Naylor then muttered something I couldn't hear over a truck braking as it approached the Red Apple Market, and he took a step in my direction.

Yikes! I needed to make myself scarce.

Taking Madison by the shoulders, I herded her back the way we came. "There's icky cigarette smoke over there, but if we head back inside," where it wouldn't look like one of us was eavesdropping, "I'm sure we can find your dad."

"Daddy!" she squealed, running up the steps when my prediction came true. "I found you."

Eric picked his daughter up, balancing her on his arm. "Hello, monkey. Were you looking for me?"

Madison pointed at me. "We were—"

"Having a good time, playing on the steps." I pasted a smile on my face while I broke into a sweat.

"Thanks for keeping an eye on her." Carrying her up the steps, he gently gave her tummy a poke. "Haven't Mommy and I told you to stay where we can see you?"

Madison heaved a sigh. "Yes."

"The next time we go somewhere, I want you to remember that."

She waved at Glenn Ferguson when he came into view. "Grampa, are you coming back to the party?"

"I'm right behind you." He winked at me from the base of the steps. "I'm just a little slower."

"I think that goes for pretty much all of us here," I said, trying to sound like my heart hadn't leapt into my throat while I snuck a peek at Rusty Naylor striding toward the parking lot.

Holding the door open for me, Eric's father-in-law extended his hand. "I don't think we've officially met. Glenn Ferguson."

"Charmaine Digby."

His handshake was firm and warm, the light blue

eyes behind his glasses calm as a still lake. But lakes often had hidden depths, and while the man oozed grandfatherly charm along with a smoking-room odor that his cologne couldn't disguise, I didn't trust him as far as I could throw him. Especially after what I'd just overheard.

"Ah, I've heard about you," he said, ushering me into the foyer.

Since I'd talked to most of his family members, I shouldn't have been surprised. But when you witness the undeniable head of the family barking an order that could have been borrowed from a *Godfather* movie, it's not the thing you want to hear.

I made what I hoped wasn't a lame attempt to laugh him off. "Are you sure you're not confusing me with my mother?"

"Marietta Moreau, right?"

Whoa. He knew exactly who I was.

I nodded like a bobblehead.

He leaned a little closer, a curl at his lips. "These old eyes aren't that bad, although you do look a little alike. No, I heard you had a Jaguar you're thinking about selling."

He knew me because of my car? He had to have talked to Eric. "Not just yet."

Dropping the smile, he retrieved a business card from his jacket pocket. "Let us know if you change your mind. I'm sure we can make you a very competitive offer."

I just hoped it wasn't an offer that I couldn't refuse.

"Good golly, child," Gram stated when I joined her

and Marietta near the corner, where Glenn and Diana Ferguson huddled by the window overlooking the parking lot. "You're as white as a sheet." Gram pressed the back of her hand against my forehead. "You're clammy, too. Are you sick?"

I grabbed a napkin from the nearest table and mopped my brow. "I'm fine. I just got a little hot in this wool suit."

"Hot!" Venting a breath, Marietta fanned herself with a funeral program. "Give it another decade. Then, you'll know what hot feels like."

Sheesh. It wasn't a misery competition. "I can hardly wait."

I didn't have the time for this. Glenn Ferguson was heading for the door.

"Be back in a minute," I said on my way to the punch bowl, where I could have an unobstructed view of the foyer.

While I filled a cup, I watched Mr. Ferguson cross his arms, looming at the door like an aging bouncer in a designer suit.

The role of enforcer didn't fit him as well as the cut of his suit. But it seemed that the authoritarian man at the door wanted the satisfaction of seeing a black Cougar leaving the lot.

"How's the punch?" a male voice asked, interrupting my thoughts.

I handed my cup to a kid-free Eric. "You tell me."

He screwed up his face as he took a sip. "It's disgusting. My kids will love it."

I looked past him at his wife holding their young son, but I didn't see a little girl in the vicinity.

Not that it was my job to watch her, especially when I was preoccupied with what her grandfather was up to, but... "Madison isn't out playing on the steps again, is she?"

In an instant he flicked on the high beams of his toothy salesman's smile. "Not yet, but I'm sure it's just a matter of time until that escape artist makes her move."

"Well, she's a darling escape artist."

"Thanks." He eased closer. "I should also thank you for looking after her earlier. Ordinarily, Bethany and I wouldn't bring the kids to something like this, but our babysitter wanted to come," he said, casting a glance at his mother-in-law. "So whaddya do? You bring the kids with you."

It felt like he was being uncharacteristically chatty.

Was it that difficult to say a simple thank you?

My gut told me *Yes*.

"Speaking of which..." Eric held out his hand to the daughter sidling up next to him. "What's up, monkey?"

"Mommy says she needs the diaper bag." She wrinkled her nose. "Connor pooped."

"Duty calls." Eric gave me the most sincere smile I'd ever seen on his face. "Good seeing you again."

Watching him let Madison lead the way to the door, it struck me that fatherhood may have mellowed Eric Caldwell. It certainly appeared that some of his pricklier edges had been softened.

He was still a prick who only deigned to speak with me because he wanted to make a sale, but he had a lovely family that he obviously adored.

"Good for you," I muttered, tamping down the unexpected niggle of envy I felt flaring in my chest. "Even a prick can be a good dad."

Steve would make a good dad.

"What?" Where did that come from?

"What just happened?" Lucille asked, pouring herself some punch. "Did I miss something?"

Yes, and I wasn't about to have a heart-to-heart about it with the biggest mouth in town.

I grabbed another cup for her to fill. "Nothing important." Just Rusty Naylor getting ordered off the premises and me letting my imagination run amok.

"Anyone show up to have some last words with the stiff?"

Other than Jessica after the room had cleared out? "Nope."

Lucille grunted. "Bummer. I'd still lay odds that our suspect was at the funeral. Might even be here in this room."

I glanced in Glenn Ferguson's direction. "Maybe."

"Been through the receiving line yet?" Lucille asked between slurps of punch while she scanned the crowd.

I glanced over at the Ziegler clan, standing near the front window, where a red-faced Kendra looked like she was about to blow her top. "Not yet."

"You'd better hurry before this wingding breaks up, 'cause Kendra's been spoutin' off like she's ready for a cage match."

"With her husband?" I didn't know Damon well, but he sure looked like a burr had gotten under his saddle.

Lucille solemnly shook her head. "Her father. According to Renee, Tami invited him to the funeral without letting her daughter know."

"Uh-oh."

"Yeah. She has a few choice words for him after all these years."

When an estranged brother of my grandfather's showed up for his funeral, Gram had made a point of instructing me that death could serve as a powerful motivator to forgive and look past old hurts.

Clearly, that was not the case today.

If I needed any further evidence of that fact, all I needed to do was look at the sour face of the reporter sneaking furtive glances at Mr. Ferris and an increasingly pissed-off Marietta. "It seems like temperatures are running hot today."

"I know." Lucille nodded with satisfaction. "Usually these things are snoozers, but not today."

"No kidding."

As if sensing the tension in the room, Glenn Ferguson guided his wife toward the back wall, where Gram was chatting with the Pembrokes.

If there were some more choice words being spoken in that gaggle of seniors, I wanted to hear them, and excused myself to deliver a cup of punch to my grand-mother.

Averting my gaze when Mr. Ferguson looked at me as if I belonged at the kids' table, I pressed the paper cup into Gram's hand. "Sorry for taking so long."

"Oh, thank you, dear." Gram nudged me toward the Pembrokes, which I knew from years of experience was my cue to demonstrate the good manners she had painstakingly drilled into me. "You remember my granddaughter, Charmaine."

"It's nice to see you again," I said, shaking Malcolm Pembroke's hand.

"My wife tells me she ran into you at the grocery store the other day." He flashed me an endearing grin. "It seems to be our destiny to run into one another—one way or another."

Gram heaved a dramatic sigh worthy of Marietta. "Which is why I will never again let my daughter drive my car."

"And why I get conscripted to act as her chauffeur." As soon as the words left my mouth, I realized I'd as good as stuck my foot in it, especially when Katherine Pembroke's eyes started pooling with tears.

I sucked in a breath. "I'm sorry. That was insensitive, given the reason we're here."

"No, I'm sorry. If it hadn't been... Colt might still be..." Biting her lip, Mrs. Pembroke shook her head. "We never should have gotten into that limo that night."

Diana Ferguson wrapped her arm around her friend. "I arranged for it, so there's plenty of blame to go around if you want to go there."

I stole a glance at Mr. Ferguson, who had clamped his mouth shut. Obviously, he didn't plan on joining his wife as a blame game partner.

Mrs. Pembroke wiped her eyes with the handkerchief her husband had offered her. "When I think of that poor boy... It's just sad." She looked at my grandmother. "Did you know that Colt was one of the young men who painted our house?"

Gram inched closer. "I hadn't even realized that you'd had it painted until I drove by a few days ago."

After she had heard it had been broken into and wanted to see it for herself. She had left out that part.

"It's tragic what happened, but your house looks

positively refreshed with the new paint." Gram gave me an elbow jab. "Doesn't it?"

What was I supposed to say? "It looks very nice, especially now with the azaleas in bloom."

Blinking back fresh tears, Mrs. Pembroke cracked a bittersweet smile. "Those boys took such good care of my azaleas. I don't think I lost a single bud."

"The last outfit that painted my house brutalized my rose bushes, so that's good to know. Who'd you use?" Gram asked.

Mrs. Pembroke turned to her husband, who shrugged. "Darned if I can remember. You recommended them," he said to his buddy, Glenn. "What was the name?"

Glenn Ferguson recommended them? Holy crap!

"Boynton House Painting," Mr. Ferguson dead-panned.

Gram gave me another nudge. "Remember that. I'll want to give them a call."

"No problem." Because there was no way I would be forgetting that name, or the man who had just provided it.

Chapter Twenty-Three

"I DON'T WANT to stay here," Marietta said, pacing in front of my grandmother's kitchen table. "Let's all get in the car and go do something."

Gram blew out a sigh as she put the tea kettle on the stove. "Mary Jo, we just got home."

She wouldn't say it, but somewhere in that sigh contained Gram's dismay that we had driven off, leaving Barry Ferris standing in the parking lot like a jilted lover.

The poor schmuck was learning the hard way that Marietta didn't like surprises, especially in the form of a stunning ex-girlfriend.

"Doesn't mean we have to stay home." My mother flashed a brittle smile at me. "It's a sunny afternoon. Everything's in bloom. We should go for a long drive and enjoy the day, just we girls."

Forget it. The only drive I wanted to do was to my apartment. Unfortunately, my wheels were in the shop, so I was stuck in the middle of this drama until Gram drove me home.

"Oh, I know." Marietta shuffled her stilettos to a stop next to the refrigerator. "We could go have dinner at that country inn you like in Clatska, Mama."

Gram shook her head. "Sweetheart, that place closed years ago, besides—"

"Fine," Marietta bit out between clenched teeth. "We'll go somewhere else. We can figure it out on the way."

"I've been on my feet for most of the last hour and I'm tired," Gram said to my mother. "I'm going to have some tea and relax, and so should you."

Hugging herself, Marietta lowered her gaze. "I don't want any tea."

"Suit yourself. I'm gonna change my clothes." Gram crossed the room, giving me an exasperated look as she headed for the stairs. "And while I'm gone I'd appreciate it if you'd talk some sense into your mother."

Since when did everybody think that was supposed to be my job?

"I resent that!" Marietta called out, following her mother as far as the foyer.

"She's right, you know." As much as I hated to admit it. But when it came to dispensing unsolicited advice, Gram was usually spot on. "You should sit down and relax."

Because Barry Ferris was sure to be arriving any minute, and we all knew it.

Groaning, Marietta dropped into the nearest kitchen chair. "You don't understand."

She had clearly forgotten that she was speaking to someone who had invested over thirty years at Marietta Moreau University. I hadn't started out as a quick study, but after developing my own relationships with most of the men who had breezed in and out of her life, I understood plenty.

The tea kettle began to rumble to a boil, so I turned off the stove and pulled a couple of mugs from the cabinet. "Sure you don't want some tea?"

"No!"

Fine. Then, she could sip on some liquid courage and keep her mouth busy in the process.

A minute later, I delivered two glasses of the fumé blanc that we had never gotten around to opening last night, and took the seat next to her.

Knowing that my mother hated to feel rushed, I gave her a heckuva lot more time to breathe than I had given the citrusy wine I was sipping.

"I imagine he's been trying to call you," I said after she finally tasted her drink.

"I wouldn't know. I turned off my phone."

Very mature. "He's still going to want to talk to you."

"Well, I have nothing to say to him right now."

"That's too bad." Because I could look out the back window and see a dark blue Nissan pulling into the driveway.

Tracking my gaze, Marietta twisted in her seat. "Crap! I should've never let you talk me into coming straight home."

It hadn't been that much of a hard sell. Probably because, in her heart of hearts, she knew it was time to take her own advice and have an honest conversation with the man.

I patted her shoulder. "It'll be fine. I'm sure he just wants to..." Apologize?

I didn't know that he had anything to apologize for.

It wasn't like my mother had told him about every man she'd ever been with. Then again, none of them lived here in town and still looked as gorgeous as Renee Ireland.

"Maybe he wants to clear the air," I said, making my way to the back door.

She bolted upright at the same time that Gram came down the stairs wearing a pair of sweatpants and an old pullover sweater—her typical gardening attire.

"Now, what's going on?" she asked, frowning at her daughter standing white-knuckled in front of the table as if she were waiting for her horror movie closeup.

"Barry's here. After I let him in, maybe you could take me home to give them some privacy." Please.

"Nobody's going anywhere," Marietta commanded.

Gram waved her off. "Says you. I'm going to have my tea and then go out and pull some weeds. Char, you may borrow my car if you'd like."

Goody.

"Okay, then, let's get this over with. Ready?" I asked my mother.

She finger-fluffed her already perfect hair. "No, but let him in."

I swung the door open. "Hi, Mr. Ferris."

His lips drew back into the bleakest of smiles. "Is it that bad that we're back to 'Mr. Ferris'?"

"Of course not." I just had a hard time calling a former teacher by his first name. "Would you like something to drink?"

"No, thanks." He fixed his gaze on Marietta. "I only need a few minutes of your time."

That sounded like my cue to leave, so I stepped around my mother to grab the tote sitting behind her on the table.

That's when she clamped her hand around my wrist. "Let's go into the living room, where we can be more comfortable."

"What are you doing?" I whispered as she led the way to the sofa.

"I'm in need of your assistance." She pointed at the end of the sofa, where I sat last night. "Sit there, please."

"You don't seriously want me here for this."

Batting her long eyelashes, she smiled saccharine sweet. "It's just for a few minutes."

"Mom, this is a very bad idea."

Ignoring me, she waved her hand at the chair to my left. "Have a seat, Barry."

When she turned on the table lamp between us and opened the blinds, he gripped the armrests as if he were bracing for impact. "Given the way this looks, I guess I should have had that drink."

"Don't be silly," she said, shimmying onto the sofa next to me. "We're just going to have a little chat."

My mother had a summer tradition of trotting her little girl out for impromptu games of *Truth or Dare* with the men in her life, so I'd had plenty of experience with these *chats*. This typically led to them getting kicked out of her house the same night, so this didn't bode well for Mr. Ferris.

While Gram and I had both been concerned about Marietta rushing to the altar with my former biology teacher, I didn't want to play any part in her decision if she suddenly opted to call off the wedding.

Despite what he told me yesterday, I was quite sure that Mr. Ferris would be quick to agree with me.

I pushed off the sofa and headed for the kitchen.

"I'm not doing this."

"You most certainly are," Marietta said, calling after me. "So, get back in here and sit your butt down."

Pouring another glass of wine, I bristled at the parental tone of her command. "You gave up the right to talk to me that way a long time ago, lady."

Gram looked up from the magazine she was reading at the table. "What'd you say, honey?"

"Nothing. Just muttering to myself."

She picked up her mug and rinsed it out in the sink. "How's it going in there?"

"It's a little tense, but they're adults." At least one of them was. "They can handle it."

"It's a little early, isn't it?" she asked, giving the wine glass in my hand a long look.

"It's not for me. It's for Mr. Ferris."

"Poor guy. You'd better make it a double."

I ordered a double for myself an hour later, when I stopped off for a late lunch at Eddie's. Only it was in the form of grilled chicken on a boring field of greens—nothing remotely as tantalizing as the cheesy calzone Rox was chowing down on while Eddie gave her a break from tending the bar.

"Oh, that was heaven," she said on a sigh, savoring the last bite of cheesy bliss. "Exactly what I've been craving."

I stabbed a dry strip of chicken with my fork. "Trust me, I can relate."

She put her feet up on the chair between us. "Sorry. I'm not trying to be a cheese tease."

"Not a biggee. After not being able to eat in your first trimester, you should enjoy."

"Yeah, but if I keep indulging my cravings, I'm going to be as big as a house." Rox glanced down at her growing belly. "I'm already well on my way."

"Stop it. You look gorgeous."

"Hardly, but speaking of gorgeous, I heard your mom showed up at Colt's service in all her glamorous glory."

News around town traveled fast.

"She was in the same graduating class as his mother, so I guess Marietta wanted to be there to pay her respects." At least that's what she seemed to want everyone to believe.

"Hmmmpf," Rox grunted, wiping the grease from her fingers.

"Yeah, I don't buy it either, but I have bigger fish to fry right now."

She stared at me from the other side of the table. "Oh, honey. You're not still having problems with Steve, are you?"

"No, everything's fine." Of course, I had yet to talk to him about what I'd witnessed at the funeral reception. "At the moment. But he's not going to like what I have to tell him later tonight."

Her mouth gaped open. "You're pregnant, too."

"No! Nothing like that."

"Then, what is it?"

"It's about something I saw at Tolliver's."

"You mean something that could make a difference in the case against Little Dog?"

Pushing my salad away, I nodded.

She leaned back in her chair. "Holy cow. This could be huge."

"I know. I don't have any proof of anything," I said, choosing my words carefully, "but I think I've stumbled onto something Colt was involved in that might have gotten him killed."

Rox's eyes widened as they locked on mine. "So, spill. What?"

"I can't get into any detail—not while there's an active investigation. But I'm pretty sure that there's a connection between the robbery at the Pembrokes' and Colt's death."

"You're the third person to come in here and say something like that to me."

"You're kidding." Although I could see for myself that she was telling me the truth. "Who?"

"That guy Seth that works at the feed store, and Glenn Ferguson."

That Seth would talk to Rox about his former coworker came as a shocker, but my breath caught in my throat at the mention of the second name. "Glenn Ferguson was in here talking about the robbery?"

"Yeah, he and some prospective client came in for lunch on Tuesday. I figured since the man was friends with the Pembrokes, he was entitled to focus more on the break-in than Colt, but still... It seemed a little cold to use it in his sales pitch."

"Not only cold, but weird."

Rox sat quietly, looking at me as if I had suddenly sprouted horns. "Uh...I guess."

"You don't think it's weird that he's using the break-in at his friends' house to sell someone a car?"

"A car? Honey, he was trying to sell him a security system."

Chapter Twenty-Four

"DO YOU WANT to know what I found out now or after dinner?" I asked while Steve cut into the steak I'd grilled for him on my balcony barbecue.

He aimed a glare at the dog nuzzling his elbow. "Being a little pushy, aren't you?"

"He thinks it should be time for him to eat, too. But it's not, so Fozzie, *sit*."

After the fur ball reluctantly dropped to the floor between us, Steve gave me a sidelong glance. "I was talking to you."

"Me, pushy? I like to think of myself as being giving. As in someone who can provide you with some important information."

"More like someone who's been poking her nose where it doesn't belong." He popped the bite in his mouth and started to work on his baked potato.

"Hey, I stuck around for that reception. You didn't, so trust me. You're gonna want to hear this."

Steve grunted something unintelligible with his mouth full.

It sounded like *I doubt it*, but I preferred to believe that his guttural utterance could have contained a crumb of curiosity, so I decided to strike while that tiny iron was at least lukewarm. And while I had an audience hungry enough to stay at my table.

"There's obviously a connection between the break-in at the Pembrokes' house and Colt Ziegler's death," I said while Steve swallowed. "And it has everything to do with Glenn Ferguson."

Steve pointed his fork at me, his gaze as sharp as a butcher's blade. "I already know that he sold the party store that Town Car last year, so I'd like you to drop this right now."

Not a chance. "I bet you didn't know that he's the one who recommended Boynton House Painting to his buddy, Malcolm Pembroke. You know, the company that employs Rusty Naylor—the thief who pulled off that robbery the night of Mr. Pembroke's retirement party."

Steve leaned close. "Enough. Drop this."

"But you haven't heard the half of it, because Glenn Ferguson engineered the robbery for the sole purpose of selling the Pembrokes a security system."

Several silent seconds ticked by before the crease between Steve's eyebrows softened. "This is your important information?"

"Yes, and it's good information, so I'd appreciate it if you'd take it a little more seriously."

"Duly noted."

That's it?

The only heat I saw in his reaction came at the mention of Rusty Naylor's name.

Crunching on my salad, I stole glances at Steve. "Glenn Ferguson is now using that robbery to peddle security systems."

"Hey, he's a salesman taking advantage of an opportunity."

"I think he created that opportunity with this real estate pissing contest he seems to have going with Malcolm Pembroke."

"Now what are you talking about?"

I stabbed one of the few bites of steak in my bowl. "According to Rox, not only did Ferguson buy that electronic surveillance company last year, he's acquired all the vacant land between his wife's party store and his dealership."

"Not a crime, Chow Mein."

"But it feels like he's trying to show that he can play with the bigger boy in town. Maybe even tried to cut that boy down to size a little by siccing Rusty on him."

"Okay. Interesting theory. Now can we drop this and talk about something else?"

"I don't see how it got Colt killed, though, unless he left something incriminating in the limo."

Steve didn't respond.

Since he seemed a little too intent upon finishing his salad, I thought I must have struck a nerve. "Colt left something behind, didn't he? That's why Georgie caught him trying to break into the car hours later."

"I'm not going to say it again. *Drop it.*"

I sucked in a breath, my pulse pounding as I felt a piece of this wretched puzzle click into place. "And because he failed, he had to pay a price."

Steve threw down his napkin and pushed away from the table. "Thanks for dinner."

"Don't leave," I said, following him to the door. "You didn't finish."

"Trust me, I've had enough."

Whimpering, Fozzie echoed my sentiment as we watched Steve stride down the third-floor hallway as if he couldn't get away from me fast enough.

"That didn't end well, did it, boy?"

I reached down to stroke his back, but Fozzie turned tail and disappeared inside my apartment.

I didn't take the rejection personally. I knew that Glenn Ferguson wasn't the only opportunist in my acquaintance.

"Not people food," I reminded the dog I found staring at Steve's plate. "Just because someone doesn't finish something here doesn't mean that it's going to end up going down your gullet, so if you plan on remaining as my guest you'd better learn the house rules."

Inching closer to the table, Fozzie licked his chops.

Taking my seat to finish my boring salad, I pulled Steve's plate closer and sliced off a bite of steak. "Besides, I cooked this to perfection, if I do say so myself. Not that any male around here would appreciate that."

Fozzie sat and nuzzled my arm.

A few seconds later, he rested his head against my leg.

"Don't think I don't know what you're doing, you con artist. Did your prior owner teach you how to milk your mark for everything she's worth?"

With a doggie sigh, Fozzie dropped down to the floor.

I pushed the salad away. "Sorry. That was uncalled for. Will you accept my apology?"

He didn't move.

"Fine. I'll sweeten the pot."

With Fozzie hot on my heels as I took the dishes into the kitchen, I tossed a marbled slice of steak into Fozzie's dog bowl.

It disappeared in an instant, so I cut off another little piece, and then another until the piece of steak I thought I'd be nibbling on tomorrow had disappeared.

"Happy now?"

After giving my fingers a big lick, he trotted to the door and woofed.

"Fine." I retrieved his leash and he smiled back at me when I clicked it on.

Yep, one of us was clearly happy. The other was becoming too easy a mark.

✳

I had hoped to see Steve's truck when I brought my grandmother home from church, but just like two hours earlier, his driveway was empty.

"Does Steve have Sunday morning practice with the peewees?" I asked, following Gram into the house.

"Not that he's mentioned. Why?"

Because my heart still hurt with the way he left last night. "Just curious."

Closing the door behind me, I hoped the coffee I smelled was because Gram had her brewer on a timer and not because—

"Good morning," my mother chirped. "Hope you're hungry, because I'm making breakfast."

Gram gave me a wary glance as she set her handbag on the kitchen table. "Any idea what this is about?"

I shook my head and followed the coffee aroma into the Marietta Moreau Twilight Zone, where I saw a sight I had never before seen: my mother wielding a spatula.

"What's the occasion?" I asked her.

"I just thought it would be nice to have breakfast with my two favorite girls."

Not only was Marietta Moreau decked out in full hair and makeup before noon, she was preparing food in something other than a toaster.

This sighting could only mean one thing: She had some big news for us.

She pointed the spatula at the coffee pot. "I made the coffee strong, just the way you like it. At least I think so. Taste it and see."

"I'm sure it's fine," I said, filling two cups.

Since my mother was staring at me the way Fozzie had been fixated on Steve's steak, I girded my loins and took a sip of inky brew that was surprisingly palatable. "It's good. Best I've had today." Also the only coffee I'd had today.

Marietta beamed. "I'm so glad you like it."

Since she seemed to be waiting for me to make the next move, I pointed at the covered frying pan smoking on the stove. "Everything okay over there?"

"The omelet!" Marietta pulled off the lid, revealing a crispy blob that could double as a Frisbee. "It's ruined, and I had so wanted this breakfast to be special."

Gram patted her daughter's slumping shoulder. "Sweetheart, you have many talents, but none of them are in the kitchen. Although the coffee isn't bad."

"Maybe we should just take our cups into the dining room and..." *Get this over with.* "Skip breakfast, at least for now."

"Great idea." Hooking arms with her daughter, Gram escorted her out of the kitchen. "Who needs all that cholesterol anyway?"

Marietta sniffed. "You're just being nice."

"I'm your mother, and you know I love you," Gram said, depositing the family drama queen into her usual chair. "But if you ever want to get up early and make another breakfast, you know where I keep the cereal."

I stifled a chuckle as I brought in our cups.

Leaning on the table, Marietta rested her chin in her palm. "There's no need to be insulting. I just wanted to do something special to make up for my behavior after we got home from that poor boy's service."

She hung her head, her extended eyelashes fluttering like spiky bat wings. "And just like yesterday, I made a mess of it."

True, but what I didn't understand was why she was acting as if this had never happened before.

Gram reached over and touched my mother on the arm. "One thing about a mess, it can always be cleaned up."

Marietta looked across the table at me. "I'd like to believe that."

If that was supposed to be my cue, I didn't know what I was supposed to say, so I slurped some coffee to block the intensity of her gaze.

Injecting a little steel into the chin she was aiming at me, she straightened. "I wanted to say that I'm sorry."

And that was supposed to make everything okay?

"I wish you'd say something," she said, her full lips curling into a fragile smile.

"Sure. Just remember that I'm your daughter, not your trick poodle."

"Chah-maine, that's not how I think of—"

"That doesn't matter. Do you still plan on marrying Barry?"

She blinked. "Yes, of course."

"Then never use me to put him to the *test* again. That will help all our relationships going forward," I said, heading into the other room to collect my tote bag.

"Chah-maine, don't go." Marietta followed me to the door. "We should talk, don't you think?"

It felt like it was twenty years too late for that. "Don't worry. We're okay, Mom."

"Are you sure?" She hugged me, enveloping me in her musky jasmine. "We could make pancakes. Well, you could."

Yeah, pancakes would fix everything.

Chapter Twenty-Five

I DROVE THROUGH the streets of Port Merritt stewing about the choices I'd made since I sat down to dinner with Steve.

While I regretted being so blunt with the mother I had just walked out on, I knew our exchange would soon be like dust in the wind to her. So if she had any dusty ruffled feathers, I knew I could count on her to perform the requisite preening without further repercussion.

The situation with Steve was another matter entirely. Given the fact that his truck wasn't parked in his driveway or outside the police station, the Roadkill Grill, Duke's, or Eddie's, I had a sinking feeling that his anger with me wouldn't blow over anytime soon.

Worse, with all the breakfast smells venting from the restaurants I was driving past, my stomach was growling, demanding to get in on some of that greasy action.

I was in no mood to get grilled like the pancakes I was now craving *(Thanks, Mom)*, so Gossip Central was out. That left the next best breakfast option in town—one that I'd heard featured a short stack special.

Doubling back to turn into the Roadkill Grill parking

lot, I spotted Lily and Anna Maxwell walking up Madrone Way and pulled over to say hello.

Lily waved and ran up to poke her head through the window I'd lowered. "Hi! Did you get a new car?"

"I probably need a new car, but no. This is my grandmother's." I smiled at Anna. "Are you out enjoying the sunshine?"

Lily didn't give her mother an opportunity to respond. "I'd rather be out walking Fozzie. Is he with you?" she asked, searching behind me.

"No, sorry. I had to go somewhere this morning and left him in my apartment."

"Are you going to be walking him later? I could come with you."

Anna heaved a sigh. "Miss Digby probably has plans for later, so let's not intrude upon them."

Lily glanced back, crinkling her nose. "Well, he has to be walked some time or you know what'll happen."

"Very true." And the longer I kept Fozzie, the more I worried about how I was going to keep accidents from happening when I had to work late. "You're welcome to join me when we go for a walk later in the afternoon. I live just a couple of blocks from you and—"

"You live that close?" Lily's eyes gleamed with excitement. "I could come over every day after school and walk him for you, just like I did for Colt."

"Lily," Anna chided, "my little entrepreneur, you're being way too pushy."

"No, it's okay." Because her daughter had just presented the perfect solution to our mutual dilemmas.

"That would really help me out." I extended my hand through the open window and shook the girl's much smaller one. "So, if you want to be my dog-walker, you've got a deal."

She grinned. "Awesome!"

"If it's okay with your mom, I'll stop by later to show you where I live, and then we can take Fozzie out for a little stroll."

"It's okay, isn't it?" Lily gazed up imploringly at her mother. "Please, please, please."

Anna nodded. "All this is okay with me as long as you agree to get back by four every day. Because we won't be using a dog-walking job as an excuse to not do your homework."

"You've got a deal!" The ten-year-old shook her mother's hand and then turned back to me. "So when are you coming over?"

After pancakes. More important, after I found Steve.

"I'm pretty sure pancakes aren't on your diet," Steve said, taking the seat next to me at the Roadkill Grill counter.

I shot him as haughty a glare as I could pull off with maple syrup coating my lips. "Are you the food police now?"

"Nope. I hear that's more hours, less pay." He grabbed a laminated menu from behind the napkin holder in front of him. "Not in my best interest."

"Same goes for annoying me while I eat."

"That goes both ways, Chow Mein."

Cringing, I put down my fork so that I could focus on what I needed to say. "Sorry, the last thing I wanted was to chase you away last night."

"Maybe." Steve set down the menu, picked up my fork and snatched the last bite of my pancakes. "But you wanted something else more," he said chewing. "And that's a problem for me."

"I know."

"I don't think you do." He poked my arm with the fork. "I can't have you interfering in this case."

I yanked it away so he couldn't launch another pronged attack. "I know. I get it, and I'll thank you to not poke holes in my sweater."

"Coffee, hon?" Janine asked Steve while she topped off my cup with some steamy brew that put Duke's to shame.

When he didn't answer right away, she shifted her gaze to me as if she had sensed the undercurrent rippling between Steve and me. "Sorry, am I interrupting?"

He unfolded himself from the bar stool. "Nope, I was just leaving."

"Don't go," I said, hating myself that I sounded like Marietta. "Stay and have some coffee." *And talk to me.*

He gave my shoulders a squeeze. "I'll take a rain-check on that."

When Steve headed for the door, Janine set down the coffee carafe and dashed after him. "Detective, wait."

He opened the door for her, and they spent the next minute talking in the parking lot.

It obviously hadn't been about his breakfast tab, and by the way Janine was avoiding making eye contact with me when she returned to retrieve the carafe, it seemed apparent that he had instructed her to keep the subject of their discussion to herself.

"What the heck was that about?" I asked.

She waved me off. "Nothing important. Just something he had asked about."

"Having to do with Colt Ziegler's death?"

Her eyes widened.

Bingo.

"Uh..." Worrying her lips, she splashed a little more coffee into my already full cup. "I don't think I'm at liberty to say."

"That's okay. Let me guess. You saw Colt stop by here for a burger the night he died."

"Wow, you're a good guesser."

I wasn't that good. Katherine Pembroke had told me as much when I bumped into her at the grocery store. "About what time was that?"

"Oh, I didn't see him. One of the cooks filling in this morning mentioned seeing him last Sunday."

No doubt Steve had gone around through the kitchen door to speak with him. Personally, I didn't see the need to chat with another witness who'd be telling me something I already knew.

Unless...

"Did your cook say anything about who Colt was with?"

"I got the impression that he was late coming on shift and didn't see much other than the two guys sitting in the front of the limo."

Someone else was sitting in the limo?

Someone who could have used that opportunity to stash something in that limo shortly after the robbery at the Pembroke residence?

I'd bet dollars to doughnuts I knew who that someone was.

※

"Char? Did you hear me?" Lily asked, interrupting my thoughts while we walked with Fozzie toward her apartment.

"I'm sorry, I was thinking about..." I didn't want to admit to this kid that I was trying to picture Rusty Naylor standing over the body of her dying friend and neighbor. "Just some work stuff. What'd you say?"

"I kinda wanted to know when I'd get paid."

"Oh." I'd been so consumed with showing Lily around the apartment so that she knew where everything was that the very important detail of payment for services rendered had skipped my mind.

"Colt paid me at the end of every week. Five dollars *cash*." She glanced up at me. "'Cause I don't have a bank account yet."

"A good entrepreneur should have a bank account. I did at your age, so you should probably talk to your mom about that. And let's make it ten dollars a week. I'll leave an envelope with the cash for you on my dining room table every Friday."

She nodded, a bright smile on her face. "Cool."

Lily seemed so happy about her raise, I didn't have the heart to remind her that I was still looking for someone to adopt the fur ball trotting between us.

When we rounded the corner and the Madrone Arms came into view, Fozzie picked up the pace.

"He still knows his old home," Lily announced, breaking into a jog to keep up with her buddy.

And I was quite sure he'd pick that grungy apartment over mine in a heartbeat. I doubted that the person belonging to the moving van parked in front of unit 3 wanted a big furry dog, though.

Unfortunately, based on the lack of response from all my *free dog* posters, no one else around here did either.

Too bad, because Fozzie was a pretty nice dog when he wasn't blasting my eardrums with barking, which he tended to do when strangers approached a little too quickly.

Ten minutes later, with Fozzie standing his ground between me and the Ford pickup that had just pulled over near the street entrance to my apartment complex, it seemed that he didn't like metal strangers either.

Steve rolled down his window. "Why the heck is your dog barking at me? He was practically licking my fingers last night."

"Maybe he senses that you don't have good intentions."

"Oh yeah? Then he's smarter than I thought."

Trying to keep a lid on the happiness bubbling inside me like fizzy champagne, I held Fozzie close. "Sit, and no barking." *We don't want to chase the nice man away.*

I smiled up at Steve when Fozzie's butt met the sidewalk. "You were saying something about intentions?"

"Actually, I think you were."

"So I was, but only because I thought you might have stopped by to pick up where we left off last night."

Steve's mouth curled into a heart-stopping grin. "You're right. I have that steak dinner to finish."

"Sorry, your eligibility for that dinner expired last night."

"You ate my steak?"

"Technically, it was *my* steak."

"Then, technically, I guess we can't pick up where we left off."

"Sure we can," I said, not willing to let him wriggle off this deliciously fun hook we were both playing with. "I'd be happy to make you something else."

"I've seen your refrigerator. All you have is lettuce in there."

"Trust me, pal. I have something else in mind for you."

He revved the engine. "Race you there."

Chapter Twenty-Six

ALMOST TWO HOURS later, Steve shifted his attention from the flat screen above the bar at Eddie's to the last slice of pizza sitting between us. "I'll split it with you."

While Steve and Fozzie had both helped me work off my caloric intake from those pancakes, if I wanted to squeeze into that bridesmaid's dress, another bite of pizza was out of the question. "It's all yours."

"Of course, we could take it back to your apartment for a late-night snack."

I batted my sparse lashes at him. "Sir, just what are you suggestin'?" I said, borrowing Marietta's fake accent.

"Exactly the same thing you were suggesting earlier."

Goody. "I beg your pardon."

His eyes darkened. "Go ahead. I like it when you beg."

If he wanted to watch me melt right before his eyes, he knew just what to say. "My mama warned me about boys like you."

"No, she didn't. And since when do you listen to your mother?"

"Good point." I angled in for a kiss, and Steve immediately deepened it.

"Jeez, you two. Get a room," Eddie said, collecting Steve's empty glass. "Or do you want another beer?"

Steve gave me a lopsided smile as he used the pad of his thumb to wipe the corner of my mouth. "I think we're done here, don't you?"

I stiffened as if he had poured my ice water down my back. "What was that?"

"Just some tomato sauce."

Swell. I'd been shamelessly playing this seduction game with pizza goo on my face?

I grabbed a clean napkin and started wiping while Steve reached for his wallet. "Did you get it all?"

"I guess."

I looked down in horror at the red smear on the napkin. "I'll be right back," I said, retreating to the ladies' room.

The lighting over the mirror wasn't great in there, but at least I had the space to myself to inspect the damage, which after an application of lip gloss appeared to be confined to my ego. "But girl, you really know how to impress a guy."

Someone in one of the stalls cleared her throat.

Perfect. Now I was making a fool of myself in front of strangers.

The toilet flushed while I washed my hands and a brassy blonde who had been no stranger of late emerged from the stall.

"Hi," Jessica said, tentatively approaching me.

"Hey." I moved closer to the paper towel dispenser to give her room at the sink.

Flashing my reflection a smile, she lathered up while I dried. "I saw you at the bar with that detective."

"Yeah, he's a friend of mine."

She reached for a towel. "I could see that. It also looked like you don't need to worry about impressing him."

Easy for her to say. She hadn't just spent the last fifteen minutes with pizza hanging from her lips. "I don't know about that, but thanks for saying so."

"I'm the one who should be thanking you."

"Me?"

Jessica's eyes glistened as she pressed her lips together for a silent second. "For being so nice to me after Colt's service."

"Losing someone isn't easy, especially someone you were close with."

"Well," she said, blotting away a tear that had spilled over her spiky lashes. "You were the only person who talked to me there. Kendra didn't even acknowledge me."

"You two haven't talked since it happened?"

Jessica shook her head. "She and her mother probably blame me for leaving Colt and—"

"No, I know for a fact that they don't." Because Tami lay the blame solely at Georgie's feet. "So please don't beat yourself up about what happened."

"I can't help it. I keep wondering if...if I hadn't left him that way..." Jessica turned away, struggling to compose herself. "Sorry. All I seem to do lately is cry."

"It'll get better. Pizza helps," I said, trying to distract her with a little humor.

"Sure." Staring into the mirror, she dabbed at her leaky eyes. "Waterproof mascara helps, too."

"Whatever works." I thought she could use some

privacy and inched toward the door. "Well, take care of—"

"Did I see you sitting with Marietta Moreau yesterday?"

"Yeah, she's my mother." I readied myself to hear something about the resemblance, at least from the neck up.

"She is? Really? You don't look anything like her."

Whatever.

Turning toward me, Jessica framed her face with her hands as if she were inviting my close inspection. "You should tell her that the mascara she sells on those commercials really works."

This night kept getting better and better.

"About time," Steve said when I rejoined him at the bar. "I thought I was going to have to send a search party after you."

"Sorry, I ran into someone I know."

His eyes tracked Jessica as she made her way to the back table, where Seth Lukin was chowing down on a slice of pizza. "Uh-huh."

"And before you get on my case, I didn't ask her a single question."

"Sure."

"Hey, she's the one who started the conversation with me, actually to thank me for being nice when I sat with her yesterday."

He smirked. "Yeah, you're so nice. Not an opportunist at all."

"Excuse me, but I can be very nice."

"So I've noticed."

And I had noticed he hadn't given Seth and Jessica a second glance.

He draped his arm around me and led me toward the exit. "Maybe you'd like to show me how very nice you can be."

"I would be happy to." Truly. "Just answer me one question," I said, waving good-bye to Eddie.

Steve blew out a breath. "It'd better not be about my least favorite subject."

"You don't seem especially interested in Seth and Jessica."

He removed his arm and pushed the door open. "Don't start."

"I just find it curious since it's obvious that he's someone who knows a lot more than he's been willing to say."

"Unbelievable," Steve muttered, the loose gravel of the parking lot crunching under his feet as he stalked toward his truck.

I ran to catch up with him. "I'm sorry. I know you don't want to hear this, but if you'd let me tell you everything I know about—"

"Why can't you trust that I've already questioned him?"

I wedged myself between Steve and the truck he was about to climb into. "I do trust you. You know that. I'm just trying to understand what happened last Sunday."

He brushed back the strands of my hair that the evening breeze had whipped into my eyes. "I'm sure you do, but I'm telling you for your sake and for Dog's—stay out of this."

"Okay, but—"

After silencing me with a kiss, he pointed at the passenger seat. "Get in. I'll take you home."

I wrapped my arms around his neck instead. "You'll come in, right? You know, so that we can share that late-night snack."

The corner of his mouth curled. "Only if you promise to be good."

"Detective, not only will I be good. I'll be nice."

＊

After spending most of my Monday morning in the stuffy copy room, I craved fresh air, so I took my break on a bench sitting in full sun across the street from the courthouse.

I closed my eyes, lifting my face skyward to soak in a little Vitamin D, and considered everything I'd seen and heard last night.

Clearly, I had been warned off the case. Again.

I understood why. Steve had to still be gathering evidence. Otherwise, he would have already taken Rusty Naylor into custody.

I put a mental check mark next to the painter/thief's name because I'd seen with my own eyes that he was a person of interest to Steve.

That hadn't been the case last night with Seth Lukin. Unlike me, Steve was always aware of his surroundings, but not once at Eddie's had he given Seth so much as a moment of pause.

Setting aside bogus alibis by well-intentioned girl-friends, my gut told me Seth wasn't anything more than a potential witness in the case against Georgie. That in itself was going to be totally depressing if Steve didn't start taking some people like Glenn Ferguson in for questioning.

"You will," I said aloud, replaying Steve's words to me in the parking lot. "You have to." Because Ben Santiago rarely lost a case.

Almost an hour later, my mother called me while I was back on my knees, doing battle with an overstuffed filing cabinet.

"What are you doing?" she asked, sounding way too chipper for my mood.

"I'm working."

"Can you take a break for lunch?"

This could only mean one thing. "You need a ride somewhere?"

"Actually, yes, but I thought we could have lunch first."

"I only have an hour, so I don't have time to go somewhere fancy."

"And you're on your diet. I know. That's why I thought you might want to grab a quick bite at Duke's and then drop me off for my appointment."

"What, like a doctor's appointment?" With one of the legal assistants at her desk ten feet behind me, I lowered my voice. "Is something wrong?"

"No, silly. It's a hair appointment. There's going to be a photographer at the interview."

"What interview?"

"Honey, you were there when I first talked to Renee about this. Don't you remember?"

Yes, but after everything that happened Saturday, I didn't seem to be the one suffering from some short-term memory loss. "Of course, but are you sure you want to do this?"

"Oh, my darling," Marietta said, injecting venom into every word. "I wouldn't miss this for the world."

Chapter Twenty-Seven

"WELL, SUGAH?" MY mother asked, using her Georgia peach accent when I came to pick her up at Donatello's. "How do I look?"

One of the gray-hairs under the hood of a hair dryer answered for me. "Gorgeous."

"Not only that, picture-perfect." In a casually tousled, every hair in place kind of way.

"Nicely done, as usual," I said to Donna, who had another client in her chair with two more waiting.

Donna finger-fluffed Marietta's fringe of bangs. "I thought so too, if I do say so myself. Of course, look at the beautiful creature I had to work with."

"You're a dear." My mother gave her a quick hug along with what appeared to be a generous tip. "Thanks for squeezin' me in on such short notice, hon."

Pocketing the cash, Donna thumbed in the direction of the ladies snapping pictures as if the photo session had already begun. "Are you kidding? As soon as the word got out that you were coming, I booked up solid for the rest of the afternoon. Speaking of which, I'd better get a move on before my three o'clock gets here."

"I need to get back to work, too." And to the post

office, where I was supposed to be mailing a certified letter for Patsy. "Let's go. Soon, please," I added, trying to get my mother to stop posing for fan photos.

After she finished glad-handing everyone in the salon, I turned to her as she slid into the car. "Are you absolutely sure you want to do this interview?"

"Of course."

"Because you wouldn't want to say anything that you'd regret."

She patted me on the thigh. "Sweetie, I think you're worrying a little too much."

Only because I didn't want to subject Gram to any blood-curdling screams after her Wednesday *Gazette* was delivered.

Marietta flipped the visor down and checked her flawless makeup in the mirror. "We're just gonna have ourselves a little chat."

Ten minutes later, she repeated the same line to my grandmother, who immediately turned to me after Marietta ran upstairs to change her clothes. "Am I the only one who thinks this is a dangerous idea?"

I shook my head. "But I don't have time to keep debating it with her." Nor did I want to stick around to hear the hissing if this turned into a cat fight.

"One last thing before I go. Georgie texted me earlier and said my car's ready. So, if you don't mind coming with me to pick it up, you'll get your car back tonight."

"No problem, sweetheart. But if it's ready now we could go, 'cause I'm quite sure your mother won't need me here."

I kissed Gram's cheek. "Nice try, but I have to get back to work."

She heaved a sigh. "Sure, leave me in the midst of impending doom."

"It'll be fine. Like Mom said, it's just a little chat."

"I seriously doubt that."

You and me both.

After mailing that letter at the post office, I knew I should make like a homing pigeon and return to my roost at the courthouse. Because if I didn't hand Patsy a certified mail receipt in the next few minutes, I was sure that the third-floor hall monitor would make it her mission to make sure this bird's wings got clipped.

I didn't need any additional hassle today, so I had every intention of turning and going straight up the hill to the courthouse. And then it struck me that I could take a three-minute detour through my neighborhood and possibly catch a glimpse of Lily walking Fozzie.

I didn't know why this felt like a must-see, but after all the misery of the past week, I longed to catch the bliss that I knew would be reflected on Lily's sweet face.

And I missed my turn.

After cruising down every street in the neighborhood, I finally spotted a girl skipping toward my building with a big furry dog. "Sweet."

This arrangement was going to work out perfectly. In all respects because I couldn't stop smiling, a girl and her dog buddy had been reunited, and I no longer had to worry about that buddy having an accident and costing me my damage deposit.

"Yep, perfect," I said, making a U-turn back toward Main so that Lily wouldn't think I was spying on her.

"Now, get back to work."

Because your ass is gonna be grass if you don't put the pedal to the metal.

Unfortunately, Glenn Ferguson was emerging from his electronics store up ahead, and my foot was no longer listening to me. Especially once he shielded his eyes from the sun and looked down the street as if he were surveying his kingdom.

He looked in my direction and then at the car a half block behind me, but it wasn't until he started pacing with his cell phone to his ear that I got the impression he was impatiently waiting for someone.

I wanted to know who, so I pulled into Eddie's parking lot where I could watch Ferguson from across the street.

I didn't have to wait long because a Ford Escape driven by his daughter, Bethany, stopped to pick him up.

"Good grief." I made myself even later because of some after-school carpool they participated in?

Only he owned a car dealership. Instead of carpooling with a family member who would be a slave to her kids' schedules, as a wheeling-dealing opportunist, wouldn't he make a point of driving one of the latest luxury models he wanted to sell?

Not only that, when Ferguson got into the car, Grandpa didn't turn around to say anything to the kids.

Something was off.

Okay, if I hadn't had any contact with Glenn Ferguson on Saturday, I wouldn't think twice about him hopping into a car with his daughter—kids or no kids. But that wasn't the case, and I knew I'd be kicking myself later if I didn't find out where they went.

"What does five more minutes matter?" I asked my-self as I pulled out on Main Street and followed them. I was sure my ass would be grass no matter what time I tried to slip by Patsy's desk.

At least I didn't have to go far to satisfy my curiosity, because Bethany was turning into the One Stop Party parking lot.

Were they planning the next big wingding?

Doubtful. More likely they had some family business to discuss with Mom working in the back room there.

I pulled into the gas station across the street, where I hoped to get a sense of their body language as they stepped out of the vehicle.

Only it didn't seem like I'd get that opportunity any time soon, because mine was the only car door that opened.

Fine. I could pump some gas while I waited.

By the time the Honda's tank was full and every window had been squeegeed clean, father and daughter had finally wrapped up their private meeting, and I watched them make their way to the party store entrance sans children.

Yep. This was definitely some sort of family meeting.

Interesting that they were having it here. At a place where the sales clerk had told me Bethany rarely makes an appearance.

"It must have been pretty important to get her to hire a babysitter and come to the store," I muttered to myself as I slid in behind the steering wheel. No sooner than the words left my mouth that a beater Dodge parked next to Bethany's SUV and a skinny guy who looked like he could be Colt's younger brother disappeared inside the store.

"Interviewing for the limo driver job?"

Considering the crowd that had already gathered, the obvious answer was *Yes*.

Waiting for a logging truck to rumble by before I merged onto the highway, I pulled out my cell phone and snapped a photo of the guy's car. I didn't know if I'd need it, but at least I had something that could come in handy if he turned out to be an associate of Rusty Naylor's.

I tapped on the stored image and zoomed in to ensure that I could make out the license plate.

The characters were fuzzy, but I could read them, so good enough.

I was about to toss my phone onto the passenger seat when I realized that I'd caught something else in the image: The inflatable gorilla had managed to twist around to face me, almost as if it were posing for the shot.

"Weird."

I didn't need my logic-minded grandfather to materialize and give me a physics lecture. It was a simple matter of the wind coming in off the bay, the speed of the passing logging truck, the surface area of the inflatable. Blah, blah, blah.

Still, it looked weird.

Even weirder, his outstretched hand pointed in the direction I needed to be heading. As in immediately, before any of the Ferguson family stepped out to find me watching them.

I didn't typically take the advice of inflatable gorillas, but it seemed like the right time to start.

✳

"How was your day, dear?" Gram asked three hours later, when I came to pick her up.

"I survived it." Only because Patsy and Frankie were huddled in a senior staff meeting that went long—mercifully for me.

"But never mind boring stuff like that." Since there was a Subaru parked out front, I eased my way toward the kitchen so that I could sneak a peek into the living room, where a photo shoot appeared to be wrapping up. "How's it going in there?"

"Charmaine, don't be an eavesdropper."

I scowled at my grandmother. "As if you haven't been listening in on them most of the afternoon."

"It's my house. I can do what I darn well please."

"So?" I asked, hearing an unexpected peal of feminine laughter.

"It's been surprisingly civil. A little tense at first." Gram stepped past me and held up a wine bottle. "But once the gals downed a little of this, they loosened up."

"Ooh, I hope that didn't loosen Mom's mouth too much." Or bring the talons out.

"She seems fine. From the sounds of it, I'd say she's been having fun."

That could also be said for little sadists who enjoy pulling the wings off butterflies. "I bet."

I didn't particularly want to hear a blow-by-blow of how my mother's meeting went with her fiancé's ex, so I jingled the keys in my hand as a not-so-subtle reminder of what had brought me here. "You want to drive?"

"And miss out on being chauffeured like a queen

bee? No, thank you. I'll get my coat and let your mother know we're leaving," Gram said, heading for the foyer, which from my vantage point appeared to be crowded with Marietta and her guests.

Gram looked back at me. "Looks like it might be a minute."

"No problem." I had fed Fozzie before I left, and Bassett's wouldn't close for over another hour, so there was no big rush other than to get out of here before my mother decided that she wanted to come with us.

A minute turned into five by the time the Subaru drove away, and Gram reappeared with her coat. "Your mother wants to come with us."

I clenched my teeth. "It's not like we're going out to do anything fun. I'm just going to pick up my car."

"You can be the one to tell her that."

"Okay, I'm ready," Marietta announced, her double Ds bouncing as she pranced down the stairs in her favorite red stilettos.

"Are you sure you want to go? We're just going to Bassett's shop to get my car."

She flicked her wrist as if she were shooing away a pesky bug. "Nonsense. We'll go to dinner afterward. I'm starving."

"You don't have dinner plans with Barry, honey?" Gram asked.

My mother shook her head. "Cancelled, but I told him I set something up for him after the interview."

I didn't like the sound of that.

Obviously, Gram didn't either because she shot me a worried glance. "I hadn't realized that he even knew about it. You know, considering all the parties involved."

"Don't be silly, Mama. I believe in total transparency."

Since when? "What are you up to?"

Marietta's glossy lips curled as she glided toward the back door. "Just a little clearing of the air." She held the door open for her mother. "Shall we?"

"Mary Jo, I have a very bad feeling that you're playing with fire," Gram said, putting on her coat.

"No, Mama. I'm making sure that a fire is out."

Chapter Twenty-Eight

"MAKE THE LEFT at the corner, Chah-maine."

I shot the uninvited back seat driver a glare from the rearview mirror. "That's not how to get to Bassett's."

"No, but it's the fastest way to Barry's and I'd like to swing by for a moment."

Gram and I exchanged wary glances.

"I saw that," Marietta huffed. "Will you just trust me to know what I'm doing, please?"

"Fine." I turned left and headed up the hill toward where Mr. Ferris lived, south of the park.

After a moment of companionable silence, my mother looked up from the red lacquered nails she had been inspecting. "Have you seen the new paint on that cute Victorian on J Street, Mama?"

"No, I haven't been up this way for a couple of weeks," Gram said. "Do we have time to swing by?"

"Of course we do. Chah-maine, take the next right and let's show it to your grandmother."

The last Boynton house painting crew member I'd seen in town had been at Colt's funeral, so I didn't see how a drive-by could hurt. "Okay." But if a black Cougar was parked in the vicinity, Gram had better not blink, because this drive-by was going to set a land speed record.

"Oh, no. They're changing that pretty burgundy to a deeper plum." Marietta clucked her tongue. "Whatever for?"

I didn't care. I was more concerned about who had arrived in the white cargo van parked out front.

Gram leaned in to look through the windshield. "A little more contrast, I guess."

"Stop the car, Chah-maine," Marietta commanded.

I only saw the one painter who had given me the car repair advice last week. A team of one certainly could have been dispatched to re-paint the trim, but with a house this size, I doubted it. "I don't know if that's a good idea. Bassett's is going to close soon and—"

"Don't be ridiculous. We can stop for two minutes so that your grandmother can get a good look at the place."

"Fine." I pulled to a stop across the street from the van. "But let's stay in the car. We don't need any more complaints about trespassing."

"Now, you're just being a stick in the mud," my mother retorted, climbing out of the back seat.

Gram reached across me to lower the driver's side window. "Mary Jo, where do you think you're going?"

Crossing the street, Marietta raised an index finger. "I'll be back in a flash. I'm just going to ask this gentleman a quick question."

Criminy, Mom, I thought, scrambling after her. Now was not the time to be hanging around, asking questions.

"Yoo-hoo, sir?" Marietta sang out as she approached where the painter was working on the front door trim. "Ah know you're busy, but may Ah interrupt you for a brief moment?"

Turning, he smiled politely. "Okay."

"Is there a problem with the burgundy paint other than the cullah?"

He furrowed his brow as if he were having difficulty understanding her rapid-fire southern accent. *"Qué?"*

"The reason I'm asking about the color change is that I have a friend..." Marietta said, trying again without the fake accent. "Well, truth be told, more than a friend who'll be painting his house soon and—"

"Rusty!" he yelled, sounding a plea for rescue from a crazy woman.

Crap, I didn't want Rusty Naylor to see me here again.

She touched the base of her throat. "Oh, dear. I didn't mean to cause a fuss."

Maybe not, but this fuss had just grown to dangerous proportions.

I hooked her arm to pull her back to the safety of the car. "We need to leave—*now*."

She shook me off. "Chah-maine, puh-lease. We can't just up and leave. I'm in the middle of something here."

And I was going to be in big trouble with Steve if he got wind that Marietta and I had returned to the scene of our not-quite crime.

"Hello," she said, extending her hand to Rusty Naylor as he rounded the corner of the house. "I'm Marietta Moreau."

"Whoa, wasn't expecting to hear that today." Grinning, he pulled a rag from a back pocket and wiped his hand. "I'm Rusty." He bowed ever so slightly as he pressed his palm against hers. "I used to watch your movies when I was a little kid."

She puckered as if his words had left a sour taste in her mouth. "Aren't you just the sweetest thing."

His smile stretched from ear to ear. Clearly, he hadn't felt the sting of her jibe. "What're you doing here?"

"Mah daughtah," she said, pulling me by my sleeve, "was just showin' me and my mama your excellent craftsmanship with this lovely Victorian."

Rusty waved at someone behind me, and my heart sank to the pit of my churning stomach when I turned to see my grandmother.

"I was hoping you'd wait in the car," I whispered.

She sniffed with disdain. "Why should you two have all the fun?"

Some fun.

"As I was telling your co-worker," Marietta said, fanning her hand in the direction of the guy who had returned to painting the door trim. "I was concerned that there might have been a problem with the paint that you're replacing because I had recommended it to someone who will soon be painting his house."

Rusty shook his head. "No problem other than the owner changing her mind about the color after she was sent some pictures by my boss."

Pictures? That could only be because of one reason. "She's not in town, then?"

"Traveling overseas, I think," he said.

That explained why I hadn't seen anyone other than a neighbor around to chase us away. Unfortunately, it also made her home more vulnerable to burglars and thieves like Rusty. Assuming Glenn Ferguson hadn't already sold the owner a security system.

Gram tilted her head at the stately Victorian as if she were admiring an oil landscape at one of the local art galleries. "Well, they say a woman is entitled to change her mind, but if it were up to me I would have stuck with the burgundy."

Rusty nodded. "Me too, lady. But I just paint the color I'm told."

She glanced back at the cargo van. "There's no name on your vehicle back there. If you don't mind me asking, who are you with?"

"Your granddaughter must not have passed along the business card I gave her," he said, fixing me with a stone-cold stare while he fished another card from his breast pocket.

I smiled sweetly. "Sorry about that. Must have slipped my mind."

Gram tucked the business card into her handbag. "No matter. I've got it now, and I'll be sure to give you a call. Especially since your company has come so highly recommended."

I didn't want her to mention who had provided the recommendation, so I stepped between them to break up this Victorian decor appreciation session. "Okay, it's time to let these gentlemen get back to work."

After waiting for Marietta and Gram to say their good-byes, I hung back to lock gazes with Rusty for what I hoped would be the last time. "Don't even think about bringing your *business* to my grandmother's house."

He stood very still as if he were trying to project a calm demeanor. "My *business?* I don't know what the heck you're talking about."

His dilated eyes suggested otherwise.

"You know exactly what I'm talking about," I said, wishing that I sounded more commanding and less like Marietta arguing with an ex-husband.

Lips parted, his gaze tightened.

With the satisfaction that my message had been received, I marched back to the car.

"Now, wasn't that worth stopping for?" Marietta asked as I slid behind the wheel.

While Gram nodded with agreement, my pulse roared in my ears like a freight train. Because I might have just caused Steve's case to run off the rails.

✳

After George Bassett Senior escorted Gram and Marietta to his office fifteen minutes later, I sat in my idling car and listened for the cowbell.

"You can sit there all day," Georgie said, leaning in through my open window. "But you're not gonna hear anything other than an engine purring like a kitten. For now, anyway."

Turning off the ignition, I climbed out of the Jaguar. "What do you mean 'for now'?"

He stroked the front fender as if it belonged to a living, breathing feline. "She's a finicky one, especially with all the miles she's got on her. Always gonna demand a lot of TLC."

If I hadn't known better, I would have thought he was describing my mother. "That sounds expensive."

"Sorry, Chow Mein. It's pretty much standard operating procedure with this kind of car."

Which meant that my ex-husband's pride and joy was going to slowly bleed me dry.

"I've had someone approach me about buying it." Since Eric Caldwell was Colt's cousin, I thought it best if I didn't use any names. "Maybe I should ask him to make me an offer before something else goes wrong."

"You might want to let me fix that door problem then, so that you can get top dollar."

I didn't need a bigger repair bill than I already had. "Let me talk to the guy and get back to you on that."

"Okay." Georgie pointed his big work boots in the direction of the office. "Want to settle up?"

"Sure, but..." Before I wrote him a painfully large check, I needed to take advantage of this alone time. "Could we talk for a minute?"

"If it's about my case," he said, shaking his head. "I got nothin' to say."

"Then you can just listen to me."

"Char, I don't think—"

"Dog, will you please shut your mouth and listen?"

With cheeks ablaze, he folded his beefy arms and made a pouty face like a giant toddler given a time out.

"I can't give you any details, but I think there's going to be a big break in your case really soon."

His jaw went slack as he sucked up all the oxygen in the immediate vicinity. "Did you get this from Steve?"

Heck, no. "He never discusses open investigations with me, and nothing is official yet. But I want you to know that there are some things brewing that are going to clear you of all the charges." Assuming that my big mouth hadn't damaged the brewing process.

Georgie's face split into a goofy grin. "You serious?"

"Yeah, I'm serious."

"When?"

That I couldn't tell him. "I don't know, but hang in there, big guy. We're trying to get you out of this mess."

"I knew it!" Wrapping me in a bear hug, he lifted me off my feet. "Thank you."

Balancing myself against his grease-stained chest as he lowered me to the ground, we both looked down at the black smudges on the pink knit tunic I was wearing.

"Oh, man," he said, grimacing, "I slimed you."

I gave him another big squeeze. "It was worth it." And then some, just to see Little Dog smile. "Just do me a favor and don't say anything about this to anyone." Especially Steve.

"Okay, but that's gonna be tough."

"You've come this far." I extended my hand. "Now shake on it and promise me that you'll continue to follow your attorney's advice and not discuss this with anybody. But me, of course."

"Deal," he said, pumping my arm with his greasy paw. "Want to go in and pay up now? I think your mom's antsy to go to dinner."

"Sure, but I may have to clean up a little first."

He handed me a rag. "Sorry again about the shirt."

"Yeah? Want to take a few bucks off my bill to replace it?"

He grinned. "I'm not *that* sorry."

Chapter Twenty-Nine

AFTER AN INTERMINABLY long dinner with my nervous mother, Gram took her home to await the arrival of Mr. Ferris after his air-clearing *date* with Renee.

I needed to have an air-clearing session of my own and headed across the street to talk to a cop about a case I wasn't supposed to involve myself in.

"Whatever you're selling, I want some," Steve said the instant his door swung open.

Taking a deep breath to bolster my faltering courage, I stepped inside. "We'll see if you feel that way in a few minutes."

He followed me into the living room. "Not what I was hoping you'd say."

As much as I didn't want to see his face when I delivered my news, I planted my butt in an overstuffed chair opposite the chocolate brown sectional I knew Steve preferred.

"Sorry to take you away from the game," I said, glancing at the flat screen television blaring in the corner.

"Never mind that." He took a seat across from me

and clicked off the TV. "Let's hear it."

"I've done something bad."

"Care to elaborate on that?"

Not especially. "You know that Victorian on J Street being painted by someone who you didn't want me to talk to?"

The tic at his jawline counting down to an explosion answered for him.

"I didn't mean for it to happen, but I said some things to Rusty Naylor today."

Steve hung his head. "Why is it so hard for you to follow simple instructions?"

"I know. I know. You have every reason to be mad, but after Gram practically hired the guy on the spot, I had to make sure that he understood that I was onto that scheme he has going with Glenn Ferguson."

Frowning, Steve scrubbed his face. "Just tell me exactly what you said."

"I warned Naylor not to bring his business to her house."

The crease between Steve's brows eased. "That's it?"

"Isn't that enough?"

"No other names came up?"

"No, I told you, that's all I said."

"How'd he act after you gave him your *warning*?"

"Confused but also a little scared, because I made it sound like I was one step away from making a citizen's arrest."

"Yeah, I'm sure you were really scary."

I bolted upright. "Hey, I can be plenty scary. And if you don't think I got his attention, think again."

Steve pushed off the sectional and wrapped his arms

around me. "I'm sure he got the message loud and clear to stay away from your granny's house."

"I don't get it," I said, feeling the tight coil of tension in my chest starting to unfurl. "I thought you were going to be furious with me."

"Who says I'm not?"

Pushing him away, I studied his face. "Nope, I've seen angry on you before. This isn't it."

His laugh lines crinkled despite his effort to maintain a respectable scowl. "I wouldn't be so sure if I were you."

"Now I'm the one who's confused," I said, trying to read him.

"All will be clear soon enough."

"Says you."

After a brief kiss, Steve held me at arm's length. "Just don't do something *bad* again."

"I promise I won't do anything bad tonight. And since you're being so nice about this, maybe even tomorrow."

"Well, let's not be too hasty about tonight," he said, slowly unbuttoning my tunic.

Just when I wished his fingers would work a little faster, his gaze narrowed and he pulled me toward a table lamp for closer inspection. "What'd you get on this?"

"You don't want to know." And I didn't want to tell him.

"It looks like grease. You haven't been moonlighting with Little Dog, have you?"

"Hardly. Although I may have to think about getting a second job if he keeps handing me repair bills like the one I got today."

"Poor you." Steve's eyes darkened as he pulled my tunic over my head in one smooth motion. "If only I could think of something we could do to take your mind off your troubles."

I linked my fingers with his and led the way to his bedroom. "Come on, you've tortured me long enough."

"Trust me, Chow Mein. Your night of torture has just begun."

The next afternoon, while driving back from serving a subpoena on a pissed-off Clatska tavern owner needed at an upcoming trial, I received an unwelcome summons of my own from my mother.

You're needed at home.

"Again?" I tossed my cell phone onto the passenger seat. "Whatever's going on, just deal with it and count me out."

No more than a minute passed before my phone started ringing.

I knew she'd keep calling until I picked up, so I pulled over near the turnoff for Gibson Lake to take the call. "What's so important that can't wait an hour for me to get there?"

"Actually," replied a woman with a soft voice. "I'm calling about the dog you have for sale."

What part of *FREE DOG* on each one of the signs I'd posted did she not understand? "Not for sale. He's free."

"Excellent. I have someone who would love to meet him. Would you be available to meet later this evening, maybe at the dog park kiosk?"

"Definitely. What time?"

After a brief pause with some muffled voices in the background, she responded with, "How about seven-thirty?"

"Perfect. I'll see you there."

After disconnecting, I sat in my blessedly quiet car while I waited for my eyes to stop burning with tears, because what I had just agreed to wasn't so perfect.

It was going to break Lily's heart.

"You took your time getting here," Marietta groused when I stepped through my grandmother's back door a few minutes before six.

I wasn't in the mood to be sniped at. "Some of us have jobs, you know."

"Excuse me, but I have something you need to see."

Somehow I doubted I'd find it as interesting as she did.

Waving me over to the kitchen table where she was sitting with Gram, my mother handed me her smart phone. "Read this email I received today."

Gram scooted her chair back. "I've already had the pleasure, so I'm gonna start dinner." She pointed at me. "You staying or am I eating alone?"

"I can stay for a while. I have to meet someone at the dog park before it closes."

"About Fozzie?" Gram asked.

Marietta tapped her phone. "You can talk about that animal later. Barry is coming to pick me up any minute, so read."

Heaving a sigh, Gram started rooting around in her refrigerator, and I turned my attention to my required reading of the day.

I recognized the sender's name—Annette Lazenby, one of Marietta's *Peachtree Girls* co-stars. "Blah, blah, blah. Daughter's having a baby. That's nice." And made me feel like everyone I was remotely associated with was busy getting married or having babies.

My mother wagged a finger at me. "Keep reading."

"Okay," I said scanning the newsy message for salient details. "So, Annette's worried about her daughter giving birth the same weekend as some wedding she's traveling to." I looked up from the tiny text that was straining my eyes. "Is that it, or is there some hidden meaning lurking between the lines?"

Marietta snatched her phone back. "Don't be obtuse. You know very well what wedding she's referring to, Gina Campanella's."

Egads. It was about that stupid wedding again. "I take it Annette received an invitation?"

"Her husband was a producer on Chad's last movie, so Gina was probably obligated to include them."

"Okay," I said, hating that my mother kept plunking me down in the middle of this wedding invitation drama. "Hopefully her daughter can wait until after Gina and Chad's big day."

Pursing her mouth, my mother leaned back in her chair. "Of course, that would be ideal. But that's not why I wanted you to read Annette's email."

Of course not.

"Her daughter's due date is June sixth, so it's safe to assume that the wedding is that same weekend."

I leaned back, adopting Marietta's posture. "Probably."

"So? Has Steve said anything about it, because I need to make plans if I'm going."

Enough. "I wouldn't plan on going."

She narrowed her eyes. "Because he doesn't want me to go with you, or—"

"Jeez, Mom. It's not always about you." I stood up to get some water. "I'm not going, either."

She trotted after me in her stilettos. "What do you mean you're not going? It's going to be the event of the summer."

"I know you think it's a big deal," I said, filling a tumbler at the tap. "But these aren't friends of mine, so I'm just fine with staying home."

Gram turned from the carrot she had been peeling. "Are you saying Stevie's going by himself?"

I didn't have the answer to that question. "Maybe."

"Maybe!" Marietta spun me around to face her, splashing water on my khakis. "Is he going or isn't he?"

"I don't know. He hasn't told me."

"Charmaine, it's been a week and you still haven't talked to him about this?"

I slammed the tumbler down on the counter, sloshing more water on myself. "I've been busy, okay?"

"Well, you don't need to get all huffy about it." My mother aimed a tapered index finger at me. "What you need to do is clear the air with that man."

I'd had all the air clearing I could take in a twenty-four hour period. "Right."

"Speaking of which," Gram said to her daughter, "how did it go last night with Barry and Renee?"

Marietta's blood red lips curled. "Like a champ. Renee now has some closure, and Barry can be a little more comfortable in her presence. And maybe someday the three of us could be friends."

"Friends, right." She needed to become a better actress if she expected us to believe that she had suddenly developed some empathy about the broken heart of an ex-girlfriend.

No, what my image-conscious mother had conducted was a two-pronged attack for personal and professional damage control.

Are you that desperate for good press or that afraid of suffering the same humiliation as Renee?

As if reading my mind, Gram gave me a parental glare. "That's actually very good news since you're all going to be living here. Although I was a little worried about you springing that meetup on him."

Smiling with satisfaction at her reflection in the window, Marietta tucked back a stray wisp of hair. "No need to worry, Mama. Everything's been smoothed over."

And just in time for the feature article Renee was supposed to write for tomorrow's *Gazette*.

The end might justify the means in the world of Marietta Moreau, but that didn't mean I had to hang with her there tonight.

"Oh, look at the time. Sorry about dinner, Gram, but I should probably go pack Fozzie's things."

"Somebody called, huh?" she asked.

"Yeah, I'm meeting her and, I'm assuming, a kid or two at the park. If everyone gets along, I probably won't have a dog after tonight."

Marietta took a sip from my water glass. "That's good news, right?"

"Yep, I've been trying to find him a permanent home

for over a week."

Gram touched the sleeve of my sweater. "I worry about you living alone in that apartment, so are you absolutely sure that you want to do that?"

I patted her hand. "I'm sure." At least I thought I was until I received that call.

Chapter Thirty

WALKING WITH FOZZIE around the kiosk at the dog park, I took another glance at the time on my phone. *Seven thirty-seven.*

"I don't know what this says about your prospective mom, but she's late," I told him.

Fozzie tugged at the leash, pulling me away from the circular path we'd been beating into the grass, and promptly watered a spindly bush.

"Yes, I know. You have places to go and bushes to pee on, but we need to wait here for a few more minutes."

While he sniffed his way around the head of the trail that led to the parking lot, I searched the grounds for a family who looked like they needed a dog and came up empty.

Just when I started to think the woman who called me was going to be a no-show, my phone rang.

"Hey," I said after I saw it was Steve.

"Hey, yourself. You home?"

"No, I'm at the dog park, waiting for someone who called me about Fozzie."

"A little late to be there, isn't it? It's gonna close

soon."

"And it's getting dark." I looked up as the light attached to the shingled roof over the kiosk turned on as if by power of suggestion. "So, I'm about ready to consider myself stood up."

"Did you have dinner?"

"Not really, I..." Seeing movement in front of a thicket of Douglas fir near the western fence line, I shielded my eyes from the overhead light. "Wait a minute. Someone's coming."

Unfortunately, not a woman. "Never mind. It's not her."

"Do you recognize who it is?" Steve said, his voice shifting into cop-mode.

"He's wearing a hooded sweatshirt, so I can't make out his face."

"Char, I want you to go to your car right now and lock the doors."

"There are other people around." At least there were a few minutes ago. "But I agree, it's time to go." I gave Fozzie's leash a tug. "Come on, you can pee some more when we get home."

Only Fozzie wasn't showing any interest in any of the nearby foliage. Standing alert like a well-trained guard dog, he growled low in his throat.

"Char, tell me what's happening," Steve demanded.

I tried to catch a glimpse of the man's face so I could convince myself that Steve and Fozzie were just being alarmists. "Not much, but we definitely need to go."

Just as I thought my thudding heart couldn't beat any faster, Fozzie started barking, and I dropped my phone into my jacket pocket so that I could use both hands to control him. "Come on. Fozzie, let's go."

I looked back at the guy and could see he was now jogging toward me. "Dog, let's go!" I yelled, sounding my own alarm.

Defiantly standing his ground, Fozzie turned up the volume of his barking.

"Criminy!" This was not the time to act macho. "Come! *Now!*" I grabbed Fozzie by the collar and dragged him forward with all my might.

Once I got him moving toward the safe haven of my car, the *fight or flight* hormones coursing through his quivering body must have dialed up a new appropriate physiological response: *Run.*

With my dial already at that setting, my job was clear: Get us into the car.

But first, hold on and haul ass.

Easier said than done with sixty pounds of muscle propelling me down an uneven dirt slope in a dead run.

My lungs straining for oxygen, I willed my rubbery legs to keep pace with Fozzie's four-legged sprint. But I only had two legs and none of his raw power.

Unfortunately, I hadn't realized how impossible my task was before I coiled his leash around my other hand so that I couldn't lose him. Because now that Fozzie's nylon collar was slipping through my aching fingers, I had all but guaranteed myself the fate of being dragged into a face-plant on the trail.

Fozzie had run off before. He could be found again.

I needed to make sure I could be found, uninjured, and preferably by Steve inside my apartment in the next ten minutes. So I twisted off two of the loops of nylon around my hand and let go of his collar, but not before an unencumbered Fozzie bounded forward and jerked me to my knees.

"Char!" a male voice behind me called out. "Are you okay?"

Ignoring the sting of my abraded knees, I wobbled to my feet like a colt walking for the first time. "I'm okay." And since this guy knew my name, I had some hope that I'd remain okay.

A muscular arm wrapped around me, holding me close to a solid torso. With my heart battering my ribcage, I twisted around so that I could look into the face of my would-be assailant.

Son of a... "Eric!"

I jabbed my elbow into Eric Caldwell's side so that he'd release me. "What the heck are you doing, running after me? You scared me half to death."

"Sorry. I was just jogging back to my car. You know, getting in a little workout while the wife and kids walk the dog."

He was wearing the sweatshirt hoodie of a typical jogger, but he had dress slacks on and wingtips, which didn't lend an iota of believability.

"Are they here? I should introduce Fozzie to Bodie."

"Yeah, they're coming."

No, they weren't. And I didn't see anyone moving in the dusky shadows of the park. Not good.

"Speaking of Fozzie," Eric said, scanning the parking lot. "Where is he?"

"I'm sure he's waiting for me at the car."

"I don't know. I don't see him." Eric took me by the elbow as if I needed an escort. "Maybe we should go look for him."

"Thanks. I'd hate to think that he's run off again. 'Cause I've got someone interested in taking him off my hands." Someone I had a feeling Eric had cajoled into making that call for him.

Crap. Crap. Crap. I'd walked right into a setup.

He flashed me a fake smile while negotiating us past the boulder that marked the start of the trail. "Hey, that's good news."

"Something that we haven't had much of since your cousin was killed," I said, praying that Steve was still listening.

Eric nodded as we approached our vehicles. "It's been a rough week."

I heard crying coming from inside his wife's SUV, dishearteningly the only other car in the lot. "Sounds like someone's having a rough time in there right now."

"You're okay," Eric said, opening the rear passenger door, revealing his toddler strapped into a well-padded car seat. "We're going through the terrible twos, and there's more crying than sleeping going on right now, especially while he's getting over a cold."

"I know a guy who takes his kid on long drives at night just to lull him to sleep." At least I guessed as much about the one I was looking at.

"Yeah, the motion of the car works like a charm."

I shuddered with the certainty that Eric hadn't stayed home Sunday night with a sick kid, like Bethany had told me. He slipped out when she was asleep and took the kid with him.

"Oops," Eric said, shaking his head while a hiss of air escaped from his lips. "He was supposed to be on a walk with my wife, wasn't he?"

"Yeah, you blew that. But the story you were trying so hard to sell was already blown because you're not that good of a liar. Or human being."

I smacked him in the shoulder. "Really? You leave your baby to sleep in the car while you beat your cousin to death?"

Eric sneered at me while sirens blared in the distance. "It was an accident. He hit his head on something when he fell."

"But you left him there to die. I bet that wasn't an accident."

"You don't know anything, and certainly can't prove anything."

"Yeah? I know that Colt's death had everything to do with the jewelry that Rusty Naylor stashed in that limo."

Eric's gaze sharpened, his eyes gleaming in the low light like a predator's. "Rusty said you were on to him. I thought he was just being paranoid, but now that we've had an opportunity to clear the air, I guess I should've taken him a little more seriously."

Jeez. Now, this jerk was making air-clearing references.

Hurry up, Steve!

Eric pointed at the empty seat next to his squalling son. "Get in."

"I'm not getting in there."

"This isn't optional. You have become another loose end, and I can't afford any right now."

"Is that what this is about? What you can or can't afford?" I asked, trying to buy time.

"Never mind that. Get in."

I racked my brain for what I could remember about

Eric in high school. "You couldn't afford much growing up, so you're gonna make sure that never becomes an issue again?"

"You make it sound like money's a bad thing. It makes life a heckuva lot easier. You should recognize that, Charmaine. I checked your credit. You can barely afford to buy a car."

I wasn't about to let Eric make this about me. "And you've got rich in-laws that are helping you. What do you need to do this for?"

"You don't know what you're talking about. Shut up and get in."

"What'd you do? Blow your money on something and you're afraid Bethany's going to crawl to Daddy and embarrass you?"

Eric clamped his mouth shut, filling his jaw with so much iron that it looked like he wanted to snap me like a twig.

You did. "That's it, isn't it?"

"This conversation is over." He pointed at the back seat. "In the car. Now."

"If you want me in there, you're going to have to pick me up and throw me in there."

"If you insist," he said, digging his fingernails into my flabby biceps.

But despite the fact that he could easily shove me in next to his son, Eric froze, uttering a string of obscenities.

Craning my neck to see what had this big man scared stiff, I saw a long shadow move in front of my car. But it wasn't until Fozzie crept closer that I could hear him growling over the ragged breathing blasting my eardrum.

"Everything's okay," Eric said in the singsong voice he had used to soothe his little boy, but Fozzie didn't sound the least bit convinced.

Good boy. "The only way that you're going to get out of this in one piece is for you to let go of me and step away. Now."

"I—"

"You don't think he remembers you? Think again."

Eric's hands came off me as if they had been spring-loaded. "I'm not touching her. See?"

When he inched back, I scampered to close the car door so that no matter what transpired over the next few seconds outside of the vehicle, the little guy inside wouldn't be harmed.

With me out of the way, Eric must have sensed that Fozzie had a straight shot to the tender appendage of his choosing. But the moment Eric reached for the passenger door, Fozzie lunged, sinking his teeth into the closest ankle.

While the bigger Caldwell male howled like the smaller one sitting in safety, an unmarked cruiser with flashing lights pulled up behind the SUV and Steve jumped out.

"Char," he shouted, drawing his revolver. "Are you okay?"

"I'm fine." I stepped between him and the snarling dog pulling the pants off of Eric Caldwell. "Please don't shoot Fozzie. He was trying to protect me."

"I'm not going to shoot him. Now, get out of the way. And Caldwell, stay down."

"Get him away from me," Eric cried out, writhing on the asphalt.

Steve's mouth flatlined while he watched Fozzie toss a pant leg in the air. "Yeah, I'll get right on that."

I turned at the sound of the patrol car rounding the corner into the parking lot. "Let me grab Fozzie's leash before somebody in the posse you've assembled thinks this is a dog attack."

"He won't," Steve said, handing me the loop end of the leash. "I heard pretty much everything you two said and briefed Howie on the way."

"So you know that Eric is responsible for his cousin's death, not Little Dog."

With his revolver trained on the guy being pantsed, Steve nodded. "Just needed some evidence to convince your boss. Now, will you please call off your dog so that I can make an arrest and we can get out of here?"

Since I wasn't the alpha dog here, I didn't know if I was capable of calling Fozzie off. "I can try, but he doesn't look like he's in the mood to listen."

"Hey, if you can't—"

"Someone hurry up and get this dog off me!" Eric screamed, dialing up the threat level at his ankles.

Not helpful. "Shut up or I'll have him bite you again."

Steve gave me a sideways glance like he might have to start shooting to get my feet moving.

"Everyone just calm down." Including me. "And give me a minute."

I slowly approached so that Fozzie could see me and gave his leash a tug. "Come."

Still tearing at the pants of the man who must have abused him the night of the accident, Fozzie ignored me.

I pulled on the leash with greater force. "Fozzie, come!"

With fight-mode fully engaged, he growled at me.

"Want me to call animal control?" Howie asked, stepping up behind me.

"No. Just stay back and let me handle this."

"Will you hurry up?" Eric whined, cursing at me while he struggled to squirm out of his pants.

I'd heard more than enough from this ass-wipe. "Eric, why don't you finally do something smart. Shut your mouth and don't move."

When he finally stilled, I gave the leash another tug. "You ready to go home, boy?"

Eyes glazed, Fozzie didn't appear to be in a state where he could hear me. "I'll take that as a no." Darn it.

I didn't want Howie to get an itchy trigger finger, so I eased close, latched onto Fozzie's collar and pulled him off Eric. "Let's go."

Growling with a mouth full of gray polyester, he turned on me as if I were his new enemy.

"Fozzie, it's okay," I said, muscling him to the other side of my car, where he couldn't see Eric. "You're okay. It's just me."

Holding Fozzie close, I waited for him to settle. "Yeah, you're okay now." At least he no longer looked like he'd clamp down on the first hand that got near his mouth, and I grabbed a handful of torn gray polyester. "May I have this, please?"

After some coaxing, he unclenched his jaw, and I was able to wrestle Eric's slacks out of Fozzie's mouth with minimal shredding. Not that I cared.

I tossed them over to Steve so that Fozzie could only focus on me and my scent. "There. The bad man's all gone." Sinking my fingers into his ruff, I was grateful to gaze into calm, glossy brown eyes. "All better now?"

He rubbed the top of his head against my chin.

"I know," I said, blinking back hot tears. "I'm happy to see you, too."

After giving Steve enough time to get Eric into handcuffs, I straightened. "Want to go for a ride, boy?" Because I sure was ready to get out of there.

With ears pricked to attention, Fozzie immediately strained at the leash.

"Okay, since you're the muscle of the two of us, you're riding shotgun with me."

Unlocking my car, I gave Steve a thumbs-up sign as I led Fozzie around the back of my car. "I'm taking him home. Unless you need me to stick around to watch the little kid until his mom picks him up."

"No, we've got it covered. Go home."

"See you later?"

"I'm going to be busy for a few hours," Steve said, escorting Eric to Howie's patrol car for transport, "but I'll get there when I can."

"I'll have dinner waiting for you."

"That's nice, but it's going to be to get a statement from you."

Of course. "Does that mean that you don't want me to order a pizza?"

"When have you ever heard me say no to pizza?"

"That's what I thought," I said with a wave as I followed Fozzie into the Jag.

Pulling out of the parking lot, I turned to my furry co-pilot. "Shall I ask Aunt Roxie to grill a burger for you?"

Fozzie woofed.

"You got it, pal." And whatever else you want.

Chapter Thirty-One

GEORGE BASSETT SENIOR was quick to greet Steve and me when we stopped by the shop early the next evening.

"I can't thank you enough for everything you did," he said, taking turns shaking our hands while Rufus danced around our feet.

"Just doing our jobs, sir." Steve gave me a hip bump. "Speaking for myself, of course."

I put my elbow in his side. "When are you gonna let that go?"

"Something goin' on that I don't know about?" Mr. Bassett's gaze traveled from me to Steve and back again. "Everything's okay now, right?"

Steve pulled me close. "Everything's very okay now that we have the right guy in custody."

"Which is why we stopped by," I said, pointing to the six-pack Steve had placed on the roof of his pickup. "We thought we should have a little celebration."

"Seems like a darn good reason to take a break." The Big Dog turned toward the garage. "Junior, you got company."

It didn't take more than a minute for Georgie to slide

out from under the old Toyota he had been banging on and come running with a goofy grin on his face. "Hey, did you hear? All the charges have been dropped."

Steve slapped him on the back. "I know, Dog. That's why we're here. Plus, I've got a present for you."

"Jeez, haven't you done enough for me?" Sneaking me a peek, Georgie hung his head. "I mean, you didn't need to get me nothin'."

"Well, don't get too choked up about it. You haven't seen it yet," Steve said, stepping to his truck.

Georgie turned to me. "Sorry, that sort of slipped out."

Wrapping my arms around the big galoot, I held him tight. "Don't worry about it. Just be happy. It's over."

"It's just hard to believe it," the Big Dog chimed in.

Steve returned with the six-pack and a baseball bat. "Maybe this will help it feel more like it's over."

Taking the bat in his hands, Georgie examined it as if it really had been the murder weapon. "I wish I had never touched this that night. If I hadn't thrown it at Ziegler, maybe he'd still be alive."

Steve shook his head. "Caldwell did this. He set the whole thing in motion the minute he concocted a get-rich scheme with an old buddy."

Georgie looked up from the bat his dog was sniffing. "What are you talkin' about?"

"Let's go to the office and have a beer, and I'll tell you as much as I can," Steve said, leading the way.

Almost twenty minutes later, when a customer showed up to collect his car, Steve and I finally said our good-byes and headed back to his truck.

"Okay, I get that you didn't want to get into a lot of detail with Little Dog since he'll probably be called as a witness when this goes to trial. But I don't understand. Where does Glenn Ferguson fit into all this?"

Steve draped his arm over my shoulder. "Chow Mein, why do you keep insisting that he has some sort of scheme going?"

"Because the break-ins were helping him with his security system business."

"You mean the *one* break-in at the Pembrokes' house?"

"Well, yes." Seeing he put it that way.

Steve opened my door for me. "That was his son-in-law capitalizing on what the Fergusons had set in motion with that retirement party."

"But I saw Mr. Ferguson with Rusty Naylor after the funeral, bossing him around like he couldn't afford to be seen with him."

"Since I was the one who arrested Naylor for stealing tools from the dealership's service department, I think it's more likely that you just saw a pissed-off former boss."

"Oh." While I climbed into the passenger seat, my brain cycled through everything I now knew about Eric Caldwell, but one big question remained unanswered.

"I kind of understand why Eric went in with Rusty to rob the Pembrokes, but why did he do that to Colt?" I asked Steve when he shut his door.

"From what little Caldwell said before his lawyer got him to clam up, I don't think it was intentional."

"What exactly did he say? Can you tell me?"

"There's not a lot to tell, but from what I've pieced together, there was some sort of altercation after Colt failed to get the Pembrokes' jewelry out of the limo."

"So, he did know that Rusty stashed something in there when he met him at the Grill."

"I think all Colt knew was the cock and bull story that Eric gave him about hiding a gift under the front seat for Bethany. No doubt Caldwell was panicking that someone here would find the stash and put two and two together, so he probably did some serious arm-twisting to get Colt to jump the fence."

"And when Georgie caught Colt by the limo and chased him out of the yard with his bat—"

"Eric had to take matters into his own hands 'cause Colt wasn't going back in there. Probably even had the dog with him by then."

"You actually think Fozzie was there?"

"It explains why he was running loose the next day. Plus, I found some cotton fibers and scratches in the back of that SUV that the wife can't account for. A roll of gauze is missing from the first aid kit that they kept back there, so I think Caldwell made some sort of muzzle to restrain the dog after Colt hit his head."

"Fozzie certainly would have been barking up a storm if Colt were in trouble."

Steve nodded. "Which Rufus would have heard, and then he would have started sounding the intruder alarm. Not the situation you want when you need to quietly hop a fence and retrieve the stolen jewelry from the limo. My theory is that Caldwell tied the dog down in the car and then dumped him off a mile away so that it would look like Colt had been struck during the initial break-in. It's the only thing that makes sense."

"Okay, so sometime between Eric's arrival with his

kid and him driving away with the jewelry, Colt hits his head on something, Fozzie gets tied down in the car... And Eric makes the conscious choice to leave his cousin there to die?" Even after my brush with the creep at the park, I found that difficult to wrap my brain around.

"I don't think he just fell and hit his head, but yes. That's pretty much how I see it."

"But how could he leave Colt like that?"

"Remember what Caldwell told you about loose ends? Colt with his injury would have been a big one."

"But he was thick as thieves with Rusty—no pun intended. Colt had to have known what Rusty was up to and he was keeping his mouth shut."

Steve gave his head a shake. "I think Colt was just the limo driver—a convenient middle man that Caldwell knew he could count on to show up at the Grill that night."

What? "No, he has to be in it to some degree. The diamond ring—"

"How do you know about that?"

"Jessica told me." And I had read a note that I didn't think it was in my best interest to mention. "She also said that she thought it had been expensive."

He shrugged. "Not that expensive."

"Because Rusty sold it to him at a big discount after some heist, right?"

"Because Colt bought it at the Valu-Mart."

I slumped back in my seat. "Wow. Was I ever wrong about him."

He patted my knee. "Shocker."

"Come on, you were probably thinking the same thing when you found out that Rusty and Colt were members of the crew that painted the Pembroke house."

"But I didn't jump to any conclusions about it."

I stuck my tongue out at him.

His gaze shifted to my chest. While I typically don't take issue with him catching a glimpse of the girls, I didn't like the grin on his face. "What?"

"Looks like you might have brushed up against Dog."

I looked down, inspecting my favorite woven shirt. "Dang, I've been slimed again."

"Want to head home to change before we go eat?"

We'd had so little time together lately, I didn't want to do anything to delay the dinner date Steve had promised me when he picked me up at my apartment. "No, I got a little too busy to do laundry last night, so I don't have much to change into besides a bridesmaid's dress, and I'm not wearing that. Let's just go."

"It's early. Maybe I should take you shopping."

Other than the Valu-Mart, there weren't a lot of clothing store options in town. "In Port Townsend?"

"Sure." He started the engine. "I need to buy a wedding present anyway."

I placed my hand on his to keep him from shifting into gear. "Whose wedding?" I asked, trying to tamp down my excitement that he was finally bringing up this subject.

"Someone I used to go out with."

Really? You're not going to tell me the truth?

Turning, he must have recognized the disappointment etched in my face because his lips stretched into a lopsided smile. "Fine. My ex-fiancée."

"Gina, right?"

The smile disappeared. "I didn't realize you knew

about her."

"Gram mentioned your engagement a while back."
Last week.

"Didn't last long. Turned out we wanted different
things."

"She's a big deal on TV in LA now, right?"

"And that's nowhere I want to be."

I wasn't sure how I was supposed to interpret that. "I
assume that's where the wedding is?"

"Yep."

"You going?"

"Heck, no. Unlike your mother, I don't need to fill
my social calendar with events I don't have a personal
stake in."

She'd be disappointed to hear that news, but I was
more than okay with it.

"It's bad enough that I'm obligated to send a gift," he
said, staring at my left boob.

"What are you thinking about buying?"

Instead of answering, Steve rubbed at the grease
smudge with the pad of his thumb. "I don't think this is
going to come off." His eyes darkened as he unfastened
the top two buttons and reached under my bra. "But
maybe if you take it off and spray it with something…"

"Detective, I think you're trying to get me naked."

He grinned. "And I think your detecting skills are
improving."

While Steve and I drove back from Port Townsend
with a wedding present and a new blouse, I reached
back to pet the fur ball sticking his head out my window.

"I still don't know why we needed to bring the dog," Steve said. "He's slobbering all over my interior."

"It's a truck. It can handle a little slobber. Besides, I didn't want to leave him alone any longer than necessary today."

Steve shot me a smirk. "He's a dog. He can handle being alone for a few hours. Besides, didn't that kid walk him earlier?"

Chucking Fozzie under the chin, I smiled. "Lily, and yes. That's working out great."

"So, why exactly is he along for the ride?"

"Because I was hoping you could take us to the dog park."

"It's closed."

"I know." That was why I wanted Steve with me. "But I forgot something there. Do you mind making a little side trip?"

"What'd you forget?"

"You'll see."

"That doesn't really look like something you forgot," Steve said fifteen minutes later, when I tossed the *FREE DOG* sign into the trash can next to the park kiosk.

"Okay, technically it's more like something I've wanted to do all day."

Leaning over, I wrapped my arms around Fozzie's neck. "I'm assuming that decision is okay with you."

Wagging his tail, he woofed.

I linked my arm with Steve's. "You heard him. Let's go home."

THE END

About the Author

Wendy Delaney writes fun-filled cozy mysteries and is the award-winning author of the Working Stiffs Mystery series. A long-time member of Mystery Writers of America, she's a Food Network addict and pastry chef wannabe. When she's not killing off story people she can be found on her treadmill, working off the calories from her latest culinary adventure.

Wendy lives in the Seattle area with the love of her life and has two grown sons. For book news please visit her website at www.wendydelaney.com, email her at wendy@wendydelaney.com, and connect with her on Facebook at www.facebook.com/wendy.delaney.908.